About the Author

G.D. Sanders has previously worked in academia. He is now retired and enjoys writing contemporary crime fiction, as it allows much more creativity than writing scientific research articles. He is based in London. *The Taken Girls,* his first novel, came out in 2018. *The Victim* is his second book.

G. D. Sanders

THE VICTIM

avon.

A division of HarperCollins*Publishers*

www.harpercollins.co.uk

Published by AVON
A division of HarperCollins*Publishers* Ltd
1 London Bridge Street
London SE1 9GF

www.harpercollins.co.uk

This paperback edition 2019

First published in Great Britain by HarperCollins*Publishers* 2019

A catalogue copy of this book is available from the British Library.

ISBN: 978-0-00-831323-4

This novel is entirely a work of fiction. The names,
characters and incidents portrayed in it are the work
of the author's imagination. Any resemblance to actual persons,
living or dead, events or localities is entirely coincidental.

Typeset in Birka by Palimpsest Book Production Limited,
Falkirk, Stirlingshire
Printed and bound in UK by CPI Group (UK) Ltd, Croydon CR0 4YY

MIX
Paper from
responsible sources
FSC C007454

This book is produced from independently certified FSC™ paper
to ensure responsible forest management.

For more information visit: www.harpercollins.co.uk/green

THE VICTIM

Part One:
JUNK MAIL

1

Did I choose you today? At the ATM as you checked your balance? Was I behind you in the supermarket? If it was you at the checkout, I liked your skirt. If it wasn't you, was it your friend, a colleague, or maybe somebody you've never met? If it wasn't you, who was it? I certainly chose someone in town today.

If it is you, I shall know before you realize what's happened. Does that seem complicated? Don't be deceived. My plan is simple and elegant. I've done my research, completed my planning and made my choices. Now all I have to do is wait. Whoever you are, I'm here, waiting for a response.

Will you be the one? Why do I ask? I ask because I don't know which of my chosen women it will be. I won't know her until she makes a choice, until she chooses herself. How will she do that? One simple everyday decision is all that's required. Take that decision, make that choice and you will have offered yourself. Follow it through and you will have let me into your life. You will be blind to the implications of your action, but be in no doubt, I know exactly what I'm doing.

Did I choose you? If I chose you today you wouldn't be aware of it. If I didn't choose you today maybe I'll choose you tomorrow, or the day after, or next week. I choose and I wait.

I'm patient. Patience is easy when I'm in control. One day soon, one of my chosen women will return the favour. Perhaps it will be you. I'm out here waiting. Waiting is easy because the outcome is inevitable. One of you will choose me; it's only a matter of time.

Perhaps it has happened already. Perhaps you've chosen me. Is your door locked? Are the windows secured? Don't bother checking. If you've chosen me, I have your key. You haven't given your key to a stranger? Are you sure? If you've chosen me you will have given me a key, invited me into your home – and into your life. You will have made the choice, but I will be in control.

I may bide my time, but don't be fooled, I'm here waiting. Delaying the moment will prolong my anticipation and bring added pleasure. When the time is right, it will happen. Even then I'll be patient, enjoying your slow realization that you no longer have a choice, that you must accept your fate. Eventually, you'll give me everything. You'll give me the act I desire – you'll show you want me by giving yourself.

Why am I doing this? It's not as bad as you might think. All I want is for you to want me. I need to see, hear and feel you giving yourself to me. I want the moment of giving more than the gift itself. But it's not that simple. There's more to it than that. To be sure of the giving I must take the gift. Although the moment of giving will be the epitome of my pleasure I shall enjoy the entire dance from comprehension to panic, from panic to horror, then submission and sacrifice. No, not submission, not sacrifice. Your willingness will not be enough. I can be patient. I shall be patient. I will be patient. I shall not take the gift until your desire to give matches my desire for the giving.

2

DI Ed Ogborne wasn't in the best of moods. She faced a day spent tying up loose ends from the team's last major case, serial abductions which stretched back a decade. It had been Ed's first case in Canterbury. They'd caught the perpetrator, but his evil deeds continued to haunt her. Revisiting the investigation wasn't something she relished, but, as the Senior Investigating Officer, she had to do it.

On her way to work, she picked up a flat white from Deakin's, hoping it would kick-start the morning. It didn't. When she arrived at the Police Station, her humour darkened immediately; there was a new addition to the CID Room door. Some jobsworth responsible for signage was clearly out to ruin her day. Above the names of her three colleagues, she was designated *Detective Inspector Edina Ogborne*.

For most this would have been a non-issue, but Ed was sensitive when it came to her given name. Edina came from her grandmother, but only Ed's parents and her grandfather had ever used it. From an early age she'd insisted everybody else call her Ed, or maybe Eddie if it were someone she knew intimately. In her mind, Edina was a homely, wholesome name; for herself she wanted something short, matching her sharply cut, blue-black hair.

After several phone calls, she eventually tracked down the man responsible for the increase in her ill humour.

'The sign on our door needs to be corrected. I'm DI Ed Ogborne, not Edina.'

'I'm sorry, Inspector, the official records show your name as Edina.'

'That's as may be, but I'm known as Ed.'

'We're obliged to use the official form of your name.'

'What do I have to do? Change it by deed poll?'

'If you wish Ed to be your official—'

'Thank you for your time.'

Ed terminated the call with the feeling she should have been more gracious. Then, with a wry smile, she put aside her increasing annoyance by thinking that the issue of her name was probably already an in-joke among her colleagues.

on how I handle things once we're alone together. I've pulled off

3

Confident but cautious – that's me to a T. Can you be truly confident if you're cautious? Let's not go there. I know what I mean. I'm confident when I'm in control. I'm confident and in control because I plan. Careful planning is where the caution comes in.

The project has been up and running for three months. I'd chosen Canterbury for the main event. It's a good-sized town, there's easy access to the countryside and I could readily lose myself among the tourists. I'd rented a small flat and spent a week or so choosing my women. The first to take the bait wasn't suitable: married and expecting a baby. How did I miss that? Sloppy work, but no problem. Statistically, it had to happen and, not long after, I got the perfect woman: single, unattached and living alone. She wanted the right things, things that made her vulnerable, and she made the right choice. She offered me access and now the incidentals are all in place; that's stage 1 completed. Soon, I'll complete stage 2 and she'll be mine; we'll be isolated together in her own home.

When that happens, we'll be at the crux of the project, stage 3, conversion; leading my chosen woman from her initial panic and horror to a position from where she'll recognize my true worth. Obviously, successful conversion will depend on how I handle things once we're alone together. The problem is, I'd no experience of that. Back in Gravesend, the stuck-up graduates at work had all turned me down. I was reduced to clubbing and copping off with the thin girl's friend. Unfortunately, they were easy, did anything, anytime, anything to please. With them it was open access and willing isolation: no conversion required. The women I want are not like that.

I'd known from the start that I'd need practice, the right experience; gaining that experience became a parallel part of the project. Confident but cautious, I took time to plan and prepare: a cheap phone, a couple of pay-as-you-go SIM cards and a dating app for which I created two fake profiles. To find the right practice woman, I'd need to meet several and check out promising candidates more than once. When it was over, if any of them complained to the police, I didn't want to be tracked down. Public places have security cameras and my bleached hair is eye-catching. I bought several simple disguises, as many as possible from charity shops. Faded baseball caps and worn beanies were good; lightweight reversible hoodies and a reversible cotton bag were essential.

My plan was to pick less attractive women from the dating app, reckoning that would maximize my hit rate. Location wasn't important; any small town in Kent, apart from Canterbury, would do. By day, I worked on the main event – my chosen women. The evenings I put aside for my practice runs – nothing fancy, just well planned. I'd let the women choose where and when we met, as long as it was a large bar, in the centre of town, and at a busy time of day.

Using my first fake profile, I went for Jackie from Rainham. She was immediately up for it. I asked where she'd like to meet and we settled on a pub near the station at six-thirty;

a time when I knew there'd be plenty of commuters dropping in for a drink after work. I arrived a little late, bought a pint, checked where she was sitting and positioned myself to observe without being seen. After a few minutes I changed my hat and jacket in the Gents and returned to my pint. It was quite touching watching her angular face, expectant, then concerned, checking her phone for messages, and finally crestfallen.

Eventually, she left the pub and I followed her home, taking great care to hang well back and to walk on the opposite pavement. She turned into a street lined with semi-detached bungalows and my heart sank. Sure enough, she lived with a couple of wrinklies, probably her parents. There was no way I'd have time to get rid of neighbours, let alone people in the same house. My practice woman had to live alone and in a spot with nobody close by.

4

The day was coming to an end and the young Detective Constables Jenny Eastham and Nat Borrowdale were the first to leave the CID Room, but not together. Jenny let Nat get well clear of the building before she locked files in her desk drawer and said she was off for an early night. Ed had noticed the atmosphere between Jenny and Nat had changed dramatically. They'd always been competitive but now there was a new edge to their exchanges. At team meetings Nat had stopped trying to catch Jenny's eye; in fact, he noticeably avoided doing so.

It wasn't her concern but, from soon after her arrival in Canterbury, Ed had wondered if Nat was the right man for Jenny. Physically, they were a strikingly attractive couple. Nat's dark hair and sharp features contrasted markedly with Jenny's fresh face and honey-blonde head. Ed's doubt came from her perception of them as people. Jenny was bright, open and honest. Nat was more closed, with a suggestion of potential danger behind his eyes.

Ed watched the door close behind Jenny before turning back to the document on her screen. A few minutes later, her second-in-command, Detective Sergeant Mike Potts, stretched, yawned loudly and pushed back his chair before levering his somewhat overweight frame to its feet.

'D'you fancy a drink before calling it a night?'

At that moment Ed could think of nothing better than a cold glass of white wine, but she was determined to finish the job she'd set herself.

'Sorry, Mike, I must finish this. I can't face one more day with these abductions.'

'Another time then. I'm off, see you tomorrow.'

Ed had just re-gathered her thoughts when the telephone rang. It was DI Saunders, calling from Maidstone.

'Hi, Brian, what can I do for you?'

'I'm calling to ask a favour.'

'Hit me.'

'We've just appointed a new DS.'

'And?'

'He's sharp, but still a bit police school. I want him to start thinking laterally, outside the box. I was wondering if—'

'Surely you can handle that?'

'Yes ... but I think you'd do a better job.'

'What do you have in mind?'

'If you could spend an hour with him, talk through the way you handled the serial abductions investigation.'

Ed thought for a moment and then decided to reward herself with a trip to Maidstone.

'Okay ... how about tomorrow? I could get over to you by nine.'

'Give me five minutes. I'll call you back.'

Twelve minutes later Ed's phone rang. It was Brian.

'First thing tomorrow's not good for him. Is there any chance you could make it after eleven?'

'Tell him I'll be there at half past.'

'Thanks, Ed, I'll make sure he's here waiting.'

'By the way, what's his name?'

'It's Dan, DS Daniel Wheadon. As I said, he's not been with us long. It will be good for him to have a chat with you.'

'No problem, but you owe me.' Ed paused as her memories of previous visits to Maidstone came flooding back. 'Remember those coffees you used to greet me with? It would be good if Dan did the same.'

'Consider it done.'

5

DS Daniel Wheadon looked younger than his 26 years. Short sandy hair, tight and wiry against his head, enhanced his boyish features. His clothes hung easily on a slim, lithe body which, as Ed would discover, was more muscular than it first appeared. He'd greeted her with a coffee in each hand and led her to an Interview Room where they sat in chairs arranged at right angles across the corner of the table.

'Right. Brian said you'd like to hear about our recent case of serial abduction.'

Dan looked a little embarrassed. 'He said I'd learn a lot from the methods you used to solve the case. It would be a privilege to hear it from the Senior Officer.'

'It was a team effort. I've got a good bunch of colleagues in Canterbury. As for DI Saunders, we didn't overlap much, but from what I saw of Brian, you're lucky to be working with him.'

'We've got on well so far.'

'Keep it that way.' Ed paused. 'Thanks for the coffee.' She took a sip and then began. 'Right, I'll take you through the investigation from the beginning. Stop me at any time if you have a question.'

Fifty minutes later, coffees drained, they'd finished their chat. Daniel picked up the empty cups. 'I'll just get rid of these.'

Ed smiled. 'I'll go to the loo and meet you back here.'

As Ed re-entered the corridor, she saw DS Wheadon standing by the Interview Room door. At the sound of her footsteps, he turned and smiled.

'It's a bit early, but, if you're not in a hurry, I thought we might grab some lunch. There's a pub round the corner.'

'I was thinking the same thing.' Ed didn't add she'd been thinking the same thing ever since Daniel had introduced himself earlier that morning.

The pub was literally around the corner.

'I'll go to the bar. What'll you have?'

'A sandwich would be good, anything but tuna.'

'Drink?'

'Tonic, ice and lemon,' said Ed, 'I'm driving back to Canterbury this afternoon.'

Familiar as she was with the drinking habits of old colleagues at the Met, Ed didn't remind him they were technically on duty, so she was pleased to see Daniel return with her tonic and a mineral water for himself.

'Cheers.' Daniel touched his glass against Ed's. 'Thanks for making time to talk me through the investigation. I'd already heard about the neat way you narrowed your search for the abductor's hideout. It's entered local folklore.'

Ed smiled inwardly, but she wasn't about to bask in perceived glory. 'As I said, I've got a good team at Canterbury.' She took a mouthful of tonic. 'How about you?'

'I came here from Medway, Chatham actually, to get my promotion to Sergeant. Still settling in, but I'm getting on well with the team – as you said, Brian Saunders is a good boss.'

'And apart from work?'

'Rugby. I used to play for Medway, now I've transferred to Maidstone. You?'

'Nothing so energetic. I work out at the gym, but since I outgrew self-defence classes, I prefer to spend my free time in a wine bar or restaurant.'

Daniel's phone rang, but he ignored it. 'Favourite food?'

'I'm open to anything, but if pushed, I'd say Italian. We're well served in Canterbury. There's a good family-run *trattoria* near the County Courts.'

With her eyes on Daniel, Ed stirred her drink, waiting for him to reply.

'We're playing a summer friendly at Canterbury next Saturday. If you're free, and fancy meeting for a meal, I'll forgo the post-match beers.'

'I'd like that. Are you sure you'll be up for it?'

'Friendlies aren't particularly gentle, but I'll make sure I'm intact.'

'Excellent. I'll book Gino's, the Italian, for seven-thirty if that suits.'

'Sounds good to me. The match will finish late afternoon. I could meet you earlier.'

'Okay. Here's my mobile number. Call me when you're free. Perhaps we could meet for a drink before eating.'

6

By now, counting Jackie from Rainham, I'd worked my way through seventeen lonely women in flat-shares, bedsits or still living at home. Frankly, I was getting anxious. Everything was in place for the main event. In less than a fortnight, I'd have to move in on my chosen woman in Canterbury. Then, just when I thought the practice run would be a nonstarter, I struck lucky; Kay from Dover, the eighteenth woman from the dating app, was up for it.

Kay was great, no need to nudge her at all. When I asked where we should meet, she opted for a pub in the town centre at seven-thirty, but then insisted we swap numbers, in case something came up. I set up a WhatsApp account because it's encrypted, but she didn't use it. I was on the train to meet her in Dover, when she texted, asking if we were still on. I replied, sure, see you there, which was exactly what I intended to do. After a drink near the railway station, I arrived at our rendez-vous ten minutes late. On my way to the bar, I caught sight of Kay from the corner of my eye. Keeping my back to her, I bought a pint and moved away to a stool from where I could see her, but there was little chance she'd notice me. Anyway, if she did look in my direction, she'd be searching for the guy in my fake profile; she'd not give me a second glance.

Kay from Dover was sitting alone, at a table by the wall. To my surprise, she looked exactly like her photo; face a little chubby with too much make-up. Her clothes, a loose top and knee-length skirt, did nothing to disguise the fact that she was more than a little overweight. Definitely not my type, but what the hell, she was only a practice run. I went to the Gents, reversed my hoodie, turned my cotton bag inside out, swapped my beanie for a baseball cap and went back to my pint.

Fifty minutes after we were due to meet, Kay was looking thoroughly miserable and she showed signs of being about to leave. I drained my glass, slipped out ahead of her and lingered across the road, checking my phone. When Kay left, she walked along the Folkestone Road towards the outskirts of Dover. I hung back and followed on the opposite pavement. When she turned into a side street, I pretended to look at my phone and saw her go into a small block of flats with a For Sale sign by the door. I watched the dark windows of the building until a light went on in a second-floor window, to the right of the entrance. Pocketing my phone, I walked further along the Folkestone Road and then circled back, to stroll past the building and check the agent's board.

Maxton House
AVAILABLE SOON
SIX ONE-BED FLATS
NEWLY RENOVATED

The next day, I rang the estate agency and – bingo. Renovation was scheduled to start in a month, when the last remaining tenant would have moved out. She might not be my ideal woman, but for this stage of my project, Kay from Dover was perfect. She lived alone and the other flats in her block were empty.

I've now been watching Kay carefully for a week, whenever I could get away from Canterbury. She works in a corner shop on the main Folkestone Road. For lunch she takes a sandwich and a bottle of water to a small park, where she sits by herself on a bench facing the gate. Outside the shop, Kay doesn't speak to anyone. It's almost too good to be true; her home is isolated and she's a loner. As soon as I'm sure, I switch to my other pay-as-you-go SIM, get on the dating app and hit her with my second fake profile. Once more, Kay from Dover is up for it and we arrange to meet next Thursday. She's chosen the same time and the same pub. I could get there early and wait for her to arrive, but, just for the buzz, I'll follow her into town.

On Thursday, I took the train from Canterbury. As we entered Dover Priory station, my phone buzzed with a text from Kay. I replied, reassuring her our date was still on. It's early evening as I walk along the Folkestone Road with plenty of time to pass Maxton House and wait, further down the side street, for Kay to leave. I know where she's going, The Three Horseshoes, so I don't need to be close as I follow her to the pub. When she goes inside, I walk straight on, to kill ten to fifteen minutes looking in shop windows before returning to our rendezvous.

Kay's at the same table. I buy a pint and take a stool close to where I sat the last time we were here. Watching her face, I almost feel sorry for her as expectation becomes concern and then the inevitable disappointment. What do the military call it – collateral damage?

I swap my hoodie and baseball cap for a plaid shirt and a

balaclava rolled to look like a beanie. After waiting for an hour, Kay leaves the pub and I follow at a distance on the far side of the road. I follow her into her side street, quicken my pace and close in as she approaches Maxton House. No need for subtlety. I pull the balaclava down over my face, tailgate her through the street door, grab the keys from her hand, bundle her up two flights of stairs, turn to the right, open the door and push her into the flat.

She's screaming, but no one will hear; there's no one else in the building. I force her onto the bed and sit on her chest to tie her arms to the headboard. She's still struggling and crying out at the top of her voice. I turn, sit on her knees, and tie her legs to the foot of the bed. When I get up to check the knots at her wrists and ankles, her screaming has turned to pleading, but she's still struggling against her bonds. The knots are fine; she won't be able to escape.

The flat's not warm, but I'm sweating and the blood's pounding in my head. I must get out for some fresh air. Before leaving, I need a sample of her writing, her mobile, her real name and the keys to the flat. I also need a pee.

In the bathroom, zipping up, I'm aware there's no longer any sound from Kay. I flush and dash to the bedroom. Kay's still on her back but she's silent and no longer struggling. Her eyes are closed. I rock her head from side to side. She doesn't respond. The silly bitch has fainted. To make her more comfortable I flip off her shoes and let them fall to the floor. Now for the things I need. I look for something with her writing on. No sweat. There's a diary on a box by the bed. I put it in my pocket. From her bag, on the floor by the entrance, I take her mobile and a bank card. Ready to go, I let myself out, pulling her keys from the lock as I leave.

Outside, I swap the balaclava for a baseball cap, leave the building and circle the block before heading back to the centre of Dover for a pizza. At a corner table, I check her things. The phone's switched on. I open the dating app. There's the meet with me, or rather my second fake profile, but no other dates. The same is true of her texts: nothing since our last meeting except the exchange earlier this evening. No complications there. I open her diary. It's schoolgirl writing, easy to copy. I get her name and signature from the bank card, noticing she'd used her real name on the dating app. After a few practice attempts, copying the writing from the diary until I'm fluent, I write a short note.

Need a break. Sorry for short notice. Back in two weeks. Kayleigh Robson.

All's going to plan. I pay the bill with cash and step into the street.

It's still early and I'm not ready to confront Kayleigh just yet. There's a pub next to the pizzeria. I drink a couple of pints while leafing through her diary. God, I thought my life was bad but hers – no friends, just occasional guys from the dating app. Some have hung around long enough to cop a shag, but none has lasted beyond a third date. What a life. Well, things have changed, Kayleigh Robson, you're going to have my company for a week or two. I won't be able to remove my mask, but I hope you come to see my worth and enjoy my company.

On the way back to Maxton House, I push the note under the door of the corner shop. The flat's still silent. Kayleigh's spread-eagled on her back just as I left her. In our struggle, her skirt has bunched around her waist. I don't want her to be embarrassed when she comes round, so I lean over the bed and ease the skirt down to cover her thighs. My fingers brush her skin. It's cold.

Panicking, I feel her wrist and neck. No pulse – nothing!

What the fuck!

Kayleigh's dead.

7

It was late afternoon. Ed had just got back to her apartment when her personal mobile buzzed with a message from Daniel. His rugby friendly had finished and he was waiting for her in the bar of a large hotel on the High Street. The County was the last place Ed wanted to meet him, but she didn't want to raise questions by suggesting he move somewhere else. Instead, she called him back.

'Hi, Daniel, I've just got home and I'm about to take a shower.'

Ed paused for a response, but he remained silent, waiting for her to continue.

'If you don't get ideas, you could come here and we'll have that drink at my place before going out to eat.'

'If that works for you. Where are you?'

Ed gave him her address and then added, 'Give me fifteen minutes.' She was just stepping into the shower when the phone rang again. With a curse, she dashed into her bedroom to answer it.

'Hi, Ed, I know it's short notice, but I was wondering if you fancied a drink?'

It was her friend Verity Shaw, who edited the local newspaper.

'Hi, Verity, a drink sounds good but I've got something on this evening. How about next Friday?'

'Next Friday would be good. I'll look forward to catching up.'

'Me too. Sorry, but I've got to dash. Bye.'

'Until next week. Bye.'

Back under the shower, Ed wondered if she'd have time to blow-dry her hair.

Daniel arrived with flowers and a sports bag, which he dropped in the hall. Neither of them mentioned it when it was time to leave for the restaurant. The bag remained where Daniel had left it until late Sunday evening when he returned to Maidstone.

8

'Are you sure it's above board?' asked Rachael.

Ostensibly to say goodbye, her boss had looked into the room at the back of the dental practice where Gina Hamilton was collecting her things. The holiday had been a surprise and Rachael was obviously curious.

'Of course. It's organized by Tuscan Sun Tours. I was sent their brochure. They're an ABTA tour company. I've even checked the travel agents in the High Street. They've got the same brochure with my holiday in it. A week in Orvieto and then Siena.'

Gina closed her locker, anxious to get home. She was looking forward to an early night before starting her holiday. Rachael, nosey as usual, wouldn't be deflected.

'What about your ticket?'

'I rang the tour company to confirm the flight number and check-in times at Gatwick. They had my name on their list for the tour. We'll be in Siena when they have that horse race, the Palio, and a seat in the stands was included as a special option. I've wanted to go ever since a guy at university described seeing it.'

'Sounds like you'll have a great time. Be careful of those Italian men.' Rachael smiled. 'We're going to miss you.'

'It's only a fortnight. Sorry I wasn't able to give you more notice.'

'Don't worry. I've lined up a locum.'

Gina bent to pick up her bag and turned to leave but Rachael stood between her and the door.

'By the way, you never said – how did you win it?'

'Last month I got one of those circulars through the door: a competition linked to a new singles club. They organize groups for dinner parties, trips to the theatre, weekends away – that sort of thing. I had to write twenty words saying why I would value membership and send my answer with a request for further details. Actually, that reminds me – not that I'm interested – I won the holiday but I still haven't received details of the club.'

'It sounds like a great holiday. Lucky you!' Rachael stepped aside. 'I'll not keep you. I expect you want to pack and get an early night. Have a wonderful time.'

'Thanks. See you in a fortnight.'

Gina took the stairs down to the front entrance and stepped into the street. At the ATM in the High Street, she introduced her card, tapped in her PIN and selected cash with receipt. Gina was impatient. Every time she entered or left the practice, her eyes were drawn to the much-polished brass plate by the door. It still read *Metcalffe and Metcalffe, Dental Practice* followed by *Morris Metcalffe, Rachael Metcalffe* and, on a newer strip of brass, *Georgina Hamilton*. How long before a new plate read *Metcalffe, Metcalffe and Hamilton*? Bleeping from the ATM interrupted Gina's thoughts. She retrieved her card, folded the cash into her purse together with the receipt, and doubled back down Guildhall for the 15-minute walk home.

9

I thought it might take a while to get through but there were only three rings before someone answered.

'Hello, Tuscan Sun Tours. Clare speaking, how may I help you?'

'I'm calling on behalf of my sister—'

'I'm sorry, Sir, perhaps we could start with your name. You are Mr ...?'

'Hamilton, Colin Hamilton. I booked a place on your Tuscan tour, which leaves Gatwick tomorrow morning—'

'Is that Tour TST247, Sir?'

'Yes, that's right. A fortnight in Tuscany, a week in Orvieto followed by a week in—'

'I'm sorry, Sir, are you sure it's TST247? I have the passenger list on screen but your name doesn't appear. There's a G Hamilton but that's a woman.'

'Yes, my sister, Georgina Hamilton. I'm calling on her behalf. I wish to cancel her booking.'

'I'm sorry, Sir, before making a change to a booking we must speak with the principal traveller.'

'If I'd got my secretary to call, you'd speak with her and cancel the booking.'

'No, Sir, as I said, I would need to speak directly with the principal traveller, Ms Georgina Hamilton.'

'And how would you know the woman you were talking to was or wasn't Georgina Hamilton?'

'We have security questions.'

'And they are?'

'Personal, Sir, and I cannot discuss a client's personal details with anybody but the client. I must speak directly with Ms Hamilton.'

'I'm privy to more of my sister's personal information than you will ever be. She may be the one travelling, but I booked and paid for the holiday as a surprise.'

'That may be so, Sir, but the holiday is booked under her name and she is the only traveller. I must speak with her if I am to make changes to the booking.'

'Clare, if we continue talking in circles I shall have to speak with your superior and we don't want that, do we? I didn't want to mention more personal information than is necessary but you are forcing my hand. I'm sorry to say Georgie, my sister Ms Georgina Hamilton, has been taken ill and she will not be able to go on the tour. She has asked me to cancel the holiday on her behalf.'

'We are very sorry to hear that Ms Hamilton is sick, Sir, but as I'm sure you'll appreciate, our procedures are in place to protect our clients.'

'I appreciate your position, Clare, but at present my sister is too poorly to come to the telephone. She has been prescribed complete bed rest and must not be disturbed. Please don't force me to speak with your supervisor. I know what—'

'I'm sorry, Sir, but we must follow our procedures.'

'Clare, please let me finish.'

I paused to ensure her silence and then continued to speak firmly but without emotion.

'I anticipated this might be problematic so I visited my local travel agent and explained my position. They told me that to cancel the booking I would need to return with Georgina's passport, all the holiday documents and the original payment details. I could do that, but I didn't make the booking at the agency; I arranged the holiday directly by telephone with your company. So Clare, am I to read the contents of those documents to you or to your superior?'

'Just a moment, Sir – may I put you on hold while I speak with my manager?'

'Please do and stress that we should resolve this matter quickly because I need to return to my sister's bedside.'

There was a click and cheerful classical music filled the earpiece. I was confident I'd get my way. I could always take the documentation to the High Street travel agent but I wanted to keep my local exposure to a minimum. The music stopped and Clare returned to the line.

'Thank you for holding, Mr Hamilton. In view of the exceptional circumstances we will accept the cancellation provided you can confirm the booking reference and Ms Georgina Hamilton's address plus details from her passport.'

I began to relay the information. 'The booking reference is T, S, T, zero, zero, two, one, three, H, A, M, zero, one.'

'And Ms Hamilton's address?'

'Thirty-two, Great Stour Court, Canterbury.'

'And the postcode, Sir?'

'It's CT2 7US.'

For Gina's passport details I had to pay close attention to

the photograph on my mobile. With that completed I thought Tuscan Sun Tours would be satisfied but no, Clare also wanted details of the original payment.

'Rather old-fashioned,' I said in a lighter voice, conveying a smile. 'It was a surprise for my sister. I paid with a postal order. I have a note of the serial number here somewhere ...'

'Thank you, Sir, that won't be necessary.' Clare paused and resumed apologetically, 'I'm afraid that for such a late cancellation we will not be able to offer you a refund.'

'The money isn't important. Georgie just wanted you to know that she will not be joining the tour.'

'Thank you, Sir. I have made a note.'

'Will that information be available to everybody in your organization? My sister is very unwell. I don't want her bothered by telephone enquiries about her failure to show up at Gatwick.'

'That will not happen, Sir. A note that Ms Hamilton has withdrawn from TST247 is now on our company-wide system. Please give your sister our very best wishes for a speedy recovery. If she returns the confirmation and travel pack we'll send a voucher for 10 per cent off her next booking.' There was a brief pause before Clare added, 'Is there anything else I can help you with today, Sir?'

'No, thank you. Goodbye.'

'Goodbye, Sir, and thank you for calling Tuscan Sun Tours.'

10

I am feeling good. It's gone well. This won't be like Dover. That was a practice run. This is for real and extensively planned. This woman is perfect – elegant, slim, sexy and with long fair hair of the kind that only models and posh girls manage to have. Back in Gravesend, when I was at Scotts, she'd have been one of the smart set, the graduates who looked down on the likes of me. One of those confident professional women I wanted but couldn't have – the unobtainable.

Things are different now. I'm in control. There'll be no put-down this time.

I've learnt a lot, come a long way, learnt how to handle people, people like the woman at Sun Tours. She'd been resistant, exercising her power – 'It's procedure, Sir.' I soon put her in her place.

It hasn't always been like this. I wasn't born with that confidence. It came when I started spending the money. I soon learnt how to get what I wanted. Not only does money make people want your custom, money also gives you the assurance not to take no for an answer. I guess a good education does the same, but that wasn't on offer when I was young. I'm bright, but I didn't pass the 11+ exam. My dad said I was a late developer. My mum, wiping her hands on her apron, and turning away to hide the look in her eyes, said she didn't know where I got it all from. 'Not y' dad – or me, that's for sure,' she'd added diplomatically.

They loved me, my parents, and I loved them, but none of us was good at showing emotion.

At school I got into computers and wanted my own. I remember the first time I asked for one.

'Dad, can I have a computer for my birthday?'

'We can't afford one, son.' His eyes, which had flicked up when I spoke, had already returned to his newspaper.

I was desperate. I pleaded. 'Birthday and Christmas combined?'

No dice. His eyes remained fixed on the sports page.

'Maybe when I win the pools, lad, but it'll have to be a big win.'

Dad never did have that big win, at least not while he was alive. He joined Mum in East Hill cemetery some six years after I'd left the Tech to work in electronics at Scotts. I inherited the house, but Dad's building society account didn't even stretch to a new computer. I planned to sell up and move to a new-build apartment, but, in the meantime, I carried on working at Scotts. It must have been three months before I went into Dad's room to clear out his things. I thought there might be something I could sell. There wasn't, but I did find his pools coupons. He'd been very tidy. They were piled in date order with the one for the week he died on top. The games had been selected and the form completed, ready to post. The season hadn't finished. I found the current coupon, marked the same lines and posted it in my name as a last throw of the old man's dice.

I won. Well ... to be fair, he won. Dad's system finally turned

31

up trumps. It was a big win, a very big win. Although I'd ticked the 'no publicity' box they tried to persuade me, but there was no way I was going to be photographed with a cheque the size of a billboard. I carried on working for another 18 months. With the cash to give a girl a good time I asked a few of the women at work for a date. There were no takers. The stuck-up graduates had *in your dreams, geek* written all over their faces. I had to lower my sights.

I started going to football and buying drinks for the guys I'd known at college. I was generous. I fixed their computers and sometimes they'd take me to a club. I took what was on offer but I wanted more, I wanted better. I wanted a bright woman, a woman who'd been to university, a graduate like those who'd turned me down. It was then I had the idea and started working on my plan. I resigned from my job, stopped going to football and gave up clubbing. I told everyone I'd inherited some money and was going on a long trip to Australia.

In fact, I went to London. I spent one night in a small hotel changing my appearance and then rented a cheap bedsit in a run-down part of town. Immediately, I put my plan into action. First, I had to identify women who took my fancy and try to get their names from their credit cards. I trawled ATMs and supermarket checkouts. It was often easier on the tube, but that wouldn't be any use because I intended to operate in small towns. I soon discovered it wasn't as difficult as I'd first thought. There was no need to have an exact name because I was patient. I had all the time in the world. I couldn't believe how many partial names I could confirm using company websites. A pattern developed. I'd follow a target back to her work and, later, back to where she lived. Some of the women even had their names by their doorbells.

As soon as I'd lined up a target who lived alone, I could have broken in, but that wasn't my plan. If I forced my way in, they'd shout and scream, the neighbours would hear, call the police and I'd be in serious trouble. Even if no one heard, I didn't want that, I didn't want rape.

I knew exactly what I wanted. I wanted my chosen woman to have time to get to know me. I wanted her to know my worth, to want me, to give herself to me. She would have to invite me into her home. She would have to trust me with a key. There must be no neighbours around. Once I was inside I knew it would take time. She wasn't going to come round overnight, so she mustn't be missed at work. It was a problem. It was a whole string of problems. How could I pull it off?

One day I came back from finding targets and trod on the answer as I came through the door from the street. So simple! So elegant! It just required patience and time. With the old man's pools win sitting in the bank I had plenty of both.

Actually, that's not completely true. The money was in the bank because that's where it went when I won it. Most is still there, but when I began developing my plan I knew I couldn't use cards, cheques or ATMs. I couldn't afford to leave traces. I didn't intend to get caught. Dad's pools system had given me a really big win. I'd never have to work again so, when it was over, I wanted to walk away and live the good life. I got plastic boxes, a good pair of walking shoes, and a mountaineer's folding shovel. Every two or three weeks I withdrew cash and buried bundles of notes in isolated spots within easy reach of Canterbury, my chosen town, where I'd already rented a flat. I took my time. Finally, with everything in place, I selected my women.

In Canterbury it's gone just as I knew it would. One of my

chosen women made a choice that offered me access. Now I've closed the net. This time it will go right. Not like last time. I've got to get Dover out of my head. Kayleigh Robson wasn't my type, not a top choice, but she wasn't my ultimate goal; Kayleigh was a practice run. My aim was to get experience of conversion, of winning a woman round. For that, Kay from Dover was a necessary component but she wasn't meant to die. No one was meant to die. I'm not into killing people. What happened was unfortunate, a freak accident, regrettable, but nothing to do with my planning. One moment Kayleigh was fine – well, she was struggling and screaming – but then she fainted. I made her comfortable before going for a pizza and a couple of pints to settle my head. When I got back, she was dead.

The last thing I wanted was to be linked to her death and caught by the police. For a moment or two I panicked – in that situation anyone would panic – but I quickly gained control and planned what to do: destroy her mobile, mine too with both its SIM cards, and scrupulously clean her flat of all traces of my presence. She had no proper cleaning stuff in the flat so I had to go shopping. In a side street, near the centre of town, I found a late-night store and bought what I needed. Back at the flat, I cleaned scrupulously. Working gently, wearing vinyl gloves, I removed Kayleigh's bonds, turned her on her side and used enough of her concealer to hide the reddening at her wrists and ankles. It wasn't perfect, but there's not been a word on the news or in the papers, so it was good enough to fool some hack of a police doctor.

Now all is calm, I'm back in Canterbury and my chosen one is perfect. I need time alone with her, time for her to see beyond the surface, time for her to get to know the real me.

Given time, she'll come to see my true worth. Later, we'll look back and laugh about the way we met. She'll thank me for being so clever. We'll be happy together.

Earlier today, I got some food and drink; it's here in her fridge. Everything's in place. I'm relaxed, sitting quietly, waiting for my chosen one to return home.

11

Alone in the CID Room, Ed glanced at her watch. There was no hurry, but she'd reached a good place to stop. Shutting down the computer, she slipped her mobile into her bag and left the Station on foot. In the city centre, she crossed the Buttermarket to Sun Street and took a window table in Deakin's where she toyed with a mineral water, wishing Verity Shaw was already there to distract her from her thoughts.

Last June, transferred to Canterbury from the London Met, Ed had been pitched straight into the disappearance of a local schoolgirl. With her new team she'd discovered the case was one of a series of abductions stretching back ten years. The perpetrator was now in jail awaiting trial. However, although the investigation was effectively wound up, Ed still woke at night with an image of the abductor in her head. She had worked on horrendous crimes with the Met, but in London she'd been able to switch off and walk away. With the abductions in Canterbury it had been different. For the first time in her career, the images stayed with her, not because she had led the investigation, but because she couldn't forget the mothers separated from their daughters. The image of the abductor returned and she shuddered at the evil he had perpetrated.

As she took another sip of water, Ed's honesty forced her to concede she was troubled by more than recurrent thoughts of the abductions. She would never let her mood influence her work, but for some months she'd felt decidedly below par. Not down, exactly, but until recently things had not been as she would have liked. Ed knew herself well enough to know the reason. There had been a long gap without a man in her life.

Men!

They'd not always treated her well; indeed, a few had treated her badly. Ed could live without them, but on balance, she would rather have a bastard in her bed than no one at all. This time, perhaps, she'd struck lucky. So far there had been no sign that Daniel was a bastard. He was fit and attentive, but he was another cop and that should be warning enough.

12

Gina Hamilton weaved through the meandering tourists on Mercery Lane and Sun Street. Quickening her pace, she left the city centre and headed home via Palace Street. Mechanically following the familiar route, she was still wondering how long it would be before the Metcalffes offered her a partnership in their dental practice.

'Bhaaarrrr!'

Gina stopped abruptly at the edge of the kerb, jolted from her thoughts by the blare of a car horn. The number of pedestrians had thinned rapidly and the street was narrowing between flint buildings and a high brick wall. From nowhere she felt a twinge of apprehension, a cold tension between her shoulder blades. She'd felt it before, as if someone were watching her, following her, but that had been weeks ago. Approaching the dogleg beside the entrance to The King's School she glanced back. The pavement behind her appeared deserted but then, before she could be certain, she'd turned into The Borough and Palace Street had disappeared from view.

Why was she feeling so jumpy? The last time it happened, Gina had been unable to fathom what had sparked her apprehension and now she was equally unable to identify the source of her unease. Annoyed that she should feel so unsettled the evening before her holiday, Gina crossed the road to pick up a ready meal and a foil-sealed glass of white wine at the supermarket on Kingsmead.

'Snap!' said a guy behind her at the checkout.

Gina jumped at the sound of the male voice and turned to face the speaker. It was some stranger with a beard.

'Sorry?'

'Snap! Your items and mine; seems like we're both facing a lonely meal for one.'

Gina wanted to end this exchange quickly before he suggested they eat their meals together at his or hers.

'Sorry, I'm in a rush. I have to get back to pack for my holiday.'

What was she doing? That was way too much information – an open invite for him to continue the conversation. Fortunately, the assistant was scanning her last item. Gina, thinking quickly, put her card back into her purse and pulled out some cash.

'I guess you live nearby?'

'Sorry, can't stop, I must run.'

Gina picked up her bag and turned to leave.

'Excuse me, Madam.'

What now? It was the assistant. Surely the tenner would cover it.

'Yes ...?'

'You've forgotten your change, Madam.'

'That's okay. Put it in the charity box.'

'I shop here a lot so I'll see you around.'

Ignoring the stranger's parting shot, Gina walked towards the exit without looking back. Once outside, she paused to put her purse back in her shoulder bag. Zipping it closed, she saw the bearded guy about to follow her out. Without thinking she half ran around the side of the building to a gap in the fence and took the short cut home via the path by the river.

Hurrying along the rough track, she began to have second thoughts. The path appeared deserted but she was aware of someone behind her, their footsteps in time with her own. Was it the guy from the checkout? It couldn't be; she was sure he hadn't seen which way she went.

Gina continued walking, but the chill of apprehension and tension between her shoulder blades, which she'd felt earlier in Palace Street, had returned. Here on the lonely path, Gina was convinced someone was following her. She turned to look back, but could see no one there. Why couldn't the bastard, whoever he was, have come up to her in the street? She could have handled that. What was he playing at, hanging back, following her?

Gina knew she should have taken the main road. It was crazy to lead him down this deserted footpath under the trees by the river. Knowing it was too late now to change her mind, she quickened her pace. The illuminated area, which surrounded her block of flats, was just beyond the next bend.

Stepping into the light, Gina forced herself to walk normally to the rear entrance of her building. She opened the door and relaxed as it clicked shut behind her. The apprehension disappeared the moment there was a locked door between her and the outside world. Peering through the glass door panel, she was unable to see anyone outside. Whoever had been following her had stayed on the footpath, hidden by the bushes. Trying to dismiss the incident from her thoughts, she walked to the entrance foyer and paused to check her post box. It was empty.

Buying the apartment in Great Stour Court had stretched her financially. Even with her minimal social life, meeting the mortgage payments took much of her income, but she was happy. She loved her new home and she'd splurged her remaining cash on having her bedroom redecorated. She wasn't sorry, but that additional expense had put a holiday out of the question. It really had been her lucky day when she entered the singles club competition. *A chance to meet and mix with bright young professional people on equal terms for fun and maybe romance.* Never had twenty – well, actually nineteen – words been so profitable. Gina had been surprised she'd won the Tuscan holiday, but she wasn't going to complain.

Taking the lift to the third floor, she planned her evening. First, she'd pack, and then have a long soak in the bath before the ready meal, glass of wine and an early night.

13

Sitting in the kitchen, I hear a key in the lock. The front door opens and closes. Bleeping starts and then stops as the alarm is cancelled. My pulse remains steady despite a brief moment of doubt. I dismiss my unease. It must be Georgina. There'd been no trace of another person and no evidence in the flat, or on her laptop, that she knows anyone who'd have access to her home. Certainly, there's been no sign of a boyfriend.

I listen as she puts her keys on the side table in the hall. Everything is ready. Georgina is perfect. All will go well. All we need is some time together, time for her to get to know me, to see my worth.

I hear her turn and then pause. She's noticed the kitchen door's closed. I'm pleased. She's bright. The first few moments could be tricky, but I know exactly how I'm going to play this. Aroused by a sense of anticipation, I wait for the kitchen door to open.

14

Gina opened the door to her apartment and heard the reassuring sound of the alarm. She stepped inside, used her foot to close the door behind her and automatically tapped her code into the pad. Silence. Immediately she felt the warm contentment she always experienced when safely home. She resisted the impulse to look at her newly decorated bedroom; there would be time for that later. Since the workmen had finished, she had gone immediately to admire it every time she came home. Tonight would be different; tomorrow she was flying to Italy.

First things first: wine in the fridge and switch the oven on. Gina put her keys and handbag on the hall table, stepped towards the kitchen and stopped, puzzled. The door was closed. Something wasn't right. She always left the kitchen door open. Gina shrugged. This morning, preoccupied by thoughts of her holiday, she must have shut it without thinking.

'I'm here.'

Gina froze.

It was a man's voice.

Without thinking, she pushed the door open.

15

Gina was face to face with a man sitting at her kitchen table. He rose to his feet and she recognized his thin, almost emaciated body and the white-blond hair that fell sideways across his forehead.

'What on earth are *you* doing here?'

'I'm sorry if I startled you, Ms Hamilton. Mr Smith, Colin Smith ... of Decorart, the interior design company. We decorated your bedroom last week.'

He held out his hand, which Gina ignored.

'Yes, yes, I know who you are. More to the point, what are you doing here *now*?'

'A problem arose, Ms Hamilton.'

'A problem? What problem?' Gina's first thought was the money. She was stretched financially, but surely that wasn't the problem? When she had bought a new dress and two tops for her holiday, she'd calculated carefully that what remained in her account would cover the decorators' bill. 'Did I make a mistake with the cheque?'

'No problem with your cheque. It was our mistake. We inadvertently overcharged you for the work. I've come round to refund the balance.'

'You didn't need to come in person. A cheque in the post would have been fine.'

'I wanted to apologize to you directly and I thought this would be a good opportunity to make sure you were completely satisfied with our work. As you know—'

'Hang on!' Accustomed to seeing this man in her flat during the redecoration of her bedroom, Gina had lost sight of what was happening. 'We didn't have an appointment.' Anger welled inside her. 'How dare you come into my home uninvited?' Spurred by a nascent anxiety she added, 'This is outrageous.' Then, before he could answer, a further thought struck her. 'How did you get in?'

'With these ...' He reached into his pocket and dangled a set of keys. 'If you don't mind, I'd like to take some photographs for publicity—'

'Are they my keys?' Gina desperately tried to think back to when the work was finished and she'd given him the cheque. Had she overlooked getting her keys back in the excitement?

The man continued to speak, ignoring her question. 'As a thank you for letting us use the photographs I've taken the liberty of putting a bottle of champagne in your fridge. I thought we might celebrate the completion of the work.'

'You've done *what*?' Gina couldn't believe what she was hearing. 'You've come into my home uninvited, you've brought champagne and you want to celebrate! This is totally unacceptable. Please leave immediately.'

Struck by another thought, Gina added, 'Wait a minute. Where did you get those keys? I took my spare ones back. Look, they're hanging on the wall.'

'I had this set cut while the work was in progress.'

'*What*? You copied my keys! You can't just have somebody's keys copied!'

'Oh, but I can. These keys are not high security. Anybody can take them to a shoe repair shop and have copies cut in a few minutes.'

'But you've no right. You can't let yourself into other people's homes uninvited. Give me those keys and my refund, then leave my home immediately!'

'It wasn't like that. You invited me in and you gave me a set of keys so that I could return when you weren't here.'

'But that was for the decoration of my bedroom. I trusted you to return my keys when the work was finished.'

'I did return your keys. You said so yourself; they're hanging on the wall.'

'Yes, but you'd already had them copied.' Gina paused, frustrated that the exchange was going in circles. 'Your behaviour is intolerable. Give me the keys you're holding and get out of my home.'

He slowly returned the keys to his pocket.

'I'd rather stay.'

'Give me those keys and leave immediately!'

'But the champagne, the photographs—'

'There's no question of photographs. You can take the champagne with you.'

'Let's not be hasty, Georgina. I may call you Georgina?'

'It's Ms Hamilton to you. Now, give me those keys and go.'

He remained standing by the kitchen table. Gina's mind was racing. A new thought struck her.

'Wait a minute. This morning I set the burglar alarm. Just now, when I came in the alarm sounded and I cancelled it at the pad. The alarm was set but you were in the flat.'

'As I said, you invited me in. You gave me a code for the alarm. I used my code to enter the flat, reset the alarm and came to the kitchen before the alarm activated. There are no sensors in the kitchen.'

This man had an answer for everything. Why was he here? When she came home to find him sitting at the table her initial fright had quickly been replaced by anger. Now a growing sense of frustration that he wouldn't leave was morphing into an ominous apprehension. Whatever he wanted she must get him out of the flat before things slipped further from her control.

'Give me the refund, give me the extra set of keys and get out!'

'Georgina ...?'

'Leave now before I call the police.'

'Don't do that, Georgina. What harm can there be in a glass of champagne?'

'I've asked you repeatedly to leave my home. Leave at once or I'll call the police.'

He began to move round the table.

'And leave the keys.'

He stopped, opened the fridge and took out a bottle of champagne.

'And take your bottle with you.'

'It's vintage.'

'Give me the keys and leave.'

He began to open the bottle.

'Right, I'm calling the police.' Gina turned back to the hall. He made no move to stop her. She heard the cork pop behind her as she went to the telephone on the hall table.

'Where are the glasses?'

Gina began to dial 999.

'No matter, I'll find them myself.'

Two rings and then that reassuring voice: 'Which service do you require? Fire, police, or ambulance?'

'Police. And please ...'

The line went dead. Gina froze and began to panic until the connection went through.

'Canterbury Police Station: please state your name and address.'

'There's a man in my apartment. He won't leave. Please, send somebody – quickly!'

'Calm down, Miss. First, your name, you are ...?'

'Ms Hamilton, Georgina Hamilton. There's a man here and he—'

'Let's take it slowly, Miss Hamilton. Your address is ...?'

'Apartment 32, Great Stour—'

'Apartment 32, Great Stour Court, Canterbury, CT2 7US.'

'Yes. There's a man—'

'You say there's a man in your apartment—'

'Yes, and—'

'—and he refuses to leave. He's used copies of your keys to access your home and—'

'Yes, how did you know?'

'—he's offering you a glass of champagne.'

Everything seemed to be happening in slow motion. Gina felt her body turn cold. Her mind struggled to grasp what was happening. Words continued to come from the receiver. She recognized the voice. The phone slipped from her hand to the floor. She heard glasses clink in the kitchen. He came into the hall. Her feeling of disbelief turned to horror as he walked towards her. She had to get away. She had to get out of the flat.

Gina rushed to the front door, turned the latch and pulled.

The door remained shut. She grabbed her keys from the hall table. He made no move to stop her. Back at the door she searched frantically for the correct key. She felt her panic increasing with each fumble, and the cold tension between her shoulder blades returned. She had turned her back on him. Any second, he could attack her. At last, Gina got the right key and pushed it into the internal lock. It wouldn't turn. She pulled it out, checked it was the right key and tried again. Still it refused to turn. The feeling between her shoulder blades was unbearable. Tearful and shaking with fear and frustration Gina turned to face the intruder.

'What's happening? What's happened to the lock? What have you done?'

Standing calmly in front of her, he held out a glass of champagne. 'All in good time. Have a drink. There's nothing to be afraid of.'

'I'm not afraid. Open this door!'

'Come –' he gestured with the champagne glass '– let's take it slowly.'

That voice ... *let's take it slowly* ... the telephone. It was the same voice as the policeman. How could he do that? She had dialled 999! Gina turned back to the door and tried the key again. No use. She pulled frantically at the latch but in vain. The door remained shut. She dropped her useless keys and beat on the door with her fists.

'Help! *Help!* In here. Please, somebody, *help me!*'

'Nobody will hear you.'

Gina pulled off her shoe and hammered on the wall. The heel dug into the plaster. She screamed uncontrollably, beating at the wall with her shoe. Gradually her blows became weaker and her screams were broken by sobs.

He stood calmly, holding the two glasses of champagne.

The strength to scream deserted her and she convulsed with sobbing. The shoe fell from her hand. Her shoulders slumped and she leant against the wall.

He remained at a distance, still making no move to approach her. Again, he proffered the glass of champagne.

Gina continued to lean against the wall, her fear and panic joined by a feeling of total powerlessness. Vulnerable and defenceless, she forced herself to look at him, pleading.

'What do you want?'

'You ... you to drink a glass of champagne with me. Come, let's sit in the kitchen.'

'Why are you doing this?'

'Come, let's have a drink. We'll go to the kitchen and talk about it.' He held out the glass. 'We'll talk as we drink the champagne.'

Gina remained leaning against the wall. Although she barely had the strength to stand, her mind sought frantically for an escape.

'My neighbours ... they'll be back soon.'

He smiled. 'Your neighbours are away for two weeks.'

'I'm due to check in at Gatwick tomorrow. The tour company will miss me and raise the alarm.'

'I cancelled the holiday. You're here until I decide to let you go.'

Gina barely registered what he said. She was flustered, desperate to convince him. 'You can't keep me here indefinitely. If I don't turn up for work, my boss will raise the alarm.'

'Come now, have a drink. Rachael won't miss you for a fortnight. You must have told her that you were going on holiday for two weeks.'

Rachael? Holiday? Renewed fear and panic made speaking difficult.

'How – how do you know?'

At first her arms and legs, but then Gina's whole body, began to shake. She crumpled and slipped to the floor. He put the champagne glasses down next to the telephone and bent to pick up the receiver. She flinched away from his movement. He replaced the receiver, turned and stepped towards her.

'Come, let me help you.'

Threatened, her strength and voice returned. 'Don't touch me! Stay where you are!'

'Okay ...' He picked up the glasses. 'I'll put your glass by your feet.'

Drained and defeated, Gina was immobilized by an overwhelming sense of helplessness. She stared blankly at an unsightly mark on the opposite wall and remembered she'd meant to ask the decorators to retouch that blemish.

Decorators!

If only she hadn't contacted them, invited them into her home, he wouldn't be here now, she wouldn't be trapped in her own home. She must escape, but the door – her key wouldn't work. She'd tried to call the police, but the phone wouldn't work. All of these thoughts tumbled in the back of Gina's mind as if behind a veil. She didn't have the strength to bring them into focus. The power to concentrate and think clearly had deserted her. Gina's eyes glazed; her brain, as if protecting her from the horror of her plight, fixed her eyes on the wall and held on to that one single thought: the blemish should be repaired.

16

In Deakin's, still musing on the men in her life, Ed Ogborne took another sip of water.

'I've got us a bottle of Picpoul and some olives.'

Lost in her thoughts, Ed had not seen her friend arrive.

'Verity!'

'Sorry I'm late, my new reporter had a bit of a run-in with a drunken husband on the Hersden estate.'

Ed didn't want to go there. Hersden was where the abductor's sister lived. Looking up at Verity, she smiled a welcome.

'Thanks. A cold glass of white is just what I need.'

'You seemed very engrossed.'

'Haunted is probably a more appropriate word.'

Verity quickly poured two glasses of wine and moved one towards Ed.

'The abductions?'

'Yeah ...' Ed sighed. 'We've done our job and the CPS say it'll come to trial next year. I've almost finished tying up final loose ends.'

'If you've put it to bed, why the brooding?'

'I can't get the images out of my head – thoughts of what those girls went through.'

Verity reached out to cover Ed's hand with her own and squeezed it reassuringly.

'You've a tough job, but I'd have thought you saw worse during your years with the Met.'

Ed nodded.

'Somehow, they weren't the same. At every turn this case has reminded me of lost children. I thought the pain would ease with time but I'm still waiting.'

'You need a break.' Verity sipped her wine. 'If you've wound up the case, you must be due at least a long weekend. Let's go away for two or three nights. I know the perfect place, it's on the South Coast, about an hour's drive from here. Rye, have you been there?'

Ed withdrew her hand and picked up her wine glass. 'I know of it, of course, one of the Cinque Ports, but I've never been.'

'You'll love it. We'll have a leisurely walk or two – Camber Sands is good – and there's good food to be had in Rye.'

'Thanks for the offer.' Ed took an olive. 'A weekend away sounds good.'

'So you'll come.'

'I'm sorry, Verity, I've got a lot on at the moment. May I take a raincheck?'

'Of course.' Her habitual half-smile had disappeared.

Both women busied themselves with their white wine and olives. Verity was the first to speak.

'How's the team? I've heard your DS Potts has been seen drinking alone in back-street pubs.'

Ed stiffened. 'My team's my business. Anyway –' she indicated Verity's near-empty glass '– Mike's not the only one who likes a drink after work.'

'*Touché!*'

Before Verity could say more, Ed continued. 'I've never seen Mike the worse for wear and it doesn't affect his work.'

Verity held up her hands. 'Sorry, it was the journalist—'

'It's a non-story.' Ed held Verity's eyes. 'Your work and mine are our own concerns unless something happens that is of public interest.'

'I'm sorry.' Verity looked at Ed apologetically. 'As I say, it was the journalist speaking.'

Ed realized she'd overreacted. They'd long since established their working boundaries. She softened her voice.

'Journalist and friend.' Ed paused, then raised her glass and inclined it towards her friend.

Verity reciprocated and both women drank enough to warrant a top-up.

'Would you like to stay here or shall we go for supper at Gino's?'

'Gino's,' Ed replied without hesitation. 'Pasta with some of their Sangiovese is just what I need.'

'I'll ask them to hold a table and open a bottle.'

As Verity called the restaurant, Ed's work mobile buzzed.

'DI Ogborne.' She listened for a few moments. 'Right, get Jenny. Tell her she's coming with me. I'll be at the Station in ten minutes.' As she spoke Ed looked across the table, waving a finger and shaking her head. 'Sorry, I've got to go.'

Verity muttered, 'Just a moment,' into her mobile and her look of surprise became a questioning frown. 'What? Why?'

'It's work. A young woman's been found dead in Dover. She appears to have been alone in her flat.'

Before Verity could reply, Ed was on her feet and walking between tables to the exit. She had no doubt the editor would use her contacts to get a reporter to the scene well before other journalists got wind of the incident.

17

Gina's chin dropped onto her chest, waking her with a start. She was slumped on the floor in the hallway of her flat. For a moment she was disorientated, then the horror flooded back. She scrambled to her feet and began pulling frantically at the lock on the front door. It wouldn't budge. In desperation, she grabbed her keys from the floor and tried each one again. None of them worked. The lock wouldn't turn.

'*No! No! No!*' Gina beat on the door with her fists, screaming uncontrollably.

A chair scraped against the kitchen floor. Gina froze. She heard footsteps coming into the hall. The cold tension between her shoulder blades returned.

'You're wasting your time. Nobody will hear you. Your neighbours are on holiday.' The voice was getting closer. 'Please don't be alarmed. Come, let's take it slowly ... let's talk it through.'

The telephone ... the policeman. No, not the policeman. She turned to face the voice. Three feet away stood Colin Smith, Decorart. His thin, childlike body and choirboy face did nothing to lessen the threat Gina felt. She took a half-step backwards and then something snapped inside her. With a cry of rage, Gina launched herself at Colin with the blind intention of beating her tormentor to the ground.

'Let me go! Let me go! Let me go!' she screamed, her fists raised to attack him.

Despite his slight build, Colin held her wrists easily and waited until her shouting became pleading and the adrenalin-fuelled rush of strength left her body. Gina sagged and he lowered her to the floor.

'I'll leave you to appreciate the situation. There's no escape. Take your time. There's no hurry. I'm here. I'll be waiting.'

Once more slumped against the wall, Gina felt numb. Her mind and body were devoid of strength. Overwhelmed by an immobilising sense of helplessness, she appeared impassive despite the thoughts raging in her head. The only sign of movement came from the tears that escaped her eyes and dripped steadily onto her crumpled shirt.

18

Glum faces stared from cars in a tailback from the ferry terminal in central Dover. The grey evening was not an ideal start to a summer holiday, but for DI Ogborne and DC Eastham, unexplained deaths came in all weathers. When they reached the far side of town, Jenny parked behind a line of police vehicles near the entrance to Maxton House, an unremarkable block of flats just off the Folkestone Road. Together they approached the uniformed officer guarding the door and showed their Warrant Cards.

'Who found her?' asked Ed.

'Parents, Ma'am. They're in the van with a WPC.'

'And the body?'

'Second-floor flat, two flights up and turn right.'

The two detectives became aware of the smell on reaching the second floor. It was far from overpowering; nevertheless, the WPC standing with her back to the door of the flat had a handkerchief held to her nose. Barely glancing at their Warrant Cards, she lowered the handkerchief to indicate fresh coveralls, overshoes, face masks and latex gloves, housed in bags leaning against the opposite wall. Despite the presence of a senior officer she was unable to hide her distress.

'Your first?' asked Ed as she pulled on the protective clothing. 'I guess it's not pleasant.'

'I don't know, Ma'am, I've not been inside.'

'Probably for the best.' Ed nodded to Jenny. 'Ready?'

The full force of the smell hit them as they opened the door and stepped inside. Ed heard Jenny gasp and knew she'd immediately wish she hadn't. Touching the DC's arm Ed said, 'If someone had told me she'd been dead for days, I'd have brought my Vicks. Remember next time.'

It was a small one-bedroom flat, with a few pieces of cheap pine furniture and a notable absence of lampshades. Blonde artificial wood flooring and dull off-white paintwork completed the decoration. There were no ornaments and no pictures on the walls. Through an open bedroom doorway Ed could see a pathologist leaning over a small double bed, examining the discoloured body of a young woman. The dead woman was lying on her side wearing a T-shirt and knee-length skirt. A duvet was folded on the floor at the foot of the bed.

'DI Ed Ogborne and DC Jenny Eastham, Canterbury CID. What have we got?'

'Dorling, Buckland Hospital. I've just about finished. You've got a young woman in her early twenties. Like many these days she's above average weight for her height. I estimate she's been dead some six to ten days. When I get her back to the lab, potassium levels in the vitreous humour of the eye might provide a more precise estimate, but I'm doubtful; putrefaction has already started. I've found no superficial signs of injury. My initial impression is SCD, Sudden Cardiac Death. Given her age it's likely she was congenitally predisposed.'

'Anything unusual?' asked Ed.

'Almost certainly she's been moved after death. The discolouration due to putrefaction is strong, but from what I can see of the livor mortis pattern, I'd say she died on her back and was turned onto her side two or three hours later. I'll need to confirm that at the post-mortem.'

'Any chance of fingerprints?'

'A week or so after death shouldn't be a problem. When can we have the body?'

'Forensics will arrange it.'

As the pathologist gathered his things and left, Ed turned to Jenny.

'If the body was moved, that means somebody was here a few hours after she died. The question is: was the same person here when she died? Either way, why didn't they call the emergency services?' Ed indicated the body. 'Why leave the poor girl to decompose in a locked flat?'

Jenny, who was standing further from the bed, kept her eyes on Ed's face. 'I can't imagine anyone being so callous.'

Sensitive to her young DC's discomfort, Ed sent Jenny to look at the rest of the flat while she stayed in the bedroom. Apparently oblivious to the smell and horror of the discoloured body, Ed bent close to examine the victim before standing back to study the position of the dead woman on the bed. After a quick glance around the sparsely furnished bedroom, Ed called Jenny to join her.

'What do you make of this bed?'

Jenny came closer for a quick look and stepped back.

'The sheet's not new, but it doesn't look slept on. Apart from the marks made by escaping body fluids, it's actually very clean, just like everything in the main room and bath-room.'

'Same in here: not only the room and the bedding, but also the head and foot of the bed appear to have been thoroughly cleaned.'

'We need to speak to the parents. Go down to the van and have an initial chat with them. I'll stay here until forensics arrive.'

With a look of relief, Jenny turned to go.

'Oh, and Jenny, check the doors for any signs of forced entry.'

19

Gina opened her eyes. She was still slumped against the wall near the door to her flat. Her back ached and her joints were stiff, but these, and other sensations, were overridden by a debilitating sense of listlessness. After fitful hours of weeping, she no longer had the strength to struggle or scream for help. He was right. No one had come. No one could hear her. She was on her own.

There were noises from the kitchen. It sounded as if he were eating. Gina felt sick at the thought of food and then became aware she was terribly thirsty. The glass of champagne was still near her feet. Without thinking, she reached and took a sip. Too late she realized it might be drugged.

'Ah, Ms Hamilton, you're awake. I'm pleased to see you've decided to try the champagne. That glass must be flat. Let me get you a fresh one.'

'I want you to leave.'

It was more a weary plea than a demand. Gina felt helpless and too exhausted to insist. The terror she'd experienced as she fumbled with her keys, the horror she'd felt when she grasped she was imprisoned and at his mercy, those extreme emotions had left her body; she could acknowledge them in her head but she lacked the energy to experience their intensity. Physically, her body had shut down.

'Please go, go and leave me alone.'

'Let's not repeat ourselves. Accept the situation. If I wanted to hurt you, I could have done it when you arrived. I could have done it any time since. I could do it now, but I have no intention of hurting you.'

Despite her weary detachment, Gina was aware his manner, in keeping with his unimposing appearance, showed no immediate sign of threat. She felt she should do something, but a total lack of physical strength left her body inert.

'I've taken the liberty of getting myself something to eat. All food I've paid for, I hasten to add. I brought it with me when I arrived this afternoon. At the moment I'm eating smoked salmon with cream cheese and bagels. They go well with the champagne. May I get you some?'

With what seemed like an immense effort she forced herself to speak. 'I'd like you to go. Just go and leave me alone.'

'Georgina ...' he replied, reprovingly.

'I'm not hungry.'

'Perhaps you'll have some later. How about some champagne?'

'No.' Suddenly, Gina had an idea and felt revitalized. 'No. No, thank you. I need the bathroom.'

She forced herself to her feet and took her bag from the hall table. As she turned to close the bathroom door, she saw him smile from his position in the hall. Her hand moved to the lock. The *bastard*! He'd removed the mechanism. Gina tipped her flat champagne into the basin, ran the cold tap and filled her glass. Drinking the water with one hand, she fumbled in her bag with the other and retrieved her mobile phone. It was off. Puzzled, she switched it on. Nothing. Her phone was dead. Gina opened it to find that the battery and SIM card had been removed. Stepping back into the hall, she waved the mobile phone at him.

'What have you done with my battery and SIM?'

'Gina,' he said with a look of mock disappointment, 'surely you didn't expect me to leave you free to contact the outside world. Don't worry. Your battery and SIM are in a safe place, together with the charger and battery from your laptop.'

Gina felt an ominous sense of foreboding. His calm assurance was becoming as frightening as the thought of what he might do to her.

'If I don't contact my friends they'll—'

'Sadly, you don't seem to be in regular contact with any friends.'

'What? How?'

'This last week I've had plenty of time to hack into your laptop while you've been at work.'

Gina's sense of isolation increased. She stepped back into the bathroom to think. Feeling weak, she leant against the washbasin for support. Determined to be rational, she forced herself to take stock. Normal access to the world had been taken from her. House keys, landline, mobile and computer; all were useless. If the people in the flat next door were away, she had little chance of attracting attention. Her flat was on the third floor. The external windows were at the side of the building facing thick leafy tree-tops. Even if she could get a window open, her cries for help were unlikely to be heard. The lock had gone from the bathroom door, leaving her exposed and defenceless. Gina's legs began to shake and she tightened her grip on the basin.

Staring sightlessly at her face in the bathroom mirror, Gina struggled to think clearly. Building logical thoughts was like trying to run waist-deep in a swimming pool. Her breathing was laboured and her mouth gaped with the effort. For the moment he had the upper hand. She was at his mercy. There was little choice but to play along, see what developed and look for a way to escape.

He was right; if he'd wanted to hurt her he could have done so already. Slowly a new thought struggled to the surface: he hadn't done so already but that didn't mean he wouldn't harm her, even kill her, sometime in the future. Gina's knees buckled and she clung to the rim of the basin. Physically she felt weak, but her mental strength was returning. She splashed her face with cold water. This man wouldn't get the better of her. She didn't know how, but she would find a way. She straightened and refilled her glass with water from the tap, determined he wouldn't win.

'There's mineral water in the fridge.' The voice drew attention to his presence, watching her from the hall. Gina shuddered.

'Tap water's fine.' She forced herself to look at him. 'I know I can't get out, but you said we should take it slowly. I'm tired. I need to rest. Just tell me what you want and we'll talk about it later.'

He looked at her carefully. Contrived or not, he appeared innocent, almost boyish.

'It's very simple. I want you. I want you to give yourself to me.'

Gina gasped. He'd spoken so calmly, as if his wish was the most natural thing in the world. But why was she so surprised? It had to be sex; why else would a man break into a single woman's home?

'If you want sex why haven't you done it already?'

A brief look of shock appeared on his face and he spoke quickly.

'No, you misunderstand. I don't want sex, that is, I don't just want sex. I don't want to force you. I don't want you to submit, to surrender yourself. Your willingness won't be enough. I want the gift of your love more than I want the act itself, but your desire to give must match my desire for the giving. You must want me as much as I want you.'

He stopped speaking as abruptly as he'd started.

Gina looked at him aghast. The man was deranged. 'Love you?' She took a step back. 'Never!'

'You're shocked, surprised, you're thinking it won't happen. You're wrong, Gina. All we need is time.'

She had to get away. She couldn't get out of the flat, but anywhere would do as long as it was away from this madman. Doing her best to adopt a professional manner, Gina stepped into the hall and faced him directly.

'I'm going to rest on my bed. Promise me that you won't come into my room.'

'We'll talk again when you're feeling better. Leave your door open, I'll not wake you.'

Gina moved past him towards her room. The moment he was behind her, the cold tension returned between her shoulder blades. Quickly, she walked into her bedroom. There was no lock on the door so she did as he'd said and left it half open. She kicked off her shoes, climbed onto the bed without undressing and pulled the duvet tightly around her shoulders. Despite the cover, her body felt like ice.

Why me? Why? Why me?

20

When they'd left Dover and were on the A2 back to Canterbury, Ed asked Jenny what she'd managed to get from the dead woman's parents.

'Very little. The husband, Tony Jenkins, did most of the talking. I didn't push Pat, the mother; she was very upset. Actually, Tony's the stepfather.'

'And the daughter ...?'

'Kayleigh Robson, 23, an only child. They're not from around here; they come from Strood.'

'Where's that?'

'Part of the Medway Towns – it's across the river from Rochester.'

'So, what was Kayleigh doing in Dover?'

'She moved out of the family home when her mother remarried. According to the stepfather, they hadn't seen Kayleigh for three or four years.'

Ed waited while Jenny negotiated a roundabout.

'If they'd lost touch with the daughter, what were they doing at her flat in Dover?'

'They had an arrangement. Ever since Kayleigh left home, her mother has paid for a mobile contract. In return, Kayleigh promised she would always call between 5 and 6 p.m. on the

21st of every month. When she hadn't called by 6.30 today, the mother tried to call her, but she couldn't get through to Kayleigh's phone. This had never happened before. She got increasingly worried and finally insisted Tony drive with her to Dover. They had a key to the flat, let themselves in and found Kayleigh dead.'

'Poor woman – to find your child like that must be an unimaginable experience,' said Ed.

The two detectives drove in silence, each with their own thoughts, until Ed added, 'We'll know more when we get the post-mortem report and hear from forensics.'

21

Gina tried to turn over in bed but couldn't; something was holding her right arm. She pulled. It tightened round her wrist. Now fully awake, she opened her eyes in time to see the Decorart man loop a cord around her other wrist and pull it towards the head of the bed.

'What the ... You *bastard!*'

Anger, not fear, rose within her. Colin was standing by the bed. She kicked out, but he stood back and her struggles tightened the cords at her wrists.

'Gently. Don't mark your skin. The cords are velvet-covered but even so you'll not want them too tight. Struggling is pointless. You'll not escape.'

'You bastard. Let me go. You promised not to come in here.'

'I said I wouldn't wake you. I'm sorry that I did. Please don't struggle. I don't want you to hurt yourself. You must see that it's pointless to struggle.'

Gina saw this only too well. The man who called himself Colin Smith stood at the foot of the bed with two more cords. Unless she could talk him out of it she would soon be spread-eagled, arms and legs stretched to the four corners of her bed.

'I know I'm in your power. You don't need to tie me down.'

'Ah, but I'm afraid I do.'

'Why? I accept that you're stronger. I know I can't escape. You said you didn't want to hurt me. I trusted you, but now you're doing *this*!'

'More to the point, Georgina, how can I trust you? I may be stronger, but I need to sleep. You must see that it would be foolish for me to leave you unrestrained while I slept.'

He bent, swiftly looped a cord round her ankle and secured her right leg to the foot of the bed. Moments later, her left leg was also tied.

'Don't struggle or you really will hurt yourself. I'm going for a short walk to clear my head. Don't worry. I'll be back soon to get some rest. I suggest you do the same.'

Gina heard him walk to the outer door. A key turned; the door opened and closed. She pulled at her bonds. They were secure. Her fear returned. Left alone in the flat she felt more afraid than when he was with her. What if he didn't come back? She'd starve or die of thirst.

Immediately, Gina felt very thirsty. Her mouth was dry. She turned her head to look at the bedside table. The near-empty glass of water was still there, but it was impossible to reach. She closed her eyes, trying to put water from her mind. The dryness in her mouth intensified. With her body stretched to the four corners of the bed, her arms and legs began to ache. She longed to turn on her side, to pull up her legs and wrap her arms around her knees.

Eventually, Gina heard him return and she feigned sleep. The dryness and thirst had disappeared. His footsteps came to the bedroom door, paused and moved through to the sitting room. Despite her bonds, she felt reassured now that he was back. She was no longer alone. He would come if she called.

Although she felt safer with Colin in the apartment, Gina

70

was still struggling to come to terms with the horror of her position. Screaming and shouting for help had achieved nothing; he'd calmly waited for her to stop. Clearly, he was confident that no one would hear her cries. With no one immediately likely to come to her aid, and no one who would raise the alarm for at least a fortnight, she had to do something. To do nothing left Colin in control. Do nothing and any change would come from him. To improve her position, she had to know what best to do. Despite her ambivalent feelings of safety and threat in his presence she must get him talking. She needed to ask questions and use his answers to formulate a plan.

Tomorrow morning she'd make a start. She'd try talking with him at length. How did he know so much about her? How did he organize getting into her home? Despite her desperate situation, part of her really wanted to know and she was certain he'd enjoy revealing how clever he'd been. Her interest would flatter his ego. She must steel herself to play a game, act a role, gain his confidence and find a weakness, a weakness that would offer a means of escape.

Tied to the bed, half dozing, half planning, it slowly dawned on Gina that her best chance of escape, probably her only chance, would involve submitting to his desires. She cringed at the thought of him touching her. Her mind recoiled at the idea of submission. Nausea threatened to overwhelm her as she fought to keep images of the likely scenario from her mind. She knew she could disengage during the physical act, but the horror of the experience would remain. In taking her, possessing her, he would rob her of her self-esteem. She might choose submission as her safest option, but it wasn't a genuine choice. The choice had been his. By engineering this situation, he was forcing her to do something her whole being screamed against.

Gina's prime wish was self-preservation, but her mind recoiled at the prospect of what survival might entail. What had he said? He didn't just want sex; her submission wouldn't satisfy him. Surrendering and giving herself wouldn't be enough. He wouldn't be content until he was sure she wanted him as much as he wanted her.

Impossible! Gina shrank in revulsion from the prospect. She could not let this man take possession of her. She would not let this man own her. There had to be another way, but what that other way might be she couldn't think. Only by getting him to talk could she find out. She must overcome her feelings and engage with him tomorrow.

These thoughts repeated in her head, at first logically, but then in abbreviated snatches of ideas, each swirling after the other in a sequence that became increasingly random. There was no progression, no developing argument, just brief flashes of horror and hope, until she slipped from consciousness to a troubled night of dreams.

22

Summoned to Chief Superintendent Karen Addler's office at 08.30, Ed had spent all of three minutes briefing her line manager on the discovery of Kayleigh Robson's body when the Super reached for her fat fountain pen and terminated the meeting with a brusque request to be kept informed.

Earlier, Ed had asked Jenny and Mike Potts to re-interview Kayleigh's parents in Strood. From Jenny's questioning the previous evening it appeared Kayleigh had moved out of the family home as soon as her stepfather had moved in. Consequently, Ed wasn't expecting any new revelations, but the follow-up interview had to be done. It would also show the police were actively pursuing an investigation. When Ed returned to the CID Room, Mike and Jenny had left and only DC Nat Borrowdale remained in the office. He looked up as she crossed to her desk.

'Forensics called. They'd like you to get back to them for an initial report on the dead woman's flat.'

Ed picked up her phone and dialled. 'Hi, it's DI Ogborne, you have a prelim on the flat in Dover.' Then was a pause as she waited for someone else to come to the phone. 'Hi, it's Ed.' After a few minutes listening, Ed spoke again. 'And you're sure there was no mobile phone in the flat?' Following a brief silence, Ed added, 'Okay, thanks,' before cutting the call and redialling.

'Mike, when you're with the parents, ask Pat, the mother, for details of Kayleigh's mobile. It may be in the daughter's name, but the mother pays the bills. Tell her we need the information in order to access the phone records; explain they could assist our investigation of her daughter's death.'

Ed ended the call and got to her feet. 'Okay, Nat, we're on our way to Dover. I'll bring you up to speed as you drive.'

When they arrived at Maxton House, Ed recognized the constable at the entrance as the one who, last night, had been inside the building at the door of the second-floor flat.

'Feeling better out here?'

'Yes, thank you, Ma'am. Before you go up, the Sarge would like a word.' She pointed to a uniformed figure crossing the road towards them.

'Sergeant Burstford, Ma'am. I'm just winding up the door-to-door.'

'DI Ogborne and this is DC Borrowdale, Canterbury CID. What have you got for us?'

'Not a lot, I'm afraid. Kayleigh Robson lived here alone. The block's due for a major refurbishment and Kayleigh was the last remaining tenant. She worked at the convenience store down the road. Some of the locals knew her by sight, but she appears not to have had particular friends in the area. At least, nobody remembers seeing her with anybody. Those who admitted knowing her said she kept herself to herself and barely spoke to people except briefly when they were shopping.'

'Did you check the shop out?'

'The owner confirmed Kayleigh worked there, but said she hadn't been in for over a week. Apparently, he found a note pushed through the door saying she needed a break and was taking a fortnight off.'

'When did he find the note?'

'First thing on Friday of last week, the 14th. Said it must have been pushed under the door during the night. He'd scribbled the date on it and kept it in a drawer. So we know she was alive on the Thursday, maybe early on the Friday.'

'Mmm ...' Ed hesitated a moment before replying. 'Probably, unless somebody else delivered the note. What about CCTV?'

'Maxton House, where her flat is, doesn't have any security cameras. Nor is this road covered, but there are cameras up there.' Sergeant Burstford pointed up to the main road. 'On the Folkestone Road, there are multiple cameras between here and the centre of town.'

'And the shop where Kayleigh worked?' asked Ed.

'They have security cameras inside. We'll check the tapes for last Thursday and Friday – should pick up Kayleigh's movements and maybe someone with her.'

'Good. We might be able to point you to some additional cameras.'

'Ma'am?' Burstford's response was tinged with annoyance. Clearly, Dover was his patch and he didn't take kindly to outsiders telling him his job.

'Relevant intel, Sergeant. Kayleigh had a mobile, but forensics didn't find one in her flat. Two of my colleagues are with the parents in Strood. They'll be asking the mother, who paid the phone bills, for details so that we can access the mobile records. With luck, we'll get intel about contacts and meetings around the time of her death.'

Burstford smiled. 'If you can identify meeting places, we can target relevant CCTV.'

'It'll be good working with you, Sergeant. Let's hope our collaboration leads to a swift result.' Ed turned to enter the building, then added, 'Two weeks without notice – that must have pissed him off.'

'Her boss at the corner shop is from an extended family. Easy for him to get someone to cover. I got the impression he wasn't sorry to see Kayleigh gone. Said she was an adult and it was her life.'

It *had* been her life, thought Ed, and it hadn't been a long one.

'Thanks. If anything else comes up, let me know. We're going to take another look upstairs.'

'Okay, Nat, what's your first impression?'

'From what I can see, it's like you said in the car: everything looks to have been thoroughly cleaned.'

'The whole flat was pristine. Of course, the sheet and pillowcase were stained where they'd been in direct contact with her body, as were the clothes she was wearing, but everything else had been recently washed.'

'Scrupulously clean flat,' said Nat to himself. Then to Ed, 'What were her hands like?'

'She'd been dead six to ten days.'

'Right. I was thinking she might have been a compulsive cleaner.'

'Unlikely. The flat had been methodically cleaned yet there were almost no cleaning items in the cupboards. Every hard surface had been wiped down with bleach, but forensics found no bleach in the flat, not even empty containers. The bins in the bathroom and kitchen were empty, and fitted with new liners.'

'Someone carefully covering their tracks, taking their rubbish and cleaning things with them,' suggested Nat.

'And someone took her mobile,' added Ed. 'Almost certainly the person who cleaned the flat and moved her body.'

'And the cleaning left no fingerprints?'

'Only hers on items at the back of cupboards, but we've struck lucky. There was a partial print in the bathroom, which appears not to be Kayleigh's, and a smudged palm print on the outside of the front door, origin debatable.'

'How come there was a stray print in the bathroom if every exposed area had been wiped?'

'Chance. The loo has a split-button flush and one half was set a couple of millimetres lower than the other. Whoever cleaned the place hadn't poked their cloth completely in and the print was left on the lower button. It was incomplete, so a fingerprint match is unlikely to be conclusive, but forensics will be able to retrieve DNA. With luck, whoever left it will be on the National Database and we'll get a match.'

'What about the smudge on the door?' asked Nat.

'Forensics will run the DNA.'

'And CCTV?'

'You heard the Sergeant.' Ed eyed Nat disapprovingly. 'It's a street of old buildings. There's no camera covering the road, let alone the entrance to Maxton House.'

As Ed spoke her mobile rang. 'DI Ogborne.'

'Dorling. I've just started the post-mortem and there's a couple of things I thought you should know immediately.'

Ed switched her phone to speaker, so that Nat could listen in.

'When we washed the body, we found ligature marks at the wrists and ankles.'

'Why weren't they picked up at the scene?'

'She'd been dead at least a week. Body discolouration alone shouldn't have masked them, but concealer had been applied to cover the marks. Like make-up, it came off when we washed the body.'

'Right, and your second point?'

'Well, the stress associated with being restrained, and whatever else happened to the poor girl before she died, probably triggered cardiac arrest. I'll confirm that in my report, but I've already seen enough from the livor mortis pattern to be certain the body was moved after death. She died lying on her back with limbs spread-eagled from her body by the ligatures.'

'What about sexual assault, traces of semen?'

'There were no signs of forced penetration, but she wasn't a virgin. However, there was no semen and no trace of lubricant.'

'Okay. Thanks for letting us know so quickly. Can you be more precise with time of death?'

'Sorry. Putrefaction was too advanced for a vitreous potassium measurement.'

Ed sighed. 'So ... we're stuck with six to ten days?'

'That's what my report will say, but from the temperature in the flat and the extent of decomposition, I'd bet on eight or nine.'

'There's a possibility she was alive last Thursday.'

'That would fit my best guess of eight or nine days.'

'Thanks, I'll not quote you.'

Ed switched off her phone and turned to Nat. 'What do you make of the pathologist's findings?'

'Kinky sex gone wrong? That would fit with the guy putting concealer over the ligature marks and cleaning the place so thoroughly.'

'I agree, but remember there was no semen.'

'He could have worn a condom,' said Nat.

'Unlikely, there were no traces of lubricant.' Ed paused. 'Of course, sadomasochistic sex might not have involved penetrative intercourse and ...' Ed paused. 'Nor does it preclude the possibility Kayleigh's partner was a woman. Let's check the bed to see if the ligatures have left cord marks.'

Both Ed and Nat were certain there were marks in the white paint, which were more prominent at the foot of the bed.

'That's consistent with her exerting more force with her legs than her arms,' said Ed. 'Legs are stronger and the cords were probably more painful at the wrists than the ankles.'

'The fact that there are marks suggests it wasn't passive restraint, which Kayleigh accepted; she fought against it.'

'Good point, Nat, and fighting her bonds could have sparked the stress that triggered the cardiac arrest.'

'Right ...'

'Even so, I don't think that confirms she was held against her will. Maybe yes, maybe no. For people into S&M, struggling against the bonds can be a turn-on.'

'One thing's puzzling me,' said Nat. 'The pathologist mentioned make-up. What were her clothes like? You said they were clean.'

'I also checked her other clothes,' said Ed. 'The ones she was wearing were the best from her small choice.'

'It's looking like she got herself ready to meet someone for kinky sex. You said there were no signs of forced entry.'

'Right. Jenny and I checked and forensics confirmed.'

'In that case, whoever was with her was probably someone she knew?'

'Most likely,' Ed agreed. 'She lived alone and there's nobody else in the rest of the building. I can't see her letting a stranger into her flat.'

'What about social media?'

'She doesn't appear to have a computer and, as you know, her mobile's missing.'

'Just like the clean-up,' said Nat. 'The missing mobile suggests someone covering their tracks. What about phone records?'

'Come on, Nat!' Ed gave the young DC another disapproving look. 'Remember? We're onto it. Mike and Jenny are with the parents in Strood. They'll get Kayleigh's number and details of the mobile contract from her mother.'

In the car back to Canterbury, Ed drafted a press release specifying a heart attack and death by natural causes. She would press the Super to hold back other details. Whoever was with Kayleigh when she died, Ed needed them to be kept in the dark. The last thing she wanted at this stage was to release a tip-off that the police were treating the death as suspicious.

23

It was late morning when Gina woke aching from her enforced position on the bed. She tried moving and cried out from the stiffness in her muscles.

'Hey! Are you there? These cords are biting into my wrists. I'm stiff. In pain. Come and loosen them. Please.'

'Good morning. I hope you slept well.'

Apart from a different shirt he looked the same as yesterday. His blond fringe seemed to be permanently fixed at an angle across his forehead.

'I'm aching all over. I can't move with these cords and I'm sore where they're tight around my wrists and ankles.'

'That's because you struggled.'

'The cords are hurting me, please loosen them.'

As soon as the words were out of her mouth, Gina was uncomfortable with the idea of him coming closer to her, close enough to loosen the cords. She felt sickened by the thought that he might touch her. She forced the revulsion from her mind, determined to suppress those feelings in exchange for immediate comfort and the possibility of escape.

Colin stood at the foot of the bed, apparently unaware of what she'd said or might be thinking.

'You must be hungry. I'll get us some breakfast – orange juice and toast.'

He left the bedroom without waiting for a reply. Gina heard him busy in the kitchen and then he returned with a tray, which he placed well away from the bed.

'First a little exercise and then we'll have breakfast. I'm going to untie one cord at a time so that you can move your arms and legs in turn. I'll hold on to the end of the cord and, if you try any tricks, I'll tie you down and leave you alone until this evening. Do you understand?'

'Yes.'

'And you promise not to try anything stupid?'

'Yes.'

They began with her left leg and, after a few minutes, moved on to her right leg and then her left arm. Before releasing her right arm, he moved the breakfast tray closer so that he could reach it while still holding the cord attached to her wrist.

'What can I pass you first, orange juice or toast?'

'Thank you. I'd like juice first and then the toast.'

As they ate, Gina steeled herself and began her campaign.

'How did you arrange all of this? You seem to know so much about me.'

'Planning and research.'

'But how? Why me?'

'Chance.'

'Because I employed your firm to decorate this room?'

'I have no firm. At least, the firm you thought you employed was fictitious. I employed a real firm myself once you had given me the keys to your apartment.'

'But I responded to a circular that came in the post. It was the same for my holiday in Italy, and that was real because I

82

checked with the tour company. They had my name in their records and on the passenger list. They sent me the itinerary and the airline tickets.'

'Of course. Like the decorators, the tour company and the holiday were real but I made the bookings.'

'But the holiday in Italy was a prize. I won it in a competition.'

'I organized the competition. The prize was chosen with you in mind. I found your dream holiday and booked it.'

'But how did you know I would win?'

'There were no other entries. Only you received the mailshot about the singles club competition.'

'Okay ... but how did you know I would enter?'

'I didn't, but I thought there was a good chance and you didn't let me down. Through me, you employed the decorators, you entered the competition and you accepted the prize holiday. That's why I'm here.'

'But how did you know Siena was my dream holiday? How did you find out so much about me?'

'Simple. You told me.'

Although it wasn't cold in her bedroom Gina felt a chill between her shoulder blades at his words.

'But I don't even know you. We've hardly met. How could you possibly ...?'

'From time to time we've been much closer than you realize. Once I'd determined how to find out about you the rest was easy.'

'That's what I'd like to know. How did you find out so much about me?'

'All in good time.'

Colin retied Gina's right arm to the bed and took the tray to the kitchen.

24

I had to get away from the bedroom. The desire to take her there, spread-eagled and helpless on the bed, was strong. I need to be stronger. Here in the kitchen with the door closed between us I've a chance to refocus. I'm not here to rape her, rape's not part of my plan. Things are going exactly as I hoped they would. No more screaming, no more crying and she didn't protest when I retied her to the bed.

So far, my plan's working perfectly. Dover was a blip, not an error. True, I did force myself into her flat, but I couldn't possibly have known it would turn out like that. With Georgina the whole operation's more ingenious. It's subtle, elegant and it's going smoothly, just as I knew it would.

All good, but there's one thing missing. It's the bloody story of my life. Only I know how clever I am, how clever I've been. My plan's brilliant. So brilliant I deserve recognition for developing it, for engineering its success. Everything's coming to fruition and I want to share my brilliance. Share it with somebody who will appreciate my skill, somebody I can impress. I've always known there'd be someone who would really be mine, my chosen one. Now I have her, I know who she is – Georgina Hamilton.

Gina. She's perfect, but I've got to be careful. When this is over, I want to walk away, to disappear. It's crucial I can't be traced. If she goes to the police they mustn't be able to find me. I don't want to hurt her. I certainly don't want to kill her. In Dover, on that practice run, I didn't hurt Kay – at least, not deliberately. Now, I don't want Georgina to die. I'm not into murder. Murder has never been part of the plan.

25

As soon as they were back in Canterbury, Ed got Nat to drop her at the Station entrance. She went straight to the CID Room to type up her draft press release and was at her desk waiting for the computer to boot up when the telephone rang. It was DI Saunders calling from Maidstone.

'Hi, Brian, what's new?'

'Just calling to thank you for taking time to talk to my new DS and to let you know you've got a new fan. Now it's not just me singing your praises.'

'Thanks, Brian.' Ed felt uncomfortable. 'From the little I've seen of him, he's going to be a good detective.'

Brian Saunders remained silent.

'You chose well, Brian, he's a great addition to your team.' Now feeling thoroughly uncomfortable, Ed lapsed into silence and waited for DI Saunders to speak.

'Yes, everyone seems to like him. How about you?' The was a brief pause, during which Ed wished she had a coffee to fill the gap, and then Saunders continued. 'How are things in Canterbury?'

'We've got a new case on our hands: a very nasty death. Right now, I need to clear a press release with CS Addler.'

'Murder?'

'A young woman, Kayleigh Robson, found dead in her flat on the outskirts of Dover. The pathologist reckons she was congenitally predisposed to sudden cardiac death, but there's evidence pointing to manslaughter.'

'Suspicious circs?'

'Her body was moved after she died and there were ligature marks at her wrists and ankles. The flat had been scrupulously cleaned.'

As she replied, Ed thought she heard Saunders reach for a mug. At least he had a coffee to hand. There was a pause before he spoke.

'S&M gone wrong? Fingerprints?'

'Only old prints of hers in out-of-the-way places that hadn't been wiped, but we got lucky. Forensics found a single foreign print missed in the clean-up. It's a partial, but we're hoping for a DNA match. There was also a smudged palm print on the outside of the entrance door, but that could be hers.'

'Any likely suspects for the rogue print?'

'That's the problem. Since Kayleigh left home she's been pretty much a loner. None of the neighbours or work colleagues have come up with anything significant about her private life. She must have had at least the one visitor, the one who moved her body, but nobody's reported seeing her with anyone, nor has anybody been seen entering or leaving her flat.'

'No CCTV?' asked Saunders.

'It's an old building, due for renovation. There's no CCTV covering her block of flats, but Dover are working on nearby cameras and security tapes from the shop where she worked.'

'Laptop, mobile?'

Ed was pleased Brian couldn't see her expression; he was

older but, during her time at the Met, she'd probably experienced as much as Saunders had during all his years in Kent. 'No computer and her mobile's missing.'

'Cases like that are buggers.'

'We're accessing her phone records, via her mother – she paid the bills.'

'I hope you strike lucky.'

This time, Ed was sure she heard Brian take a mouthful of coffee. 'We need it. If we don't get a match for the DNA, or an unexpected breakthrough, the investigation risks running into the sand.'

'As I said, cases like that are buggers.'

'While waiting on the CCTV and phone records, our next step is to go fishing with a press release. At this stage I want a simple death by natural causes and a request for anyone who knew her to come forward. If the Super agrees, I'll hold back details of the restraint and clean-up so whoever did it should think they're in the clear.'

26

Colin returned to the bedroom and placed a chair from the kitchen beside the bed. Despite the horror of her position and the revulsion she felt for him, Gina was determined to put her plan into action. She looked at him enquiringly.

'You seem to know a lot about me. Are you going to tell how?'

'I know a great deal about you, Ms Hamilton, Georgina Hamilton, or may I call you Georgina?'

'If you must call me something, call me Gina. And you ... what should I call you?'

'I told you: Colin.'

'Okay, Colin, you've got me in your power. When I found you in my kitchen, I panicked. When I discovered I couldn't escape I was terrified. When you told me you wanted sex, I was outraged, but I felt better.'

Gina tried to adjust her position on the bed with little effect. The cords at her wrists and ankles precluded all but the smallest movements.

'At first, I couldn't understand why I felt better, then it came to me. The outright panic had gone. I was calmer. You'd removed the unknown and there was a chance I could cope.

You hadn't hurt me and you said you weren't going to hurt me. I didn't feel good, but I was feeling better, feeling better, that is, until this!'

As if to illustrate her point, Gina tried again to wriggle into a different position but the cords held her arms and legs stretched to the corners of the bed. If Colin noticed her efforts he made no comment. She stopped trying to move and continued with her plan. Determined to maintain an air of resigned calm, she managed to keep her voice conversational, certain this was the best way to play it. She must find his weakness and devise a way to escape.

'You've told me what you want and I'm coming to terms with that, but ...' Gina looked directly at Colin while keeping a check on her natural tendency to flirt with men. 'I'm also intrigued ... How did you find out so much about me? How did you pull the decorating scam?'

Colin, who seemed perfectly at ease in the straight-backed kitchen chair, took a moment to reply.

'Planning and research: I had the idea but couldn't do anything about it until now. I didn't have the money and I didn't have the time. I had to work. And then I had a ... an unexpected inheritance ... from a distant relative, a great-aunt. I gave up work and put my plan into action. After a trial run in another town, I came here, to Canterbury.'

'Why choose Canterbury? Why choose me?'

'Canterbury is a good-sized town. You stood out from the crowd.'

'But you didn't know me.'

'I didn't know anybody in Canterbury; that was one of the attractions.'

'Then how did you pick me?'

'It wasn't just you, I chose ten women, and then you picked yourself.'

'I don't understand.'

'If you'd stop asking questions, Gina ...' He paused and the slight edge, which had appeared in his voice, had gone when he continued. 'Let me do the talking, I'll explain.'

'I'm all ears, but first undo these cords. They're uncomfortable.' The look on Colin's face told Gina she'd made her first mistake. It was too soon, far too soon.

'Come now, Gina, at this stage in our relationship that wouldn't be very sensible, would it? I'll slacken the cords at your ankles so that you can shuffle up the bed and rest against the headboard.'

'Thank you.'

Colin loosened the cords and Gina worked her way up the bed so that her head and shoulders were supported by the headboard. The change of position also loosened the cords at her wrists but her arms were still held away from her body. Colin made sure that the cords wouldn't slip off over her hands.

The change of position felt wonderful and Gina was aware that Colin had just said something interesting: 'at this stage in our relationship'. So he must envisage their relationship changing. Perhaps there would come a time when she'd not be tied down.

'I'm puzzled. If you picked ten women, what led you to me and how do you know so much about me? You said you knew nobody in Canterbury.'

Colin's hesitancy, despite his obvious desire to talk, reinforced Gina's growing confidence. He was obviously formulating his ideas, deciding how much to tell her. She was on the right track. Keep up the pressure; probe and wait. He might let something slip.

'You said I picked myself. How did that happen?'

Colin remained silent, apparently lost in thought.

Gina waited, looking at him attentively.

She's trying to rush me, trying to trip me up. That's not going to happen, I'm in control. I just have to be careful, take my time, not give her any information that could lead to my arrest. I've used fictitious names, paid for everything in cash and not used my home address. All she can possibly know is what I tell her and what I look like. Much good may that do her. What I look like is not what I looked like before and not what I'll look like again.

Things are going well. The two of us are alone together, just as I planned, but we need more time to get to know each other. She needs time to discover my worth, to appreciate how clever I've been. Once she's got to know me there'll be no need for subterfuge. Until then, I've got to be smart. I'm naturally cautious. If I'm careful, I'll be safe. As long as I watch what I say, watch what I tell her.

Where should I begin? I mentioned an inheritance. Well ... that was a lie, but it's an easy lie to remember. I'll keep lies to a minimum, focus on the best bits, my master plan for the selection of women and the inevitability that one of those women would choose me.

It had been a long silence. Gina stirred on the bed, trying to regain Colin's attention. He didn't look up so she spoke.

'Colin, I'm waiting. I can be patient, but I'm dying to hear how you orchestrated all this. And ... I want to know, why me, why did you choose me?'

Finally, Colin raised his head. 'As I said, you chose yourself. My plan worked because I didn't want one individual woman; I wanted a particular type of woman.'

'What type of woman?'

'A woman I didn't already know who was young, professional and attractive. I started with ten. There was a good chance at least one in ten would take the bait.'

Gina maintained her interested expression, but inwardly she bridled – 'take the bait' – what arrogance! How could she have been so foolish?

Colin settled to talk, altering his position in the chair. Unlike Gina, he had that luxury.

'I'd go to a busy part of town like the open spot between Sun Street and Burgate.'

'The Buttermarket,' offered Gina.

'Right. I'd stand, or sit, with my gaze unfocused, as if I were deep in thought. At first, I did this because I didn't want to be noticed scanning the faces of passing women, but I soon discovered that the right woman would select herself. Suddenly she would be there in the crowd, sharply defined among the softer outlines of those around her.'

'How come?'

'I was never sure. Perhaps a flash of sunlight or the breeze catching her hair. I'd wait until she passed and then follow at a distance. For me to be successful it was better if she used her card at an ATM or at a supermarket checkout. I'd stand behind her with a good chance of seeing her name on the card.'

'Surely it was difficult to read the name at a glance.'

'I didn't need her full name. Sometimes I didn't need her name at all. I'd follow her back to where she worked and then back home in the evening.'

'But if you followed me—'

'When I followed you.'

Gina shivered involuntarily. 'Okay, *when* you followed me, you would have seen two women's names at work, Rachael Metcalffe and Georgina Hamilton, but here, at Stour Court, none of us have our names by the outside door.'

'If I'd seen even part of your name on your card that wouldn't have mattered but, in your case, I didn't see your card at all. You paid with cash when I was behind you at the supermarket checkout.'

'How did you know it was me and not Rachael?'

'The electoral register in the library. There was no Metcalffe at Great Stour Court, only a Georgina Hamilton and she was in Apartment 32.'

Gina felt foolish. It was so obvious, she'd lost ground.

'Okay, but how did you arrange the decoration and the holiday in Siena? How did you know I'd want those things?'

'I had to ask you.'

'But we never spoke –' Gina shivered again '– or did we?'

'We didn't speak, but you're forgetting the lifestyle questionnaire.'

'That came from a university. It was anonymous.'

'The university was a fiction. I sent each woman the same questionnaire, but each one had the questions in a different order. Three women replied and it was easy for me to identify the senders by checking the question order.'

'If you got three, why choose me?'

'As I said, you selected yourself.'

'What do you mean?'

'You chose to complete the questionnaire and your answers gave me the information I needed. One of the three women who responded was planning to marry, but two of you lived alone and had no steady relationship. You provided an easy access to your home.'

Gina gasped, 'The decorating!'

She felt a cold chill creep across her body. It was all so normal, an ordinary part of everyday life. So much so that she'd not once been suspicious. Gina shuddered. Things one might do any day, without much thought, had led to this: an intruder in her home, who'd tied her to her bed, and she was completely in his power, completely at his mercy.

'Exactly. *Are you planning any major expenditure in the near future? List up to three in priority order.* You put down two: first, to have your bedroom professionally decorated and, second, to see the Palio in Siena. There was another question asking you to indicate the probability you would use certain services. For singles club you put, "Possible".'

'But the addresses for the questionnaire and the singles club where I posted the letters? For the decorators, Decorart, I actually telephoned the office!'

'All I needed were some correspondence addresses and careful planning. Only you received the half-price introductory offer from Decorart and the competition entry from the singles club.'

'But what if I hadn't responded?'

'I would have started again with another ten women. Time is on my side. I have all the time in the world.'

'And my neighbours, how did you know they'd be away?

They didn't mention to me that they were going on a trip.'

'James and Caroline Monkton are away because I arranged it. I got their names from the electoral register. I guessed they wouldn't be able to resist a free holiday in Portugal even if it meant visiting a timeshare village because it categorically stated there would be no hassle and no obligation to buy. I was right. They responded immediately. So, as soon as your singles club competition entry arrived, I arranged your trip to Italy and their trip to Portugal, making sure the trips coincided.'

'And the timeshare company went along with it? That doesn't sound very likely to me.'

'One of the things I discovered, nobody questions your motives when you splash money around. I put the money up front for the holiday visit and the timeshare company obligingly got rid of Caroline and James for me.'

'What about the front door? I used my key to get in but I couldn't use it to get out.'

'While you were at work yesterday I changed your lock for an identical replacement, but I put your old key barrel into the outer part of the new lock. Now your key works on the outside, but only my new one works on the inside.'

Gina didn't follow the technicalities but that didn't matter. Her plan was working; she'd got him talking.

'And my telephone?'

'I trained in electronics and it's also a hobby. After fixing the lock, I added some extra bits to your phone line. If you dialled a number with more than three digits you'd hear the engaged signal. I did that just in case you called a friend before you found me or when I refused to leave.'

'But when I dialled 999 and spoke to the police it was your voice.'

'Dialling 999 prompted automatic dialling of a number with an answer machine. I'd pre-recorded the exchange you heard. Given the state you'd be in, I reckoned you wouldn't recognize my voice initially, nor would you notice if some of my responses didn't exactly match what you had said.'

Gina gave him a look of admiration, part genuine, part feigned. 'You seem to have thought of everything.'

'I have thought of everything.'

'Not everything.' Gina smiled. 'What about those bagels and cream cheese?'

'Bagels, cream cheese and champagne?'

'Thank you, Colin, I think I'm ready for the champagne now.'

While Colin was getting the champagne, Gina thought back over what he'd told her. She was astonished how easy it had been. With time, money and some technical knowledge, gaining access to a woman who selected herself was inevitable. Actually, you didn't need any technical knowledge; the policeman on the telephone was just Colin showing off, icing his cake because he wanted admiration. Gina was still tied to the bed, but she felt better, confident she was getting the measure of her adversary.

27

The four Canterbury CID detectives were at their desks. Except for the tapping of keyboards and the occasional rustle of paper, the room was silent. Yesterday, the investigation into the death of Kayleigh Robson had drawn a blank. When visited by Mike and Jenny, the parents had not added anything to what they'd already told Jenny at the scene. Police questioning of neighbours and nearby businesses in Dover had revealed an even bleaker picture. Kayleigh had barely interacted with neighbours or work colleagues and nobody remembered ever seeing her with anyone else.

DNA from the partial prints aside, Ed and her team were pinning their hopes on CCTV footage from Dover and the assessment of Kayleigh's phone records. As the SIO, Ed had given their Single Point of Contact officer details of Kayleigh's phone and they were waiting for her billing data from the ISP. When she had mentioned this to the team both Mike and Nat had grinned broadly. SPOC *Star Trek* jokes were getting tired but the acronym never failed to raise a smile. Ed felt herself smiling at the memory of their faces. It was an all too brief respite from their concern that they were no closer to identifying the person who'd been in Kayleigh's flat. Ed stood up and then sat on the corner of her desk. She needed to push the investigation forward.

'Kayleigh Robson, everyone. The Super has sanctioned a press release for 12.00 hours, saying death as the result of a heart attack, i.e. by natural causes. The pathologist has to confirm, but he believes she was congenitally predisposed to SCD, Sudden Cardiac Death. At this stage, we don't want to tip off whoever moved her body that we know more. I'll need to talk to her parents before the news is out. Jenny, give them a call to make sure they'll be in this morning.'

Jenny picked up her desk phone and started to dial while Ed continued speaking.

'Nat, both Jenny and Mike have already seen Pat and Tony Jenkins, Kayleigh's mother and stepfather, so I want you to come with me to Strood. Mike, while we're gone, get onto Dover and see if they've managed to get anything from CCTV relevant to Kayleigh Robson.'

'Who's leading the investigation down there?'

'Sergeant Burstford.'

'Jack Burstford? Well, I'll be ... I haven't seen Jack in years. Why, it must be—'

'Excellent, Mike. It's good you know him. Unless there's a rapid match for the fingerprint DNA or until we get Kayleigh's phone records, CCTV is all we've got for a potential lead. Do what you can to chase it up.'

'Will do.'

Jenny put down her phone. 'Her parents will wait in until you arrive.'

'Okay, Nat, let's go. You take the wheel – practice for your advanced driving course.'

The car's tyres bumped gently over strips of tar between the rippled concrete sections of road surface. Nat pulled to a stop in front of a small pebble-dashed bungalow with a vivid blue hydrangea between the bay window and a sagging front fence. When Ed pressed the bell, melodic chimes summoned a man to the door.

'Mr Jenkins? I'm Detective Inspector Ed Ogborne and my colleague is Detective Constable Nat Borrowdale. We're here to—'

'Come in, come in. We've been expecting you. Tea? Coffee?'

'Tea would be good, thank you.'

'Right, take a seat in here.' The man, presumably Kayleigh's stepfather, opened a door to the front room. 'I'll just get Pat.'

A few minutes later, Pat appeared with four steaming mugs of tea and a saucer of sugar lumps. She placed the tray on a central coffee table. 'Careful, they're hot. We take ours black. Tony's got milk if you'd like it.'

With the teas sorted and introductions completed, Ed directed her words to Kayleigh's mother.

'Mrs Robson—'

'Pat ... I'm Pat Jenkins now.'

'Of course. Sorry ... Pat, we haven't met before so, first, I want to extend our condolences for the loss of your daughter. As the Senior Officer, I'm here to explain the report we've received from the pathologist who attended the scene.'

'Pathologist? What ...?'

'He was there, like a doctor, to certify the cause of death. At present, Kayleigh's death is unexplained.'

'Unexplained? Mrs Jenkins began to look agitated. She reached for her husband's hand. 'What do you mean, unexplained?'

'I'm sorry, this must be difficult for you.' Ed leant forward in her seat. 'I need to inform you about the circumstances surrounding—'

'She was my daughter, my only child. I want to know everything.'

'Kayleigh died because her heart stopped. The pathologist believes she had a condition that meant she was more likely to suffer cardiac arrest than most people her age.'

Mr Jenkins put his arm round his wife's shoulders and turned towards Ed. 'Why unexplained? Why do you say her death was unexplained if the doctor says it was a heart attack?'

Ed took a quick taste of her tea. She glanced at Nat, who seemed to be ignoring his, and then turned back to face the parents.

'We have evidence that indicates someone was with Kayleigh when, or soon after, she died.'

Mrs Jenkins tightened her grip on her husband's hand. 'You mean she was killed! Murdered!' Her eyes widened in anger.

'No. Not murder, but we need to speak to the person who was with Kayleigh in order to better understand the circumstances surrounding her death.' Ed looked from husband to wife. 'My colleagues have already asked but, now you've had more time to think, are you sure you don't know anyone Kayleigh was seeing?'

'She had her old school friends when she was here.' Mrs Jenkins's eyes were becoming red-rimmed. 'Nothing serious ... with boys, I mean. She went out, but she wasn't what I'd call a very social person.'

'And when she went to Dover?'

'She cut herself off,' said Mr Jenkins.

'Tony!' His wife looked at him, her face creased with pain.

'You can't say that, love. She called us without fail ... until ...'

Ed was about to suggest they took a break, when Kayleigh's mother took a deep breath and continued.

'She was a good girl. She called us every month, like she'd promised, but she never talked about those things, never mentioned a boyfriend.' Pat sniffed, holding back her tears. 'I was worried about her. And now ...' Finally, the tears came and Mr Jenkins pulled his wife to him, her head on his shoulder.

'We both were ... worried, that is. Ever since I've known her, Kayleigh's spent most of her time moping in her room. She hardly ever went out and I guess that continued after she left and went to Dover.'

Mrs Jenkins raised her head, but spoke without looking at Ed. 'It started when her father left. I thought it were natural for her to be upset, but not for so long. It didn't seem right, a young woman not wanting to meet people, to have nights out with friends. I had a word with her, suggested she see the doctor, but she just turned on me. "Not everyone's like you, down the pub every other night. And I certainly don't want some GP loading me with pills!" That wasn't my Kayleigh – she was a good girl. That Kayleigh wasn't well but, try as I might, I couldn't get her to do anything about it.'

The pain and guilt in Mrs Jenkins's voice prompted a general silence during which she straightened in her seat and looked directly at Ed. 'What happens now?'

'At midday today, we're going to issue a statement to the press asking for anybody who may have seen or heard something to come forward. The press release will simply say Kayleigh died from a heart attack, natural causes. There will be none of the other information that I've told you about. We don't want to alert the person who was with her until we've been able to speak with them.'

'You're expecting them to come forward?' asked Mr Jenkins.

'Maybe, maybe not. If not, we'll have to track them down. In that case, you've given us access to Kayleigh's phone records and they should be a great help.'

Ed stood and extended her hand to the parents. 'That will be all for the moment, but someone will be in touch to keep you abreast of what's happening. Once again, we're very sorry for your loss and we'll be doing our best to clear up the unexplained aspects of your daughter's death.'

Back in the car, as Nat executed a neat three-point turn, Ed said, 'As soon as we're back, chase up those phone records. They could be our only key to who was in Kayleigh's flat.'

28

D over was a hiccup; here in Canterbury I'm laughing. Ten women chosen and each one a bright, attractive professional. I'd have been happy with any of them, but Gina was the standout and Gina chose me. Okay, she didn't choose me to be her life partner. In fact, she didn't choose me at all, she chose Decorart to fix her bedroom, but that was the beauty of my plan: one small everyday choice that would change our lives, hers and mine, for ever.

It will happen. Given time, Gina will come to see I'm the man for her. I've seen the admiration in her eyes, heard it in her voice. Despite herself, she's impressed. Give her more time with the two of us alone together and she'll be genuinely drawn to me. Exactly how we'll spend our lives is still a blank, but I'm easy. I'll have her, that's the main thing. Everything else is peripheral. As for our future together, I'll be happy to follow her lead.

As much as I want her to want me, I mustn't rush things. I have to wait for that moment to come naturally. It *will* come, I know it will, and when it comes it will have been worth waiting for. When I first saw her, walking in the sunlight, I was aware of her gloriously long hair and the sensuality beneath her professional appearance. Yesterday, there'd been spirit in her anger. When she really wants me, Gina will be a conquest worthy of my planning and my patience. I'm in control and everything is going just as I planned. Soon, I'll get my reward. Sometime soon, she'll want me as much as I want her.

When Colin went to prepare cream cheese and bagels, Gina was surprised he'd left her leaning against the headboard with some slack in the cords. The moment he was out of sight, she tried to slip her arms free, but the cords were tied too snugly at her wrists. Escape was impossible.

She might still be captive, but Gina was no longer despondent; she'd regained control of herself. Panic and terror had given way to rational thought. Her plan to get Colin talking was working. However, the more Colin said, the more Gina felt he was unlikely to slip up. The possibility he would offer her a chance to escape was receding. Colin was on top of things, he'd thought this through – or had he?

As much as Colin was on top of the physical situation, his view of the outcome was crazy. The man was unhinged. *'I want the gift of your love.' 'Never!'* she'd replied. *'You're wrong, Gina, all we need is time.'* The man was mad, totally deranged. Their time together was finite. At the end of two weeks, Gina would be expected back at work. If she didn't appear at the dental practice, Rachael would contact the police and Colin would be caught. If he made his escape, she could describe him. The police would track him down.

Surely Colin must come to the same conclusion. Running from the scene would be too risky. Buying her silence would be little better. He said that he didn't want to hurt her, but only if he killed her could he ensure her silence and guarantee his escape.

Faced with possible death, there was no choice: Gina must accept his terms. She must convince Colin that she wanted him as much as he wanted her. The thought made her nauseous. Despite the powerful motivation of self-preservation, her body recoiled at the thought of surrendering to Colin. But why should she feel sicker at the idea of sex with Colin than with other men who'd been in her life? The answer was simple: with Colin she had no choice.

A champagne cork popped in the kitchen and Colin appeared with a tray.

'Bagels, cream cheese and, especially for you, *Mademoiselle*, a glass of our finest champagne!'

'*Merci, Monsieur.*'

29

With the food finished, Colin emptied the bottle into their glasses. Gina was feeling the effect of the champagne and, judging Colin must feel the same, she decided to take the initiative. Confident the situation could be turned to her advantage, she attempted to move the relationship onto a lighter note, almost flirting.

'It wasn't me you wanted then?'

'What do you mean?'

'You said your master plan was based on probability. You identified the type of woman you wanted, not individual women you found attractive. You didn't want me. Any woman would do as long as she was my type. If you don't want me as person, why should I feel flattered? Why should I feel desired? Any one of a hundred women like me would do.'

A look of alarm appeared in Colin's eyes.

'No. It wasn't like that. You've misunderstood. It was ... The probability was ... It was like a dating agency. Take a large group of women and there is bound to be one who is right for you.'

'Am I the one for you, Colin?'

'You would have to be. I would have to want you to go through with it.'

'Oh, so you wouldn't kick me out of bed?'

'You're twisting my words.'

Colin's eyes flicked away from her face as he searched for a counter argument.

'I could leave anytime.'

'But you're still here.'

'Yes.'

'So you want *me*, do you, Colin?'

'Yes.'

'You want me ... *Georgina Hamilton* ... not just someone like me?'

Colin was becoming more and more agitated. This wasn't the way he'd planned it. She was asking the questions. His control had slipped. She was playing games. He might appreciate a worthy adversary, but he needed to be on top. Tied to the bed she might be, but she'd won that round of verbal sparring and he would need to recover his feeling of control.

Gina realized she mustn't push it too far; at some point he must dominate and she must beg him to take her. She was wondering how she would recognize the right moment when the agitation left his face. His eyes narrowed. He stood up and, without a word, grabbed her ankles and pulled her flat on her back. Her skirt rode up round her thighs. He ignored her protests. Swiftly he retied her bonds. Soon she was firmly spread-eagled once more. His expression was icy as he turned and left the room. Gina called after him to no avail. She heard his key in the lock. The front door opened, closed, and he was gone.

She was alone.

Gina shivered. Her apprehension had returned with his change of mood. With his departure, apprehension turned to fear. What would happen if he didn't come back? She mustn't dwell on this. Gina tried to control her thoughts. He'd not be gone long. She'd pushed too fast, pushed him too hard. While she was helpless she must allow him complete control.

Questions, questions, questions. This time she's gone too far. Twisting my words, thinking she's being clever. Well, I've got a surprise for you, Ms Hamilton, I'll show you who's in control. Of course, she'll not know it's me. She'll think it's for real. She'll not know what's happening, not know what's hit her. Little Ms Hamilton, alone in her apartment, in her home where she's always felt safe ... she'll be petrified.

In the corner of a pub, I drain my glass and look at my watch. Eight-thirty, still too soon. I'll leave her to stew a bit longer. Empty glass in hand, I elbow my way to the bar and, now with a full pint, excuse my way back to my seat. To pass the time I eat a cheese and pickle sandwich, disguising its lack of freshness with mouthfuls of lager. After the last mouthful I glance at my watch. Almost nine. I've waited long enough. Picking up my half-empty glass, I walk to the payphone.

Gina woke with a start. Her landline was ringing. She moved to answer it and the cords bit into her flesh. Memories flooded back. She'd pushed him too far, too soon. He'd gone silent, not replied, then walked out, leaving her tied to the bed. Not a word, no promise to return. She was alone.

The ringing stopped. Silence. It must have been a wrong number. She tried to relax. Silence and then the phone started to ring again. On and on it rang in the darkness. On and on as if someone knew she were there, knew she was listening.

It was Colin! She knew it was him, reminding her of her helplessness, reminding her that he was in control. He was free, out there in town, while she was his captive, obliged to wait alone in the darkness.

Spread-eagled on the bed, Gina felt exposed, vulnerable. Her mind was racing. She counted slowly to ten, breathing deeply. She must ignore her plight, stick to her plan, gain his confidence, turn the tables and escape. But try as she might, Gina couldn't ignore the ringing telephone and its implicit message.

I know you're there. I'm in control.

The ringing stopped. The silence and darkness closed around her. She wanted him back. She wanted him here with her. With him beside her there was hope. Without him she was alone. She wanted to curl into a ball for comfort but the bonds held her exposed and defenceless in the dark.

In the silence Gina became aware of a presence, a sound in the far corner of the room. What was it? She listened intently. Nothing. No, there it was again, very faint, wind howling round an isolated house. Now there was nothing, nothing but the sense of something there in the dark. Silence, but not silence, and then, there it was again, growing louder. It wasn't a distant wind. It was someone breathing out through an open mouth. The sound continued, changing in pitch and volume, human, but not human. There was no intake of breath, just a continuous flow of air from within. Flowing out from within what? No one could breathe out for so long.

Suddenly the room was filled with light.

Blinded, Gina closed her eyes. Terrified, she cried out. There was no reply. The breathing, if that's what it was, had stopped. She strained her ears. The silence continued until ... what was that? Gina thought she could hear a soft movement on the carpet. She strained to listen more closely. There was nothing, nothing at all, just silence and the blinding light. She was imagining things. She squinted through her lashes. Gradually her eyes became accustomed to the light. There it was again. Something was scratching. No ... not scratching. What was it? A cold panic gripped her body.

It was the sound of dry scales slithering on the carpet – a snake!

Terrified, she cried out in horror and lifted her head, struggling to see what was on the floor near the bed, but sprawled as she was, her view was restricted. Suddenly, just as she decided she must be hallucinating, there was a new sound. Again, it was very faint. The new sound appeared to be coming from the left corner of her bedroom. It was a voice softly calling. At first it was no more than a breath, but then she recognized the voice was breathing her name.

Gina ... Gina ...

Then it was a little louder and coming from the right.

Gina ... Gina ... I know you're there, Gina. Why don't you answer me?

Suddenly the voice was a shout from beneath the bed.

GINA!

She shrank back against the mattress, clammy with her own sweat, unaware that she was screaming, abject terror forcing the sounds from her body in an instinctive act of survival. The light went out and the soft slithering sound returned; dry scales moving over the carpet but this time the thing was under her bed. The strength to scream deserted her, her muscles betrayed her, she whimpered in the darkness, wretched and alone.

The telephone began to ring.

Spasmodically her body shook. In her head she cried out for him. She was his. Only he could save her.

The ringing stopped.

The silence returned.

Alone in the dark, she could cry no more. Unable to think, she waited.

Exhausted, she ached for his return.

30

Alone in the CID Room, Ed was working late. The other members of her team had long since left. After hours spent going over the meagre evidence they had so far from Dover, she was beginning to wonder if they would ever solve the mystery surrounding the death of Kayleigh Robson. Who had been there? Who had moved the dead girl's body? Why had she let them in? Life is about choices, so is detection. Where should she direct the team next?

With no CCTV coverage of Maxton House, the officers in Dover had concentrated attention on nearby cameras with little success. There were sightings of Kayleigh, but she was always alone, never with someone. Never with anyone who might have left her dead in her flat. Significantly, Kayleigh was not found on camera after 20.43 on Thursday, 13 June, when she was seen walking home alone along the Folkestone Road. This suggested she died later that evening or, if she'd remained in her flat, sometime during the next 48 hours. However, if death occurred then, on Friday 14 or Saturday 15, the seventh and sixth days before her body was found, why had no one seen her on the streets, why hadn't she arrived at work on the Friday morning? Was she being held captive in her own home?

In the absence of relevant evidence, Ed dismissed this line of reasoning as speculation. She was hoping Kayleigh's phone records might give them pointers to specific times and places. Until then, Ed had identified two cameras and a time window as their best chance of moving the investigation quickly forward by identifying X, the person who was in the flat at the time of Kayleigh's death.

The owner of the convenience store had been adamant that Kayleigh's note had not been delivered before he closed for the night, at 22.00 on the Thursday, but the note was there when he reopened at 07.55 on the Friday. Kayleigh was last seen on camera passing the shop on her way home at 20.43, so it was unlikely she came back to deliver the note herself. Working on the most probable sequence of events, Ed reasoned X had delivered the note sometime between 22.00 Thursday and 07.50 Friday. If the scenario had been a clean-up after a sex game gone wrong, X might have written the note to gain time. Ed had asked Jenny to organize a comparison of the writing; Kayleigh's mother should have something, at least a birthday card.

In the hope of identifying who delivered the note, Ed had got Mike to ask Dover for copies of the relevant CCTV footage: from across the road opposite the shop where Kayleigh worked and from security cameras in the shop itself. Jenny could help Mike scan the CCTV when it arrived.

The team was on the case, and there were possibilities, but Ed knew from experience that such possibilities often failed to deliver. Unless there was an unexpected breakthrough, their chances of cracking the case were dependent on finding a match for the DNA recovered from the partial prints left at Kayleigh's flat and that was a long shot. Getting a match would require X to have had a brush with the law and for X's DNA to be on the National Database. Those chances were slim because, apart from Kayleigh's missing mobile, there had been no signs of a break-in or burglary. As Brian Saunders had said, such cases were buggers.

Ed was not in the best of moods as she logged off and collected her things. Back at home, she opened a bottle of white wine and poured a large glass. Sitting at the kitchen table, with the glass and bottle to hand, Ed toyed with a cold slice of quiche and the contents of a small packet of wild rocket to which she'd added balsamic and olive oil. Much later, the bottle all but empty, she buried herself beneath the duvet and endured a fitful night's sleep.

31

Gina hadn't heard Colin return. She must have dozed, exhausted by fear and panic at the incessant phone and noises under the bed. It was a few minutes before she became aware of his hand lightly touching her thigh.

The hand was insignificant. Determined to escape, she'd overcome her disgust at the thought of him touching her. Success was paramount and to achieve it she'd take any path to exploit a potential weakness. After the horror of being alone, she felt protected by his return. With him beside her she felt safe. Her fears of the unknown sounds, of being abandoned, left to die, were a fading memory. Her immediate world had changed for the better. Gina relaxed, prepared for what might follow.

The hand became significant. It felt different against her thigh, questioning. She wondered what he would do. His hand didn't move. She remained still, her eyes closed. What should she do? What did he want? He said he wanted her but wouldn't force her. He said he wanted her to give herself to him. No, he wanted more than that, he wanted her to want him as much as he wanted her.

From the way Colin was behaving, what he was saying, he appeared to be so convinced of success that failure and its consequences hadn't crossed his mind. What did he think success would bring?

Suddenly, Gina was in his head. Colin saw the two of them becoming lovers, lifetime partners who'd met under strange circumstances. Their meeting might have been strange but it had been a blessing because they were together and destined to remain so. As he saw it, their meeting had awakened a need, a desire in Gina's mind of which she'd been unaware. He fulfilled her need, and, for him, Gina was all he'd ever wanted. They would be happy together. Okay, perhaps happy ever after was going too far, even for his deluded mind, but they'd be together and every year they'd toast the anniversary of this bizarre episode, the anniversary of the meeting that had kindled their relationship. The man was mad! After what he'd done to her, how could he possibly believe she would come to think of him in that way?

Occupied by her thoughts, Gina had forgotten the hand. It was still on her thigh. He might be mad, but here was his weakness and she was ready to exploit any weakness that offered a chance to escape. If she didn't give him what he wanted, death was the likely alternative. She didn't want to die. If she had to convince Colin she wanted him as much as he wanted her she would do so, no matter the sacrifice. Gina focused on the intensity with which she'd wanted him to return and shifted that feeling to wanting him physically, allowing the emotional arousal she felt at the thought of imminent death to fuel a physical desire for the man beside her on the bed.

She feigned slowly waking, afraid his hand would move away. His hand didn't move until she opened her eyes, but by then she'd moved her hip against his leg.

'Mmm, you're here. I missed you. I was afraid. When you left, I was alone in the dark, I wanted you back.'

He began to move.

'No, don't go away. Stay on the bed. Hold me and don't leave me alone again.'

For a moment he hesitated, wondering if she were back to playing games.

Gina moved again. As far as her bonds would allow, she snuggled her body against his.

'Mmm, that's better,' she murmured. 'Don't leave me again.'

His hand returned to her thigh. Neither of them moved until his hand started slowly upwards.

'Mmm, not yet, just hold me for a while.'

He slid his left arm under her shoulders, but seemed uncertain what to do with his right hand. He lifted it from her thigh and Gina became hyperaware of her body, tuned to every sensation, waiting for this next movement, his next touch. Would it be her breast? No. His right hand settled lightly on her stomach and, as he leant towards her, he moved it further around her waist.

'Mmm, yes, like that. Hold me close and tell me you won't ever leave me alone again.'

Ostensibly, Gina relaxed against the lean muscles of Colin's body, but inside she cringed at what would follow. Only by giving herself could she hope to escape. She could switch off during the act but the memory would be with her for ever. Only if she found a way to totally obliterate Colin from her life would she ever be completely free.

32

I don't know what to think. What did she mean? *Tell me you won't ever leave me alone again.* For ever? Surely, she didn't mean for ever? Not yet, not so soon, not for ever. Okay, not for ever, but she doesn't want me to leave. She doesn't want to be alone. She wants me to stay with her. My shock tactics have worked. Now she knows who's in control. I'm in control. She respects that control. She's realized her weakness, experienced her need, and now she wants me beside her. It's just as I thought. All I ever needed was time. We're getting closer. The moment will come. We're almost there. Soon she'll show that she wants me as much as I want her.

33

It was daylight when Gina woke, still tied to the bed, still in Colin's arms. With her eyes closed, as if still sleeping, she moved against him, subtly at first, and then more overtly, until she felt him respond. Straining at her bonds, she twisted towards him. Her breast touched the back of his hand and she stopped, motionless, as if the contact were a surprise. Colin didn't move, but Gina could feel the tension in his body as she stretched her neck, turning her face to his.

'I can't reach you.'

Colin put his hand to her cheek, twisting her head towards his face. The cords bit into her wrists. Gina didn't wince, but offered her lips. He raised himself on one elbow and their mouths came together. Suddenly, he was on top of her, lifting her skirt, pulling her pants to one side. Still balanced on one elbow, he freed himself from his trousers. Gina arched to meet him. The tension that had built between them was released. Colin's movements quickened and his breath came rapidly through an open mouth.

'No. No. Turn me over to finish.'

Colin struggled to turn Gina's body.

'Now, quickly, do it now. Turn me over.'

'I can't.'

'Loosen the cords on one side.'

Caught in a surge of passion, Colin freed Gina's left arm, then her leg, and she rolled onto her stomach.

'Now! Take me *now*!'

Seconds later, Colin fell sideways onto his back, breathing deeply. Gina snuggled against his chest, matching her breathing to his own. His eyes closed, his breathing slowed.

Gina waited until she was sure Colin was sleeping. Gradually, she moved her left hand to the cord at her right wrist. Working slowly and gently, she transferred the cords from her limbs to his. Colin remained asleep. With the cords in place on his right arm and leg, Gina turned her attention to his left arm, looping the cord round his wrist and drawing it slowly towards the head of the bed. Alerted by the movement he began to stir. Gina grasped the cord with both hands, and, bracing her foot against the bed, pulled sharply. Colin wasn't a heavy man; Gina managed to shift his whole body to the left and the cords around his right limbs tightened. Quickly, before he grasped what was happening, Gina tied the cord from his left wrist to the bed head. Now, with only his left leg free, Gina smiled with satisfaction. From her own experience, she knew that in a short time, he'd be completely spread-eagled.

'What the fuck? Gina? You bitch!'

Colin kicked out with his free leg and pulled violently at the cords. They held firm.

'Don't struggle.' Gina kept the smile from her face, but not from her voice. 'It's pointless, and you'll only hurt yourself.'

'Get these ropes off me!'

'Oh, I don't think that would be wise, do you, Colin?'

'This isn't—'

'Isn't what? Funny? A game? How it was supposed to be?'

Colin looked at Gina, perplexed, unable to believe what had happened. She saw her chance. The final cord was already looped around his free ankle. Gina grabbed it, pulled his left leg straight and tied it to the bottom of the bed.

Now breathing rapidly, Gina checked each of the cords was securely tied to the bed and then ran into the hall. Colin's keys were on the hall table. She selected the key that didn't match her own, stepped to the front door and pushed his key into the internal lock.

It wouldn't turn.

Gina pulled the key out and tried again. Still it wouldn't turn.

The cold tension returned between her shoulder blades. She glanced back down the hall. There was no one there. Of course not, Colin was tied to the bed. Gina compared the keys again. His ring had two keys, one that matched her door key and one that was different. She was convinced she'd used the right one. For a third time she tried the new key in the lock. Still it wouldn't turn.

Gina dropped the keys, stepped to the hall table and started to call the police. With 99 showing on the display, she stopped. It was useless. Memories of her earlier attempts to escape from the apartment flooded back. The landline was useless, just Colin's voice and his mocking *let's take it slowly*. Gina leant against the wall, struggling to keep calm, struggling to think logically, struggling against the fear that she would be forever locked in the apartment with Colin. She looked from side to side, willing herself to find a means of escape. Through her growing panic she slowly realized something was wrong, something small, something beyond the horror of her imprisonment.

Something was odd. Something that should be there wasn't. It was the spot on the hall wall, which she'd hammered with her shoe, the spot where the heel had dug into the plaster – there was no mark! The damage had been repaired.

Colin!

Gina gasped, hesitated a second, then almost ran to the bathroom. Yes ... the door lock had been replaced. Her mobile, which she'd left in pieces, had been reassembled. Without thinking, she dialled her home number and the landline in the hall started ringing. Cutting the call, Gina went to the front door and tried her key instead of Colin's. It turned easily and the door opened. Gina exhaled with relief and stepped outside.

Immediately, the tension left her body. She almost laughed at the release. Colin was tied to the bed and she'd escaped from the apartment. Gina felt a surge of triumph. She was free! She was in control.

Confidently, she stepped back inside the apartment, closed the door and went to her bedroom. Colin didn't speak. She felt his eyes on her back, but no cold tension started between her shoulder blades. She took clothes from the wardrobe and underwear from her drawer, carried them to the bathroom and took a long soothing shower. Then, dressed for the street, Gina returned to the bedroom and the pathetic sight of Colin, spread-eagled on the bed with his shrunken manhood exposed to the world. He remained impassive, only his eyes following her movements as she rechecked his bonds. Satisfied, Gina turned her back and, without a word, left the apartment.

34

The bitch! I couldn't believe what was happening. I still can't believe it. I thought Gina had seen my worth. I thought we were good. When she became provocative I was only too pleased to go along with it. What man wouldn't? Now this – tricked, tables turned and *she's* tied *me* to the bed. And tight, bloody tight; there's not much room for movement. I can roll my shoulders, arch my back and clench my buttocks, but my arms and legs are held, fully stretched to the corners of the bed.

Raging at her was pointless.

This reversal – it's not my fault. No one would have seen it coming. Impossible to predict. Forget it. Water under the bridge. Move on.

Focus. What's next? What does she want?

The moment she swept out, and the door closed behind her, I thought she'd be back with the cops, but now I'm not so sure. Gina's bright, she'll think it through, she'll understand there are two sides to every story.

If she walks back in here with the police, what will they see? Me in a humiliating position; okay, let's not dwell on that. What the detectives will come to see is what I tell them. *Officer, I'm sorry, this is all very embarrassing, but I'm sure you can see what's happened. It's a sex game gone wrong. I simply don't understand what Gina, Ms Hamilton, is doing. Up 'til now she's been very happy with our relationship.* Get that in early: a relationship. We were in a relationship.

What can she say to contradict me? If she tells the truth, will anyone believe her? I got into her home, tied her to the bed, but she escaped and tied me to the bed instead. Would you believe that? I certainly wouldn't. I may not be big, but I'm strong. The police would see that and I can substantiate the nature of our relationship. *I assure you, officer, we've known each other for some time. You can easily check. Recently, I arranged for this room, her bedroom, to be decorated and I also booked a holiday with Tuscan Sun Tours for her as a surprise present. Unfortunately, Gina decided at the last minute that she didn't want to go, so I had to cancel.*

My arms, raised unnaturally above my head, are starting to feel uncomfortable and I've got an itch. Fortunately, it's on my back; rolling my shoulders brings some relief.

If I'm reasonable, and speak politely to the police, setting out the evidence, what can she say?

Officer, look what he's done. I'm sure that's the line she was planning to take. *My mobile, my laptop, my landline; the locks on the doors to the apartment and the bathroom.* Sorry, Georgina. While you were sleeping, I reversed all those changes. Your mobile, laptop, landline and door locks are all working normally. But you're bright, Gina, you know that, don't you? I heard you checking, heard the landline ring. And there's more, which I'm sure you'll fathom when you give yourself a moment to think.

I've kept the receipt for copying the key to your apartment when you decided I should have one. I also have receipts for food and drink in the fridge plus the bottles and packaging in the refuse bin; all evidence of our cosy evening together. Oh, and by the way, don't think the Decorart flier, the university questionnaire and the singles club competition entry will support your story. I searched carefully and destroyed all trace of them.

Let's face it, Gina, worst-case scenario it's your word against mine. I can hear you now, getting increasingly desperate as you did when your key wouldn't work. *Please, officer, please. Ask my friends. My colleagues at the dental practice. They'll tell you that I'm not in a relationship with this man.* Sorry, Georgina. You don't have such close friends and I'm sure you've not told Rachael about me.

I'm sure Gina will be thinking all this, well, most of it, and she'll come to the same conclusion: there's no mileage in reporting me to the police.

Things aren't good, but they're far from bad. I took my eye off the ball. Just a momentary lapse of concentration and I'm the one tied to the bed.

Fuck, the itch is back. I try moving my back more vigorously, but the cords are too tight. Bitch! At least I gave her a bit of slack so she could alter her position.

When she's worked out there's no point in going to the police, what next? Gina's an intelligent woman. That's one of the things I liked about her. Perhaps I'm underestimating her. Perhaps she's just making a point. But now she's made her point, surely that should be enough, there's no need to continue. When she returns, it'll be time to untie the bonds and laugh at how clever we've been, how suited we are, how well we go together.

Yes ... that's what'll happen. But come on, Gina, you could've done it sooner. That would've been the fair way to play it, the civilized way. But no, it seems you want more. You want to make me suffer.

Why? To what end? Not payback? Tit-for-tat is so petty.

I wince, my thoughts interrupted by the cords. They're beginning to bite into my wrists. I shouldn't have struggled, but I didn't believe she'd go through with it.

Gina, you must come back soon.

I try to relax, to stay calm, but cry out with pent-up frustration. The spot on my back has started to itch intensely and there's no way I can scratch it.

I lie still, resigned, waiting for Gina to return.

35

Taking the path by the river, Gina made her way via Palace Street to the city centre. The high she'd felt after turning the tables on Colin had gone. She'd thought the future would be simple. Her imperative had been to escape Colin's control, escape from the flat and go to the police. She would lead them to her home; Colin would be arrested, tried and sentenced to prison. But now, as she walked the familiar route to the dental practice, it dawned on Gina she'd been wrong. The scene that would greet the police at her apartment would be a problem. She needed time to think.

At the brasserie on the corner of Sun Street, Gina took a corner table by the window and ordered orange juice, caffè latte, baguette, butter and confiture. It struck her how similar this breakfast was to the one Colin had given her. Colin! Where was he now? Alone tied to her bed with his pants and trousers round his ankles. Thankfully, the image was erased by a waiter bringing her breakfast.

Gina reached for the coffee, her mind racing, weighing possibilities, probabilities and consequences. She might be free, but Colin was still a problem and, try as she might, she could not arrive at a welcome solution. Despite her revulsion at the thought, logic forced her back to a choice she never imagined she would countenance. Counting on proximity to force her hand, Gina paid the bill and retraced her steps to Great Stour Court.

When she entered the apartment, there was no sound from the bedroom. Gina could see Colin's thin body on the bed, his white blond fringe still swept sideways across his forehead. He gave no sign that he was aware of her presence. She stood for a moment, studying his features, and then walked into the kitchen to think things through one last time.

Gina sat at the kitchen table with a glass of mineral water, drinking slowly, her fingertips wet from the condensation. On finishing the first glass, she got more water from the fridge. Eventually, she stood, placed the empty glass in the sink, walked into the hall and dumped her bag on the side table. She half-turned, hesitated for a moment and then, her mind made up, she returned to the kitchen for something she needed before confronting Colin. He was where she had left him, stretched out on the bed with his trousers around his knees. It was a humiliating position, but Colin showed no sign that he felt it.

Raising her skirt, Gina climbed onto the bed and straddled Colin's thighs. His face registered surprise, then puzzlement. He appeared confused, apprehensive, but apprehension slowly turned to arousal as she moved against him. He began timing his movements to hers. As their breathing quickened, Gina reached back and pulled something from the waistband of her skirt. The light glinted from a blade as she rested it lightly against his chest. Colin froze. His eyes widened in fear. Gina smiled and drew the point of the knife gently down his chest, barely cutting the skin. Bright drops of blood appeared. She laid the knife flat on his stomach and felt the cold metal between them as she bent to kiss his lips. Gradually, Gina increased the intensity of her actions until Colin became lost in the moment. Abruptly, she sat up, grabbed the knife and, raising it high, slashed down. The blade severed the bonds at Colin's right wrist, freeing his arm. Gina leapt from the bed and ran into the kitchen.

Slipping off her clothes, she stood naked, facing the door, her buttocks touching the edge of the table and the knife clenched in both hands. There was a noise in the hall. The kitchen door swung open. Colin took one step towards her, then he saw the weapon and stopped. Gina raised the knife high above her head and struck. As the blade arced down towards his chest she swivelled, turned her back, and plunged the knife into the far end of the table, stretching her body before him.

'Now! Now! Take me now!'

Moments later, Colin levered himself upright and sank to the floor. Looking dazed, he slumped against the wall of the kitchen as if all the strength had been drawn from his body. Gina opened the fridge, poured two glasses of champagne and topped them up with orange juice.

'Whether you want this or not, you deserve it.'

'Your hands are bleeding.'

'So's your chest.'

'Is it? I hadn't noticed.'

'Nor me ... my hands, I mean.'

'I ... I don't know what to ...'

'Drink this and then we'll take the bottle to the bedroom.'

Gina led the way. She stretched luxuriously on the bed while Colin refilled their champagne glasses. He stood the bottle on the floor and began to untie the cords, which were still attached to the bedposts.

'What are you doing with those?'

'I'm getting rid of them.'

'Don't do that. Put them in the bedside drawer. You never know, we might feel inclined to use them again sometime in the future.'

'The future?'

Gina turned on her side. 'You're not going to leave me alone again, are you?'

'I ... I hadn't thought ...'

'About the future?'

'My head was full, filled with wanting you.'

'And mine, with wanting you, but you didn't make it easy.' Gina held a hand out towards him. 'Close the drawer and come here.'

Colin climbed onto the bed and Gina pulled him down by her side and snuggled into the crook of his arm. She cupped his chin and turned his head towards hers, kissing him affectionately.

'What do you mean, I didn't make it easy?' asked Colin.

Gently, with her fingertips, Gina traced the line of the knife-cut on his chest.

'We were in an impossible situation. You were in control. If I'd offered myself, I would have been surrendering. I couldn't do that because you'd said that you didn't want sacrifice. You wanted me to want you as much as you wanted me. You called it the gift, but what you really wanted was mutual respect and mutual desire. I couldn't show my respect and desire from a position of weakness.'

Gina repeated her soft lingering kiss; affection with desire held in check. Her eyes were closed. Moving her head to Colin's shoulder, she placed her lips near his ear.

'You made it hard. I didn't want to go against you, but I was desperate for you to know I really wanted you. Back there in the kitchen, I could have killed you, but I offered myself, begged you to take me: mutual respect, mutual desire.'

Colin started to speak but Gina put fingers to his lips. 'Shhh ... stay quiet. Take me now, gently ... gently with affection.'

36

Ed was walking across the car park towards the Station entrance, a coffee from Deakin's in hand, when Chief Superintendent Karen Addler's white BMW turned sharply and stopped in her path. The Super began speaking before her driver's window had fully opened.

'Ogborne, why no advance with the body in Dover?'

Ed began to answer, but Addler cut her off with a peremptory wave of the hand.

'I was talking with the Chief Constable last night. He's concerned there's been no progress. We both are. I don't want your team failing to deliver with this one. We don't need it to drag on like the abductions.'

Ed had become used to the Super's manner, but Addler's readiness to see slow progress as the fault of her staff continued to rile.

'I agree entirely, Ma'am, but the case is proving exceptionally difficult.'

'The Chief Constable and I want action, not excuses.'

Ed thought the car park was an inappropriate place for a case review, but she was not going to let the exchange come to an end without first making her point.

'Ma'am, the dead woman, Kayleigh Robson, was a loner.

Loners are notoriously difficult. It's impossible to learn anything but mundane aspects of their lives. Without a breakthrough, we're dependent on identifying the DNA retrieved from the rogue fingerprint. We know it's male, but there's no match on the National Database and none with her work colleagues or—'

'Prioritize, Ogborne. The Chief Constable and I want this sorted.'

'Yes, Ma'am, as do we all. My priority now is a familial DNA search. I was coming to see you today. I need you to request approval from the NDNAD Strategy Board.'

'Consider it done.'

'Thank you, Ma'am.'

Ed's words were lost as the car window closed and Addler accelerated into her reserved parking.

Nat and Jenny were alone in the CID room when Ed entered. She was crossing to her desk when the telephone started to ring with an external call. Ed snatched up the receiver and settled in her chair.

'Hi, Ed, it's Brian.'

'Brian, what can I do for you?'

'How are things going with the Dover case?'

'Dire. Our appeal for people who've known Kayleigh during her time in Dover fell on stony ground. It seems she really was a loner and nobody's come forward with anything useful about her private life. We haven't got a single lead to whoever was in the flat and moved the body.'

'What about the DNA from the partial print?'

'We know it's male, but it didn't match her work colleagues or her boss. However, it did match DNA extracted from a smudged palm print on the outside of the door to Kayleigh's flat.'

'It seems likely that whoever was in her flat pushed open the front door at some point, then forgot about it during his clean-up.'

'It looks that way, but the DNA's no help; there's no match on the National Database.'

'As I said, such cases are buggers.'

'Tell me about it. This morning I had Addler on my back, in the car park of all places! She practically took my toes off with her BMW. Lucky she didn't get a lapful of my coffee through her window.'

'Either way, sounds like Karen's had an earful from the Chief Constable.'

'On the bright side, it gave me a chance to get my request in without waiting for her to allocate an appointment window.'

'Request?'

'With no match for the Dover DNA, I want a National Database familial search,' Ed said. 'Addler will seek approval from the Strategy Board.'

'It's a long shot.'

'Unless we get a break, the investigation risks running into the ground.'

'Apart from your run-in this morning, how *is* your Super?'

'You know our Karen, forever mixing her metaphors by firefighting choppy waters while keeping both eyes on career progression and staying chummy with the Chief Constable.' Ed took a sip of coffee. 'From an unnecessary remark this morning I think the serial abductions have become a particularly sore point for her. The case attracted intense media interest and she insisted it was all channelled through her. There were a few interviews and she got her photograph in the locals but nothing in the nationals.'

'Not enough PR to satisfy Addler's ambitions then. From what I saw, you won the column-inches stakes by way more than a head.'

'It was my first case in Canterbury, and the new-cop angle made for a better story.'

'And, with your short dark hair, you're more photogenic.'

'Brian!'

Immediately, Ed regretted reacting. She imagined Saunders smiling into his phone.

'Seriously, Ed, the journos got the right officer. You earnt the press coverage.'

When she didn't respond, Brian wound up the conversation.

37

Gina and Colin were sharing lunch in her kitchen. Fingering the hole made by the knife she'd plunged into the kitchen table, Gina was the first to break the silence.

'We need to think about what we do next.'

Colin looked up expectantly.

'What did you have in mind?'

'My colleagues at work, friends, parents.'

'There's something you want to tell them?'

'Show them.'

'What do you mean?'

'I may have few close friends and I don't use social media, but when I return to work, my colleagues will expect to see some photographs of my holiday. The same goes for friends and my parents when I next meet them.'

Colin forked a piece of feta and leant forward as he raised it to his mouth so that any oil drops would fall on his plate. 'What do you have in mind?'

'I need photographs of me in Siena. I particularly need shots of me at the Palio – I've made such a big thing of going to see it.'

'It's a bit late for that. The Palio starts this coming Saturday and the race is on Tuesday. Perhaps I could take some shots of you and paste them into suitable images of the town and the race.'

'I'd rather be there.'

'It's run again in August. We could go then.'

'I'm supposed to be there now.'

Gina looked morosely at her plate, and silently prodded her salad, before raising her head and catching his eye.

'Remember when you told me about the timeshare in Portugal?'

'Yeah ...' said Colin, cautiously.

'You said, if you have money, you can get almost anything. Surely, you could arrange for us to go to the Palio this weekend?'

Colin hesitated.

'Come on, Colin, do it for me. Let's do it in style. If the Palio starts on Saturday, let's fly out Friday and hire a car.'

Colin hesitated for a few more seconds and then relaxed.

'Better than that,' he said with a smile, 'I'll hire a limo and a driver.'

Gina moved round the table to stand behind his chair. Bending, she put her arms round his neck and whispered in his ear.

'Thank you, darling, I knew you wouldn't let me down.'

38

'Are we any closer to identifying X, the guy who was in the Dover flat?'

It was now six days since Kayleigh Robson's body had been found on her bed in Maxton House. The Dover police had questioned potential witnesses and scoured local CCTV without success. To move the case forwards, Ed had established three lines of inquiry for her CID team to follow: the hand-written note to Kayleigh's boss; footage from particular CCTV cameras she thought worth a second look; and Kayleigh's mobile phone records.

This morning, she'd gather the team together in the Incident Room to review progress.

'Let's start with the note. Jenny, what can you tell us?'

'Pat, Kayleigh's mother, had birthday cards from her daughter going back years and also homework pieces Kayleigh had written while still at school. To my eye, the writing is immature and hasn't changed much over the years.'

Jenny placed two plastic-covered samples face-up in the centre of the table. None of her colleagues gave them more than a cursory glance.

'As you can see, Kayleigh's writing looks very similar to the note and the signatures look identical. However, in a preliminary report the handwriting specialist said the note wasn't written by Kayleigh; the forgery is good, but her writing style is relatively easy to copy.'

'Thanks, Jenny. On the sex-game-gone-wrong scenario, the note was probably written and delivered to the shop by X, the guy who was with Kayleigh at the time of her death and who left his prints on the loo and the door. Mike, do the CCTV tapes – the ones we selected to cover delivery of the note – throw any light on who X might be?'

'Not good news, Ed. The store has three security cameras. Two point up aisles towards the rear of the shop and are useless for our purpose. The third camera is trained on the counter, with the street door and windows in the background. And that's one of the problems: you can't see the bottom of the door. It's impossible to know when the note was delivered. The other problem is that the door and shop windows have posters stuck to the glass and lots of reflections. People walking by are largely obscured and reduced to blurry shadows. For the shop itself, that's it, just those three internal cameras.'

'What about an external camera?' asked Nat. 'Many places have a camera outside, above the entrance, to show the shop door and adjacent pavement.'

'Not this one,' said Mike. 'If only.'

Jenny, who had helped Mike analyse the CCTV, took over.

'We were hoping for better from a camera across the road, which gives an excellent shot of the shop front.' Jenny caught Mike's eye and he nodded for her to continue.

'Unfortunately, many vehicles on the Folkestone Road tend to be large – buses, lorries and the like. To make matters worse, vehicles are frequently stationary because of nearby traffic lights. Both Mike and I have studied the footage between

20.43 on Thursday the 13th, when Kayleigh was last seen, and 07.55 on Friday the 14th, when the owner arrived to open his shop and found the note. There's no sign of anyone at the shop entrance, pushing a note under the door. When it happened, and whoever did it, must have been hidden by a stationary vehicle.'

'Sod's law,' added Mike.

'Sod's law indeed, Mike, that's a chance missed. Thanks, Jenny. Let's hope we've got something useful from Kayleigh's phone records. Nat?'

'The real Sod's law,' said Nat forcefully, 'is that we didn't recover Kayleigh's mobile. Without it, we can't download her texts.'

'It doesn't take an Einstein to know you'd need to destroy her mobile to cover your tracks.' Mike turned to face Nat directly before continuing. 'X probably burnt the SIM card, smashed the handset and scattered the bits in Dover harbour.'

'Hang on, Mike,' said Ed. 'Kayleigh's mother told us that she paid the monthly fees for a dating app. As SIO, I gave SPOCs the details and we've had the billing data from her ISP. Nat, you've been looking at it, what have we got?'

'Lots of info, numerous data points, but nothing to pinpoint who X is or where she met him.'

Nat smiled at his colleagues and paused until he had their full attention. It was apparent he felt he had a major contribution to make and had given some thought to how he'd play it. When he spoke, he'd clearly committed the information to memory.

'Kayleigh Robson was a loner – and lonely. Apart from calls to her mother on the 21st of each month, and occasional calls to her boss at the shop, there's very little phone activity.'

'I'm not surprised,' said Ed. 'The poor girl suffered a massive loss of self-esteem when her biological father walked out of the family home. Pat, her mother, said Kayleigh stopped going out with friends. It seems that behaviour continued, perhaps worsened, when she took herself off to Dover.' As she spoke, Ed looked at Nat and decided his expression was confident rather than smug. Confidence was fine, but she was alarmed her young DC was beginning to show elements of Mike Potts's longwinded style.

Nat ignored Ed's interruption concerning Kayleigh's possible psychological state. He was absorbed by the mechanics of his findings. 'The dating app haven't released information from their private channels, but Kayleigh appears to have had very few takers.'

Now it was Mike who interrupted. 'If you haven't got her dating app communications, how can you come to that conclusion?'

Nat smiled. 'There are clusters of calls and texts to unknown numbers. These clusters occur at intervals since Kayleigh got the app two years ago. Each cluster involves communication with a single phone number, which is unique to that cluster. By unique, I mean the number doesn't occur at other times in the billing record.'

Now it was Jenny who interrupted. 'Let's be clear, you're saying these clusters of communication with unique numbers are exchanges associated with hook-ups she made via the dating app?'

'That's what I've deduced from the billing data. It seems a reasonable deduction and there were just seven such clusters in the last two years. Only two of the communication clusters lasted more than a few days. I assume the longer clusters involved repeat dates with the same guy, but neither lasted more than a few weeks. That's why I say she was lonely.'

It was a good analysis, but Ed felt Nat was milking it and she was about to move him on when Jenny beat her to it.

'Any recent clusters, during the period leading up to Kayleigh's death?'

'There were two single SMS exchanges with different mobile numbers, both pay-as-you-go. They were the sixth and seventh contacts that I've deduced relate to hook-ups made via the dating app.'

'Dates and times?' asked Mike.

'Dates, times and *locations*,' replied Nat with a smug smile. 'Monday, 3rd of June at 17.53, Kayleigh, the calling party, was accessing a mast that covers her flat. The phone used by the other person, the called party, who responded immediately, was accessing a mast that covers the railway station in Aylesham. I've called that contact C6.'

'Where's Aylesham?' asked Ed.

'It's on the main line from Canterbury to Dover,' said Nat. 'The other SMS exchange occurred ten days later on Thursday the 13th of June—'

'The day Kayleigh died!'

Nat continued without acknowledging Jenny's interruption. 'On the 13th of June at 18.20, Kayleigh's phone was accessing the mast that covers her flat while the mobile of the other party was accessing a mast that covers Dover Priory railway station. I've called that contact C7.'

'Only seven dates in two years.' Whatever his thoughts, Mike didn't elaborate.

Ed brought the meeting back to the essentials. 'C7 is clearly a person of interest regarding the events of Thursday the 13th and, if C7 and Kayleigh were planning to meet, C7 could be X. Find C7 and we could have the guy who was responsible for Kayleigh's death.'

'It's so frustrating,' said Jenny. 'Without downloads from Kayleigh's phone, we don't know who he was, or when and where they met.'

'Not exactly,' said Ed, 'we can make some educated assumptions. On Thursday the 13th of June, the last day Kayleigh was seen alive, at 18.20 she exchanged texts with C7. If we assume they were planning to meet later that evening, given their locations, it's likely they'd settled on a public place in the centre of Dover.'

'Shall I get onto Jack Burstford?'

'Yes, Mike, the team in Dover are best placed to identify central locations where Kayleigh would have been likely to meet a first-time date. Ask them to check security camera tapes between 18.00 and 21.00 on Thursday the 13th. If they spot her, get them to check the same time on Monday the 3rd. We'll need copies of relevant CCTV for the two meetings and also from cameras between where she meets the men and her flat in Maxton House.'

'What about the railway station at Aylesham?'

'Good point, Mike. Ask for the security tapes from 17.00 to 20.00.'

'It'll take Dover a few days, at least, to get that together.'

'No matter, we're moving forward.' Ed pushed her chair back from the table. 'Well done, everyone, great work!' She got to her feet and the meeting began to break up.

Halfway to the door, Ed turned to face her colleagues and added, 'I'm off for the weekend. Without the footage from Dover we're at an impasse. We'll not get the tapes until early next week. As soon as they arrive, I want the four of us to go through them with a fine-tooth comb and finally identify the men Kayleigh met before she died.'

Ed left the building and, standing at the far side of the car park, called Daniel's mobile.

'Hi, Daniel, you said you weren't working this weekend, so I've booked us a surprise two days away: seaside walks, pub lunches and good restaurants in the evening. I'll pick you up from work on Friday and drive you down myself.'

'Sorry, Ed. I've got rugby practice on Friday.'

'Okay, I can pick you up after that and we can have a late supper at the hotel.'

'Sounds good, but I can't miss another drink with the boys.'

'Oh ...' Momentarily deflated, Ed considered the options. 'Right, I'll tweak the reservations. Join me in Camber Sands for brunch on Saturday – I'll text details of the hotel – and we'll spend Saturday night at a different place in Rye.'

'You're on, but seeing as we'll both have our cars, why not make it two nights in Rye and we'll drive to work early Monday morning.'

Ed smiled. 'I'll look forward to it. Bye.'

It was 11.30 on Friday, 28 June, when Ed thought, *Sod Daniel, I'm going to have my long weekend anyway*. Twenty minutes later, she shut down her computer and downloaded a novel to her Kindle. At noon, when she left the Station and walked to her car, Gina and Colin were already thirty minutes into their Club Europe flight from Gatwick to Pisa. By the time the flight attendant served a second glass of champagne, Ed was driving out of Canterbury on the Ashford road via Chartham and through Brookland, to cross the county border into East Sussex.

39

Colin was woken by a drum. He groaned and pulled the pillow over his head. By the time Gina was fully awake, the first hesitant strokes had accelerated into a rapid, almost military tattoo. She was reminded of the times she stayed up late with her parents to watch Hogmanay from Edinburgh. The sound was similar but not the same. Edinburgh had the sharp, taut crispness of military drums, a precise, rhythmic machine gun's call to arms. In Siena, the sound coming from the narrow streets was no less intricate, no less rhythmic, but it was deeper and less constrained. Gina felt the strokes in her belly like bass notes in a club. By the time she reached the window, the lone drummer had been joined by a second from the opposite side of the Campo. Rival *contrade* marking their neighbourhoods, letting the others know they were there.

Yesterday, when they'd arrived at the airport in Pisa, there was a car waiting to take them to Siena. Colin had been reading the guide books and wanted to stop at San Gimignano, but the car park outside its massive walls was full. Their driver offered to leave them for an hour, to walk up via San Giovanni to the Piazza della Cisterna, but Gina was content to photograph the towers from a distance. This trip was all about the Palio. Soon after they arrived in Siena, their car stopped outside a battered wooden double doorway. Colin tipped the driver and went to collect the keys from an ice-cream shop on the corner. Gina felt a bit miffed; she'd been promised a view over the Piazza del Campo, yet here they were in some narrow backstreet.

Once through the battered entrance, they climbed three flights of stone stairs before Colin stopped and opened the door to the rented apartment. He asked Gina to wait while he put their cases inside. With her expectations raised by the flight and the chauffeured car journey, this wasn't the arrival Gina had been expecting. Colin returned to carry her, eyes closed, over the threshold and through to the front of the building. Standing as directed she heard him open a latch and then felt warm air on her arms. He adjusted the direction of her gaze before speaking.

'Okay, now you can open your eyes.'

Gina recognized the view immediately. She was looking across the shell-shaped Campo directly at the Palazzo Pubblico and the Torre del Mangia. Resting her hands on the window-sill and leaning forward she could see the entire sweep of the piazza, where seating, padded barriers and packed earth were already in place for the race. She turned to Colin with a smile of thanks.

'It's wonderful, absolutely perfect. I don't know how you managed it at such short notice, but thank you, thank you, thank you. You've made me very happy.'

'We aim to please.'

'You've succeeded.'

Gina turned back to look at the view. She expected to feel Colin behind her and she would have turned in his arms to kiss him. Instead, she heard him open a door and call from the rear of the apartment.

'I'm going to have a quick shower while you take in the view. I'll be out in a few minutes. Then I suggest you enjoy a long soak in a cool bath before we go down to the piazza for something to eat.'

From the window Gina watched as hundreds of candles were lit on the restaurant tables surrounding the square. The sight provoked a surge of anger, frustration and a sense of loss. Never had she seen anything more romantic. With the piazza prepared for the Palio, here was everything she'd looked forward to for years, but not like this. The location was perfect but the circumstances were wrong. Gina sighed, but remained resolute – there would be other visits, happier times.

40

The drummers were still hidden within the narrow streets of their *contrade* but their rhythms filled the piazza. It was the opening day of the Palio, and the owner of the apartment, Umberto Sinagra, arrived to escort them to the first event. He greeted Colin like an old friend, before turning to Gina and, bending low, lightly brushed the back of her hand with his lips.

'*Signora Gina, molto piacere*. Come, I take you to the *tratta*, the allocation of horses to the *contrade*.'

Umberto, as he insisted they call him – *you are in my apartment, you are my guests, we are amici, friends!* – led them onto the street, through a narrow gap in the banked seating, across the *tufo*-covered track and out into the sloping centre of the piazza. They stood among a group of local people, facing a platform, in front of the Palazzo Pubblico.

The crowd seemed to know the quality of the horses. The drawing of a good horse was met with delight by the successful *contrada*. The allocation of a less favoured horse drew a collective sigh from the unlucky *contradaioli*, who were jeered by their rivals. As the last horse was led away, Umberto insisted they join him for a *caffè corretto* in his favourite bar.

'There were only ten horses, but our book says there are

seventeen districts ... err ... *contrade*.' Colin looked earnestly at their host. 'How does that work?'

Umberto nodded appreciatively and motioned them towards a table.

'*Signora Gina*, you would like a pastry?' Without waiting for her to reply, Umberto raised his arm and called to a woman behind the counter, '*Federica, un pasticcino per la signora*.' He turned back to Gina. 'Go, point to what you like. I tell *Signor Colin* about the horses.'

Gina stepped quickly to the counter, collected a croissant-like confection, oozing custard cream into its fold of paper, and returned to her seat.

'As I say, it is chance, but not complete chance. Every year there are two races. Each *contrada* will get a horse for at least one of those races. The seven who didn't get a horse for the last race are automatically in the pool for a horse this time. The other three in today's pool were drawn by lot from among the ten *contrade* who were in the last race.'

'And we've seen the ten horses are allocated by drawing lots. From the reaction of the crowd, I guess some are better than others.'

'*Esatto, Signora*. But it is not always the fastest horse, or the most ... *agile* ... how do you say ...?'

'Agile,' said Colin.

'Nimble,' said Gina.

'*I fantini* – the jockeys – they have whips, and not just for their own horse, they can use them on the other horses and on their rival jockeys.'

'So, it's no holds barred,' said Colin.

'Pulling at a rival's reins is not allowed, but a jockey can interfere with another jockey, or his horse, in other ways. But

150

what you see is not the whole story. *Il Palio* can be won and lost through secret deals between the *contrade* before the race. On Tuesday, watch the start and you will see some jockeys, following the instructions of their *contrada*, blocking other horses rather than trying to get a good position. It is good to win, but if you have a poor horse and cannot win, it is good your main rival should lose.'

'It's cutthroat between the *contrade*,' said Gina.

'No throats are cut these days, *Signora*, but it is ... err ...'

'No holds barred,' said Colin.

'Except for your rivals' reins,' said Gina.

'*Esatto!*'

'What happens between now and the race?'

'Many things. This evening will be the first *prova*, a trial run. As a welcome gift, I give you tickets for two seats in the stands so you can be close to the action, but on Tuesday, you should watch the race from your window.'

That evening, Gina and Colin sat side by side in the front row of a stand looking across the Campo to the Palazzo Pubblico, which was still bathed in late sunshine. Their anticipation had been heightened by the bright banners, the parades of people in mediaeval costume and the incessant drumming, but when the *prova* began, they felt a sense of anticlimax. From reading about the race, they'd expected to see the ten horses and their bareback riders galloping neck and neck round the track. A few did run side by side, but others hung back and then galloped round alone. Colin reminded Gina that this was a trial run, a practice for horse and rider. Things would be different in the race on Tuesday.

Their initial sense of disappointment didn't last long. The

people in the stand were tourists and their behaviour contrasted with that of the local Senesi who thronged the centre of the piazza. Their seated companions were curious, but strangely detached, watching the event largely through the viewfinders of their cameras, collecting evidence they were there. Across the track, things were different. There was no disguising the emotion of the Senesi. The involvement of the local crowd grew as the *prova* progressed and, by the end, the emotion reached levels of naked confrontation.

Colin glanced at Gina. Her knuckles were white where she gripped the top of the barrier in front of them; her mouth was slightly open and she was breathing deeply with her eyes fixed on the unrest in the crowd.

With the trial over, the *contradaioli* swarmed onto the track. Each *contrada* gathered around its horse and rider to lead them back to their stable. One by one, the tightly packed processions turned out of the piazza into the narrow streets leading to their home neighbourhoods. Eventually, just two groups remained, moving in opposite directions round the track. At any moment Colin expected them to peel off down a side street, but they continued to advance.

'What are they *doing*?' Gina had turned to Colin, her body rigid with anticipation.

'I don't know, but they're pretty fired up.'

Gina smiled. 'Remember what Sinagra said? If you can't win, make sure you stuff your enemy.'

'Well, these guys look ready for anything. If they don't stop soon, they're going to be face to face, right in front of us.'

The two *contrade*, each headed by a burly man leading the horse, continued to move forwards until they were nose to nose in front of Gina. They were so close, the leaders' faces appeared like close-ups on a cinema screen. Colin put his arm protectively around Gina's shoulders. Her whole body was tense with expectation. The animosity expressed by the posture of the men and their followers, the looks in their eyes, the vehemence of their taunts, were such that Gina was transfixed. It seemed as if violence would erupt any minute, but, at no sign Colin could detect, the moment passed, the intensity dropped, and the rivals disengaged, turning and making their separate ways out of the piazza.

As if released, Gina leapt to her feet, pulled Colin to her, raked his lip with her teeth and urged him back to the apartment.

41

Feeling a little tired after her weekend with Daniel in Rye, Ed arrived in the CID Room to find Mike Potts already at his desk. 'Anything from Dover, Mike?'

'Burstford and his team have played a blinder! Security camera tapes of Kayleigh Robson waiting in a pub and street CCTV of her walking home.'

'Which dates?'

'Both Monday the 3rd and Thursday the 13th. Dover have scanned the tapes to ensure they have Kayleigh, but they've left detailed analysis to us. Each of the two evenings, around 1930, she turns up at The Three Horseshoes, a busy pub in central Dover. According to Burstford, she leaves alone and nobody appears to follow her home. He thinks we might pick up someone in the tapes from Dover Priory railway station and match them with somebody in the vicinity of Kayleigh later in the evening.'

'Good thinking. Also, the Aylesbury station tapes: they might throw up someone boarding the train to Dover. You call Jenny and I'll get Nat. We need them here asap so the four of us can analyse the tapes in detail.'

Later that day, the four detectives met in the Incident Room to discuss what they'd found on the CCTV.

'At this stage, we need a narrative of what happened on Monday the 3rd, when we believe Kayleigh met C6, and on Thursday the 13th when she was due to meet C7,' said Ed. 'Mike, you and Jenny looked at Monday the 3rd, what can you tell us?'

Mike looked at Jenny. 'You made our notes.'

Jenny began from memory but increasingly checked her records for precise times. 'Our analysis starts with the security tapes from Aylesham station. At 17.53, C6 received and replied to a text from Kayleigh. She was in or near her flat and he was at Aylesham. At that time, a train to Dover was in the station. A few women with shopping and some children alighted, but only two people, an old couple, boarded the train. So, no sign of a man who might be C6. We assume he was already on the train, going to keep his appointment with Kayleigh somewhere in Dover.'

'What about the tapes from Dover Priory station?' asked Nat.

'The train from Aylesham arrived at 18.13. Several men got off who could have been C6, but we haven't been able to link them with Kayleigh later in the evening.'

'What about Kayleigh, Jenny?' asked Ed. 'When does she come into the picture?'

'The team at Dover found her in The Three Horseshoes, a busy pub in the centre of town. Mike and I logged her arriving at 19.26. She glances around the bar, buys a drink and sits at a small table, one for two people.'

'Who joins her at the table?' asked Nat. 'What does C6 look like?'

'Sod's law again,' said Mike. 'Nobody joins her. Whoever she was supposed to meet didn't show up.'

'We don't know that for certain,' said Ed. 'C6 may have been there watching Kayleigh, but not approaching her, not speaking to her.'

'Whatever,' said Jenny. 'Poor Kayleigh just sits there alone, getting more and more agitated, checking her phone, until 20.20, when she leaves and walks home.'

'Does anybody follow her?' asked Ed.

'A few people left just before and just after Kayleigh, but none we could match with people who came into the pub up to 15 minutes before her or 20 minutes after her.'

'It was the same with the tapes we looked at from Thursday the 13th,' said Nat. 'After the 18.20 SMS exchange, when she was at her flat and C7 was at Dover Priory station, Kayleigh arrived at The Three Horseshoes at 19.21. She sat alone with a drink, no one approached her and she left at 20.30.'

Ed took over their report. 'We looked at men on the Dover Priory tapes around the time the texts were sent, but found it impossible to match them with the men who entered or left the pub before and after Kayleigh did. So C7 remains unknown.'

'Kayleigh's not what you'd call a stunner,' said Nat. 'From my analysis of her mobile activity, she had very few takers on the dating app. Perhaps C6 and C7 turned up to give Kayleigh the once-over, didn't like what they saw and scarpered.'

Jenny rolled her eyes to the ceiling, but Ed pushed on, keeping the meeting on course.

'Don't forget, there was a man in Kayleigh's flat on Thursday the 13th at the time – or soon after the time – she died. That was the evening she went to meet C7. Did he watch her and then follow her home?'

'If he's bright and planned to do that,' said Nat, 'he might have changed his appearance from time to time.'

'The problem is that we have no idea what this man looks like,' said Mike.

Ed sighed. 'A DNA match would have given us a rapid breakthrough. We didn't get one, not even a partial familial match, which means our perpetrator hasn't had a brush with the law, nor have his immediate family.'

Jenny reverted to her mantra, quietly saying, 'There must be a way to catch this guy.'

'I agree,' said Ed, 'but we face problems. We're looking for a respectable guy with a penchant for kinky, if not outright S&M encounters. Kayleigh was a loner with no close friends and, crucially, we don't have her mobile phone.'

'If only she'd had a computer,' mused Jenny.

'Remember, her mother paid for the phone. Even living in a flat due for renovation, I doubt Kayleigh's income would have stretched to a laptop. No matter, if she'd had one, I reckon it would also have gone missing.'

'He's covered his tracks completely.'

Ed shot Jenny a quizzical glance. 'Not completely. We've got DNA from the finger and palm prints.'

'But there's no match on the National Database, not even a familial one,' objected Nat.

'One may turn up,' said Jenny, hopefully.

Mike expelled air through his nose. 'That's a pretty forlorn hope and without a match we're sunk.'

42

I knew Gina was a sexy woman. When I first saw her, walking along Burgate, the words *sexy and professional* flashed into my mind. That's probably why I chose her – it made her stand out in the sunshine. I'm certainly glad I did, but yesterday, after the trial run for the Palio, she surprised me. We almost had our first row. How do you avoid something like that? Give and take? Since she saw my worth, I seem to be the one doing all the giving. It sometime feels as if she's just using me, but that can't be right – she saw my worth, I've heard the admiration in her voice, I've seen it in her eyes.

What happened might seem like nothing, but it irked me and I can't get it out of my head. It wasn't a misunderstanding, but a difference of opinion. Fair enough, they happen, but I was the one backing down yet again. Gina can be very determined and very persuasive. She's a strong woman. Perhaps that's what I like about her.

I'd booked a table on the piazza. It looks lovely when the sun goes down and they light the candles. The plan was to go straight from our seats in the stands to a table outside our chosen restaurant. Well, that was my plan.

To tell the truth, the trial run for the race wasn't what I expected. I'm interested in the way things work. I wanted to

158

know all about the Palio, but the guidebooks gave little idea of what it's really like. Our landlord Sinagra explained a lot more, but even he didn't prepare us for the behaviour of the locals. They were really up for it. Two rival groups met in front of our seats. I expected a fight to break out any second but, suddenly, they backed down. Perhaps they were saving it for later.

By then, I was ready for a leisurely meal, but not Gina. The raw emotion of the locals had really got to her. I'd put my arm around her shoulders to reassure her and was surprised to feel how tense she was. The passion of the encounter, the barely controlled aggression a few feet from where we sat, had left her physically aroused. Gina felt like a tightly wound spring, a spring on a hair-trigger awaiting release. By the time the two guys stood nose to nose just an arm's length in front of us, she had already put her hand on my thigh. As soon as the two groups separated, she wanted to go back to the apartment. Nobody was looking when she pulled me to my feet and pressed herself against me. I thought a kiss would satisfy her, but she sucked my lower lip between her teeth.

'Come.' She grabbed my hand. 'I want you back in bed.'

'But the table's booked for—'

'Fuck the table. Actually, let me rephrase that, not the table but me. Colin, I want you to—'

'Okay, okay! Just let me tell the restaurant we'll be half an hour late.'

Her eyes widened and her raised brows switched rapidly to a frown. It was as if I'd insulted her.

'Don't you dare! Make it an hour – at least.'

Back at the apartment, to show that I was really up for it, I suggested we video ourselves on my mobile. I liked the idea, but Gina wasn't keen.

'Colin ... I don't need a video! I get aroused just thinking about you. When we're together, all I need is to see you, feel you and hear you.'

Today is race day. When Gina woke I suggested we follow Umberto's advice to watch from the apartment. She agreed immediately and seemed particularly excited at the prospect. After breakfast in the bar, we went to the local *salumeria* for salami and cheeses, grilled vegetables in oil, bread and wine. We carried the meal to our room overlooking the piazza.

The drums had started early and they continued throughout the day. By five, the centre of the Campo was packed with spectators, younger tourists taking selfies and videoing events with their phones. Flags of the competing *contrade* waved high, in great figures of eight, above the bright colours of the historical processions that circled the track. Our vantage point above the crowds was great. I certainly got that right. Gina couldn't stop talking about it. She took pillows from the bed, wedged them on the windowsill and spent the afternoon there, leaning out to look at the scene below. Occasionally, she would reach back for food and wine.

After two more hours of pageantry, the track cleared, ready for the start. Nine of the jockeys and their horses jostled for position against the rope, while a blue-clad rider waited at a distance, ready to charge the line and start the race. Gina turned towards me, provocatively sucking a fingertip glistening with virgin olive oil. Smiling, she offered each of her other fingers, salty from salami and cheese, to my mouth. With the last one still between my lips she stretched her head to kiss me. The combination of her tongue and her finger together was a new sensation.

Gina turned away, leant further into the widow and raised her hips. 'I'm not wearing anything under this dress. When they start, take me before the race finishes.'

I stepped behind her, lifted her dress and pulled it off over her head. Leaning over her back, I held myself poised as we watched for the start of the race, eyes fixed on the rider in blue, anticipation heightened by the tension rising from the crowds below. The blue rider waited. The other jockeys manoeuvred for position. Still the blue rider waited. Then the moment came. Two rivals were poorly placed and the blue rider urged his horse forward.

I felt Gina brace herself. The rope dropped. The race had begun. As the horses started their third lap of the Campo, Gina increased the urgency of her movements. The horses were approaching the finish when I began to cry out. An explosion signalled that the leading silver grey had crossed the line. Gina and I rose together. Another grey, in second place, hit the inner barrier; both horse and jockey fell. Gina stood in the window with me at her back, her hands clutching each side of the frame. I kissed Gina's neck, stretching over her shoulder to reach her lips. My hands slid down her body, pulling her tight against me.

'*Oh, yes … yes.*'

Gina's words were almost wistful. She seemed completely out of it, reaching back to curl her fingers in my hair. Had I not been holding her, she might have fallen to the crowds below.

The sounds of our passion were lost in the tumult from the piazza. Horses were engulfed by *contradaioli* crowding onto the track. Our bodies were hot and our skins wet where they touched. Gina leant further into the window, allowing the cooling evening air to envelop her naked body. Cupping her breasts to steady her, I looked down into the piazza as two rival *contrade* came face to face by the green waters of the *Fonte Gaia*. Shouts from the first fist fights reached me as, passion spent, I sank to the floor, pulling Gina down to the welcome cool of the tiles. She relaxed against me and our bodies become one, alone in our own private world. Air from the open window brushed our skin.

'God ...' she said and then, as if it were the only thought in her head, 'We must do this again.'

43

It was Monday morning, early, and DI Ogborne was the only person in the CID Room. She stared at her computer screen, going over and over Kayleigh Robson's death in Dover. Other than knowing it was a man, whoever was with her at the time of her death remained a mystery. Drawing a blank on the DNA was a bugger, but it fitted the hypothesis that Kayleigh's death had been a case of S&M sex gone wrong. There was no evidence she'd been a willing participant, but willing or not, the missing man faced a potential manslaughter charge. He'd failed to summon aid, failed to report the death and left the scene, probably taking Kayleigh's mobile with him. That said, in all other aspects of his life he could be a law-abiding citizen, in which case there was little chance he would commit an indictable offence in the near future. If they could discover who he was, the DNA would nail him, but without a breakthrough, the chances of an arrest were zero. As Saunders had said, such cases were buggers. Nothing was working in their favour. They needed a breakthrough, but Ed couldn't see how they would get one.

44

We arrived back from Italy Friday evening. Gina didn't want to go out, so we came straight to her apartment and spent the entire weekend indoors, chilling with DVDs and takeaway meals. It was just like I'd imagined the two of us living together. Actually, moving in hasn't come up yet and I sense it's a bit too soon for me to put it to her. Today will be more typical of our relationship – at least, as it is for the moment. Gina went to work, taking the holiday photos to show her colleagues. I went for a walk along the river and shopped for food. While waiting for Gina to come home, I watched the Tour de France.

It's now eight in the evening. We're eating dinner in the kitchen. Gina pan-fried some salmon, while I opened a bottle of Chianti and prepared a salad. Halfway through the meal, she put down her fork.

'Friday the 21st of June was a very special day for me.' She smiles as she looks at me. 'It was the day you came into my life.'

'You came into mine weeks before, when I saw you in the sunshine, walking along Burgate. Later, you called to say you wanted your bedroom decorated.'

'I didn't know you then. For me, our relationship didn't begin until that Friday. And, as for the way it began—'

'I'm sorry it started as it did.'

'No, you shouldn't be sorry. I don't see how it could have been any other way.'

'What do you mean?' I didn't like the implication. 'Are you saying I'm not your type?'

'Since we met, I've realized I've based my choices far too much on first impressions, on looks and accent.'

'You don't like my looks or my accent?'

There was an edge was to my voice. Gina does this to me sometimes.

'I didn't say that,' she replies quickly, a soft sadness appearing around her eyes.

'So, what's changed? What's important for you now?' The edge is still there.

'Personality and compatibility.'

I relaxed and smiled, knowing the edge will have gone. At the same time, I felt uncomfortable, aware Gina flips me at will.

'When did you decide they were the important things?'

'It began here in this flat, but I became certain while we were in Italy. I've been thinking about it a lot. I want to take things slowly. I don't regret the experience of our first few days together, but I want those memories to recede. I want a more normal period of getting to know you.'

I stopped eating. Taking things slowly isn't what I wanted to hear.

'What do you mean, slowly, more normal?'

'Up 'til now, it's been unbelievably intense. Until today we've been together 24/7. Let's bring that down, back off a bit.'

I didn't like this at all, and I knew the edge would have returned to my voice when I next spoke.

'You don't want to see me?'

Gina reached across the table and took my hand.

'Of course not, I want to see you ... just not every day.'

'So, when?'

'I'm happy when you're here, like this evening, but let's make it two or three times a week for a while.'

'And?'

'And then, in a month or so, we could have a weekend away together.'

I wasn't taken by her suggestion, but as I went to reply, she put a finger to my lips, stood and drew me by the hand to the bedroom.

Under the duvet she snuggled her head into my shoulder and murmured, 'Do you remember the Palio?'

'You surprised me.'

'Tit for tat.'

'What?'

'Tit for tat. You surprised me, when I came home from work and found you sitting at my kitchen table.'

My muscles tensed; my whole body stiffened. Gina lifted her head and kissed my cheek.

'Don't worry. All's well that ends well.'

'Has it ended well?'

'It hasn't ended yet. I'm sure it will only get better.'

Once more I relaxed, liking the idea that we have a future. I was about to say as much, but after the slightest of pauses, Gina continued.

'It was intense though, wasn't it, in Italy, I mean?'

166

'The Palio?'

'The Palio and ...'

I was caught by surprise. 'Oh, at the window, watching the race.'

Watching the race wasn't exactly the image in my mind.

'The race –' Gina nuzzled my ear with her nose '– and doing it with all those people down below in the piazza.' She nibbled the lobe of my ear. 'Didn't you find that exciting?'

'Yes ... though they weren't exactly looking at us, they were watching the race.'

'Well, I guess most of them were, but I was very aware somebody might have been looking up, looking at us.' Her arms came around my chest and she pulled herself tight against my body. 'Of course, I was turned on by you, but the possibility someone might be watching made it extra exciting.'

Gina had never spoken like this before. I held myself still, poised in her arms, wondering what might come next.

'Should we do it again?'

'The next race isn't until August. Anyway—'

Gina interrupted me, turning my head and brushing my nose with hers before speaking.

'For me it wasn't so much the race, it was the excitement of thinking someone might be watching us.'

'Kinky ...'

Gina rolled away, settling her head back against the pillow.

'Maybe, but I'd like to do it again.'

Gina's always a surprise. I wasn't sure where she was going with this, but her words were making me horny – she had me hooked. I turned so we were face to face.

'There's a word for that. I've heard it can be dangerous.'

'No. I don't mean driving out to some lonely spot where people go to watch.'

'What *do* you mean?'

'Just doing it outside, in the open, where, by chance, somebody might catch sight of us. I don't want to be on the back seat of a car with strangers drooling at the windows.'

My mind was racing as I tried to keep up with the implications of what Gina was saying.

'It sounds like you've given this a lot of thought.'

'Not really. At work today, showing the girls the photos, I thought how much I'd enjoyed our trip and then it was like a flashback, you and me in the window, the explosion as the winner crossed the line. I was thinking about it again, as I was walking home, but if I can't tempt you ...'

I watched Gina's eyes soften. She was looking at me with a touch of sadness. It's a look I can't resist.

'Where did you have in mind?'

Her face brightened immediately.

'Somewhere in the middle of town, but it would have to be in the early hours of the morning when there's nobody about.'

'Doesn't that defeat the purpose?'

'No. The point is somebody *might* walk by. Someone *might* see us, we can never be sure. Maybe they will, maybe they won't. That's the added thrill.'

I was listening, but I wasn't convinced.

'You're saying, late at night, we go somewhere in the centre of town and – just do it?'

'We could but ...' Gina moved her lips close to my ear. 'Wouldn't it be more exciting if we did a bit more than that. You know ...'

'No.'

'Well, I could be walking alone and, at the right spot, you could come up behind me, grab me and pull me to the ground. I'd struggle, but I wouldn't scream, and you'd force yourself on me.'

I'll admit, hearing her say these things was really turning me on. It was a fantasy I'd entertained from time to time. Not rape – I'd never do that – but role-playing was different. I never thought I'd experience it for real. Gina is full of surprises of late. Did she really want to do this?

'And then?'

'We'd continue to behave as if we were strangers. You'd leave me and go back to your place. I'd come back here. A couple of days later, we'd meet here ... in bed, and ... we'd ... talk ... about ... it.'

Gina punctuated her words by touching my leg with her knee and moving it, inch by inch, up my thigh. I was aroused, but I wasn't completely sure I wanted to put her plan into action. The indecision must have shown on my face because Gina withdrew her knee, turned on her back and stretched sensuously under the covers.

'Hmm ... Just talking about it is making me horny.'

Using her foot, Gina slowly pushed the duvet from our bodies.

We talked about it several times until Gina had an elaborate scenario just the way she wanted it. Each time I could feel her words turning me on and I grew increasingly eager to go along with her plan.

Part Two:
FIGHTING BACK

45

Ed was woken by her work mobile.

'DI Ogborne.'

It was the night sergeant.

'I've got a young woman at the desk. Claims she's been raped in the city centre. By the look of her, she's in a bad way. There's nobody with her. Says she made her own way here.'

'Put her in an interview room and get someone to stay with her, a WPC if you can. Don't give her a drink, or let her smoke, or go to the loo if at all possible. Get Jenny and Anna Masood. Tell them I'm on my way. I'll be there in ten minutes.'

The time on her phone was 03.24.

Ed left her car in Chief Superintendent Addler's space and ran into the building.

'Where is she?'

'I put her in Interview Room 3. Carol's with her.'

'Good.'

'Jenny's on her way and the MO will be here in 15 minutes.'

Ed was already down the corridor.

'Thanks, Carol. Perhaps you could stay with us.'

Carol nodded from her position by the door.

Ed sat at the table across from a young woman who was slumped in a chair, head in hands. Her long hair and clothing were in disarray although she'd made some attempt to straighten her skirt and torn top.

'I'm Detective Inspector Ed Ogborne and this is PC Carol—' Ed turned to look at the young police constable.

'Davis. PC Carol Davis.'

Ed smiled her thanks and turned back to the woman.

'There's a female medical officer on her way. She'll be here shortly. For the moment it's best if you do nothing, so as not to disturb any forensic evidence.'

The woman raised her head to look at Ed.

'I thought I would ... was ... was going to die ... that he w-would kill me ...'

Her words faded to silence as she struggled to express horrors too great for her small, hesitant voice to articulate.

'He was ... strangling me ... with my bra ... but ... then ...'

The woman's voice failed completely and she covered her face with her hands as if trying to block images from her mind.

Ed leant across the table and spoke calmly.

'You're being very brave. We all appreciate how difficult this must be for you. Take your time. We're here for you. You've done exactly the right thing in coming to see us. We've people who can help you, support you.'

The woman lowered her hands and looked pleadingly at Ed.

'I can't believe it ... what's happened. It was all so ... quick. Why? Why me? Why choose me?'

Ed opened her notebook. 'I know this is hard, but we need to ask you some questions. We can stop and take a break at

174

any time. Just say if you need a moment. Are you okay with that?'

'Yes.' The word barely reached Ed across the table.

'Good. First, can you tell me when this happened?'

'I'm not sure ... When he stopped ... err ... finished ... I came here.'

'Can you tell us *where* it happened?'

'In the Buttermarket ... near ...'

'And you came straight here?'

'Yes.'

'If we said it happened half an hour ago, would that be about right?'

'I suppose ... It seemed to go on and on ... but ... probably it was over very quickly.'

The woman had been looking down at the table, but now she raised her head and looked straight at Ed and in a slightly stronger voice said, 'I came here as fast as I could. I knew I should do that.'

'You did exactly the right thing and you're being very brave.' Ed paused then added, 'So it happened about 30 minutes ago?'

'About that, perhaps a bit more.'

'I'm sorry to push you, but it would be good for us to get a description out to our police patrols. Could you give us some idea what the person looked like?'

'Everything was so ... fast. I don't ... I was shocked ... scared.'

'Did you get any impressions, anything at all?'

'Thin ... but strong. Wiry, I guess you'd say.' The woman turned her head to stare blankly at the corner of the Interview Room. 'And his hair ... very blond ... almost white.'

'What about clothes? Did you notice anything in particular?'

175

'Dark ... running gear ... like sweat pants and a top.'

'Do you remember any logos or other markings?'

'Sorry ... No ...'

Suddenly the woman's demeanour changed. She straightened in her chair, her voice strengthened and her eyes looked accusingly at Ed.

'I was being strangled ... with my bra.' She leant forward on the table as if to emphasize with her body what she didn't have the strength to do with her voice. 'He was strangling me with *my bra*. I was *terrified*.'

'You're being very strong and what you've said is going to be a great help.'

Ed stood up. 'We'll go into the details in a minute. I'm just stepping out of the room for a moment. Carol will stay with you.'

Ed got the description out to Uniform and then requested CCTV records from all the cameras covering the Buttermarket before returning to Interview Room 3. The young woman looked up wearily as Ed sat at the table.

'Our patrols are out looking for a man matching the description you've just given us. Chances are he's off the street by now but we might pick him up.'

'But if you don't?' The woman leant forward, looking at Ed intently.

'You probably don't know this, but there are several CCTV cameras covering the Buttermarket. A combination of images from each of them should give us a very good video of the incident, which could help identify and convict your attacker.'

'That's what I want, the bastard behind bars.'

This was the first time the woman had spoken with force.

'Are you in any pain?'

'Yes ... no ... it doesn't matter. I just want the bastard caught and sent to jail.'

'If you're sure ...' When the woman didn't respond, Ed continued to speak gently and reassuringly. 'As I said earlier, I'm Ed Ogborne and my colleague is Carol Davis. Can you tell us your name?'

'Gina ... Georgina Hamilton.'

'May I call you Gina?'

'Yes.'

'Good. Okay, Gina, we have to ask you about what happened, but as soon as possible, you'll need to be examined by—'

The door opened and the MO entered the room.

'—a medical officer.' Ed half turned towards the door. 'Here she is now. Anna, this is Georgina Hamilton.'

The MO nodded a greeting to Ed and walked to the table.

'Hello, Georgina, I'm Dr Anna Masood. I'd like you to come with me for a while. I'll examine you, take some forensic samples including your clothes, we'll get something else for you to wear, then you can get yourself cleaned up and come back here to DI Ogborne.'

Ed followed Gina and Anna into the corridor and walked towards the exit. At the front desk she met Jenny rushing into the building.

'Sorry, boss, I got here as quickly as I could.'

Ed wished her team would stop calling her boss. 'No problem, Jenny. The victim is with the MO. I'm going to move my car out of the Super's reserved space. Go to Interview Room 3 and relieve the young PC, Carol Davis. I'll be back in a minute to bring you up to speed.'

46

My stone to your scissors; my scissors to your paper; my paper to your stone; whichever move you make I'll cover, cut or blunt you.

It's not something I'd admit, Colin, but between you and me, credit for the way you got into my home. I'd have been pleased with that move, a touch of class, but battles are battles, you've not won the war. Apparently, you've time and money. They'll get you a lot, but you'll never better someone who'll do anything short of murder to win.

Men! Always so sure you're right, it makes you so easy to manipulate. Poor Colin, you thought you were in control, but I turned the tables. You should have seen the signs, the writing on the wall; you should have got out while you still could. You didn't take your chance; too sure I'd come to see your worth, lost in your own fantasy. No matter, had you cut and run, you wouldn't have got far. I'd have come after you.

Your first mistake was believing your own delusion, your second was choosing me, Gina Hamilton. It's a risky business choosing a stranger; you don't know their history, you don't know what they're capable of. I decided long ago, whatever it took, I'd always come out on top.

Learning to get my own way took time. With Mother it

occupied my entire childhood, while with Rachael it was a matter of months, but with you, Colin, it was different, with you there was a deadline, undeclared, but real nonetheless. With you I had to act within days.

You had no chance – with your schoolboy sex fantasies, I could play you with my eyes shut. As it happened, most of the time my eyes *were* shut. Why do you think that was, Colin? Rapture, ecstasy, sublime satisfaction? Really? Then that's another schoolboy fantasy to add to the rest. My eyes were shut because I couldn't bear to look at you, couldn't bear to see what I was doing.

I didn't show it, but it was a worrying time. Had I adopted the right strategy, chosen the right tactic, picked the right moment? I knew, if things didn't go your way, and quickly, I'd die; perhaps slowly and painfully, abandoned to my fate, or, more likely, suddenly, perhaps smothered, maybe strangled. You bastard, Colin! I had no choice – you forced me to use sex to turn the tables. It worked, but I'll not forget what you made me do.

When I left you tied to the bed, I stepped out into the world with every intention of going to the police. Then, as I walked into town, the negatives began to stack up. Yes, I'd turned the tables, but you, a man, were tied to *my* bed, in *my* home, and I'm a woman. You may be a skinny guy, but you're strong. Could I, a mere woman, have tied you to the bed against your will? I needed to think. In Sun Street, I stopped to consider my position over breakfast.

We all know about the treatment lone women get when reporting a sexual assault to the police. Mentally I'm strong, I could face a lack of sympathy, possible indifference, as long as you were arrested, found guilty and sentence to years behind bars. But if I were to report you to the police, what then? Back at my apartment, what would the police make of the sight of you tied to my bed? Would they, the courts, a jury, ever believe the truth? Your defence counsel would have a field day.

Are we really expected to believe this outlandish story of how my client is supposed to have tricked his way into Ms Hamilton's apartment and held her captive? Can any reasonable person believe this young woman physically overcame my client and tied him to her bed against his will? I put it to you, isn't it much more likely, as my client maintains, that he and Georgina Hamilton were in a relationship, a relationship that involved consensual sex games? Then the time came when, for whatever reason, Ms Hamilton wanted the relationship to end. My client accepted the situation, but Ms Hamilton wanted more. Here, today, in this court, her accusations against my client are a means to that end. Georgina Hamilton's story, this whole farrago, is her revenge.

Revenge!

That's what I wanted, Colin, revenge.

Eating breakfast in the brasserie, I struggled with my options – none were attractive. When I came to a decision, I was far from happy with my choice. The prospect revolted me, but it was the only route I could see to a satisfying outcome. It's never been easy. Making sure you come out on top whatever the setbacks. Making sure you get what you want can be hard. I experienced this with Mother. I learnt to cede a skirmish in order to win the battle, to surrender a battle in order to win the war. I don't think she realized it, but my mother taught me a lot. Watching her was an education.

At home, Mother was dominant. She always got her way

where my father was concerned. As I grew older, I saw my mother was using my father, using him to get what she wanted. Perhaps, all along, Mother had used Father for her own ends. Did she love him? Not that I could see. Did he love her? Perhaps at one time he'd loved her, but, in my eyes, he merely tolerated and supported her – anything for a quiet life.

Did they love me? In his own way my father did although his ability to express emotion was never strong. Did Mother love me? All I know is she would do anything for me, anything to get me out of her hair. Her aim was for me to be a model child, a model schoolgirl, a model student, to be everything that would enhance her position in the neighbourhood. Just as she used my father, Mother was using me.

From the time I could walk, I'd been packed off to play-school and kindergarten, then boarding through prep and at a minor private school for girls. These experiences gave me an early independence. No one would have said I was obstinate, but I'd learnt my mother's lessons well; inevitably I got my own way. If I didn't, I'd get my revenge. Once, I'd been invited on holiday with my best friend, Amanda. Mother was especially difficult, giving a string of reasons why it wasn't possible, so I exacted a particularly satisfying revenge. Mother desperately wanted to be elected Chair of the school PTFA. I told Amanda my mother was only standing because she felt pressured to do so and asked if her mother could discreetly intervene. The lobbying was so successful that my mother comfortably lost the election. Devastated by the disappointment, and what she perceived as a cruel slight, Mother promptly withdrew from all school-related activities.

The PTFA was our watershed moment. Once she'd lost the election she knew I'd won. From that point, our mother-daughter relationship changed. Whenever she sensed I intended to oppose her, she'd back down. I was on top. It'd taken time, but back then I was young and still learning. And the holiday? A direct request from Amanda's mother and I was allowed to go without further objection.

Neither I nor Amanda had close friends, other than each other. At first, I wondered why we were drawn together; but later I understood that, like my mother, we both used people for our own ends. They say opposites attract, but we were very alike; not physically – Amanda was dark and sultry – but in our attitude to life. I guess we knew exactly where we were with each other and therefore felt comfortable together.

The day I left for uni, Mother insisted Father should drive me. When we turned into the parkland campus of the university, we followed the signs and soon arrived at Barratt Building, one of four halls of residence located in the university grounds. Father helped me carry things to my room and we returned to the car together. Back at the wheel he lowered the window.

'You're no longer my little girl, Georgina; you're a woman poised to make her own way in the world.'

He'd caught me by surprise with such an uncharacteristically personal speech. I'd not been a little girl for years. I certainly hadn't felt like a little girl during the summer with Amanda in France.

I bent to kiss his cheek. 'You'd better make a start. It's a long drive back.'

'Don't forget to call Mother this evening, tomorrow morning at the latest. And … be careful, Georgina.'

'Don't worry, Daddy, I'll be fine. Speak to you both tomorrow. Bye.'

It was three-thirty. I just had time to unpack before changing into my grey shift for the Dean's Reception. The dress was new and my ticket to womanhood. At school, Amanda had been the first to do it. Others followed, but when I heard their reports of underwhelming experiences at the hands of naive sixth-formers, I decided to save myself for a more sophisticated introduction.

It hadn't happened during the summer holiday in France despite Paul, Amanda's father, raising my hopes; he was there without his new girlfriend and we were sunbathing topless by the pool. Paul was sitting nearby in the shade and I was aware of his eyes on my body. As a test, I turned onto my back and he didn't look away. That night, I left the door of my room ajar, but Paul failed to come to my bed. Frustrated, I decided that rite of passage would be a priority for my first days at uni. My new grey dress signalled I was ready and it gave me the confidence I'd pull a suitable guy. He didn't have to be the man of my dreams; as long as he had assurance and experience and wasn't totally gross, I'd give myself.

The Dean welcomed new students with a sherry party in the Georgian country house at the centre of the grounds. It was hot and humid when I joined the gathering in the ballroom. The wooden floor gleamed in the late afternoon sunlight that entered through a wall of French windows. Beyond the windows a wide terrace gave access to a croquet lawn.

Moving among his guests like a sovereign on a small-town walkabout, the Dean paused here and there to exchange a brief word with an awkward fresher. Unstintingly generous on this, his first and only social meeting with undergraduates, he had immaculate catering staff, men in white jackets with black trousers and women in black dresses with white aprons, move through the throng dispensing glasses of sherry.

The heat was oppressive, the faces unknown, and sipping sherry became a nervous tic for many of the new students. Within the first quarter of an hour, I and others found ourselves well into a second glass. At this point the true purpose of the Dean's walkabout became clear as he swept out of the ballroom and across the terrace to the croquet lawn with the first two freshers who had expressed any acquaintance with the game. He was followed by a few postgraduates and academics who'd been invited to share the burden of conversing with the new intake.

Within the ballroom, the ice broken by fortified wine and the tension relieved by the Dean's departure, groups of new students began exchanging names and experiences. On the edge of one group, waiting for an opening, I reached for another glass from a passing tray. As I raised the drink to my lips, a bronzed hand stayed my arm.

'Go easy on the sherry is my advice,' said the blond owner of the hand. 'I noticed you as soon as I arrived and I've been watching you ever since. Unfortunately, I couldn't get across until now. Form required me to humour my PhD supervisor, but at last he's off with the Dean playing just well enough to lose by a narrow margin. I'm Nicholas Wilmslow, Nick to my friends, a postgrad in Chemistry. And you, apart from being the most attractive of this year's intake, are ...?'

Startled by his sudden appearance and his smooth self-confidence, I could only blurt out my name as if back at school: 'Georgina Hamilton.' I not only felt like a schoolgirl; far worse, I sounded like one. Quickly, I added, 'Gina ... Gina Hamilton,' before lapsing silent.

'Hello, Gina.' Nick took the sherry glass from my unresisting grasp. 'You'll not be needing this. If you're thirsty I'll get some

184

iced water. If not, let's get out of this stuffy heat and take a stroll under the trees beyond the lawn.'

Still tongue-tied, I felt myself propelled by Nick's firm grip on my elbow through the French windows, around the croquet lawn and into the cool of the trees. Once in the shade Nick slowed his pace and released his grip on my arm.

'Now, Gina, tell me all about yourself and then I'll give you the benefit of my years at this place.'

Behind us in the ballroom, there was the sound of breaking glass, followed by an ominous thud as the first of three new students, overcome by heat and sherry, fell face down on the polished wooden floor. I heard of these mishaps later that evening and silently thanked Nick for saving me from a similar fate.

When we parted, Nick invited me to join him the following evening in town for a meal to mark the start of term. At first, I thought it too soon; Freshers' Week was an opportunity to meet students in my year. I hesitated, but when Nick added there would be a group of students going, I reasoned there would be plenty of time to meet my peers later in the week.

'That would be lovely.'

'Great, meet me at the squash courts at 7 p.m. tomorrow. Wear the same dress and don't be late.'

I arrived early and remember standing in a pool of light by Nick's open-top sports car. At the Dean's reception he'd been so charming and attentive, I was already thinking he would be the one. Nick was fit, assured and sophisticated. I'd thought of him last night in bed and they were not the thoughts of a little girl. My father's parting words had confirmed what I'd felt in France: I was a woman poised to make my way in the world.

The doors to the squash court opened behind me. I turned and smiled confidently, knowing my grey dress would catch the light. Nick returned my smile and I decided he'd be the one. Tonight, I would go to his room and allow him to take me in his arms. He'd think me swept my off my feet, surrendering to his charm.

'Jump in.' Nick stepped over the low-slung door of his sports car, dropped behind the wheel and started the engine.

I walked round the car, opened the passenger door and got in beside him. 'Where are the others?'

'They'll meet us there.'

At the restaurant, Nick spoke of his summer spent driving around Italy. 'A splendid country, fine cities, fabulous art, good food and great wine. Siena was magnificent. I'll never forget the evening light in the Campo as the setting sun colours the walls, the shadows darken and the restaurants light hundreds of candles on their tables in the piazza. As for the Palio – what an atmosphere, what a spectacle!'

'What's the Palio?'

'A bareback horse race in the Piazza del Campo. I'll tell you about it, but first let's order some food.'

Nick talked me through the menu. My father was giving me a generous allowance but, aware I should budget for the whole term, I chose carefully. His friends did not materialize, but I was more than happy listening to Nick's stories. With coffee he ordered a *digestivo* which, thinking of my budget, I declined. When the bill arrived, he surprised me by saying it was customary for students to split it down the middle.

Back at campus, Nick drove beyond the Barratt Building and parked outside the postgraduate block. He leant towards me, his lips searching and finding mine. The contact was soft, generous, but not prolonged. Raising his head, he looked directly into my eyes. 'Are you a virgin?'

'No,' I lied.

Nick smiled. 'Let's go up to my place.' He reached across my body to open the car door, kissing me again as he did so.

In his room, Nick left me in darkness to switch on a table lamp. His third kiss was as generous as before but longer and more demanding; a sense of urgency held in check. His fingertips brushed my shoulders. I pressed against him, feeling his body through my thin dress. He moved his hands under my arms so that his wrists touched the sides of my breasts. My legs felt weak, but I held still, waiting. He pulled back so that his hands were at my breasts. Smiling and holding my gaze he slipped the narrow straps from my shoulders and pulled the dress down.

'Take off my shirt.'

My fingers fumbled with the buttons. He pulled it over his head and my breasts touched his chest. He moved slightly from side to side. His hands eased the dress over my hips and we let it fall to the floor. He slipped out of his remaining clothes and pulled me gently to him. As we kissed his fingers fluttered like butterfly wings against my back, up to my shoulders and down to the base of my spine.

The night, with Nicholas Wilmslow in the postgraduate block, was everything I'd ever imagined. What's more, the rite of passage had been achieved just as I'd planned, on my own terms. Comfortable in the warm afterglow, I knew I wasn't attracted to Nick as a person, but as a lover he was perfect. I'd been right to wait and I'd chosen well. Curled against his back, I was looking forward to future nights together.

Early the following morning, Nick ushered me swiftly from his room. 'I've got a lot on this week.'

'When will I see you next?'

'In the Union Bar.'

No day, no time, and no kiss as he closed the door behind me.

Three days passed before I saw him again. He was at the bar, talking animatedly with another fresher. From the table where I was sitting with five less than stimulating peers, I watched Nick leave, his bronzed hand firmly on the girl's elbow. Any small sorrow I might have felt at seeing him go was swamped by the fury that he should dump me and do so in such a cowardly way. The memory of Nick still rankles; of all the people who've crossed me, he's the only one against whom I've not exacted a satisfying revenge.

That first term at uni passed quickly. The course was going well and I'd established a group of friends who could afford to live as I'd been accustomed to living, but all of this, my entire way of life, was threatened when I received a call during the last week of term. I was in my room finishing some coursework. The call was from Mother, simultaneously tearful, angry and bitter, as only Mother could be.

'The stupid fool!' She took a deep, sob-laden breath. 'It's all been lost. My life is ruined. I can never show my face again.'

'What's happened? Who's done what?'

'Your ridiculous father, he's lost everything.'

'How? Mother, what's he done—'

'All the money, all my savings – gone! He's even taken money from work.'

'Why ... why did he do that? What's happened?'

'Gambling, on the stock market—'

'I know he invested—'

'At first, maybe, at least, that's what he claimed, but then he said he was onto a sure-fire winner, Japanese Government Bonds, but he had big losses—'

'Their economy was hit. Daddy couldn't have predicted the earthquakes and typhoons.'

'But that's when he took money from work. "Don't worry, darling, I'll recoup my losses and more. The economy will recover." But it didn't—'

'More earthquakes and typhoons.'

'He's lost our money, my money, he's lost the company's money.'

Her tears had stopped and Mother no longer had the strength to be angry, but the bitterness remained.

'To think I married such a pathetic bastard. I'm ruined. The sad old man has destroyed my life. The life I've always wanted, the life I had until the pathetic fool gambled it away.'

The line went silent. Mother's rant had come to an end. I heard her pour a drink.

'Term's almost finished. I'll come home as soon as I can.'

'You'd better, you'll need to clear your things. The house is on the market – we'll be gone in January.'

When I told her, Amanda was pragmatic. She didn't waste time on sympathy. 'At first, when my parents split, it was okay, but as soon as I turned 18, the house was sold and my allowance dried up. My idea of a good time at uni went out of the window. Even living frugally, I was looking at mounting debts, just to finish the course.'

189

Gina gestured round the room. 'What's with all the new clothes and stuff?'

'Frugal's not my thing, darling. I got a part-time job.'

'What part-time job pays for that?' I pointed at the 20-inch iMac on her desk.

'Sex.'

She looked at me confidently, daring me to judge her. Typical Amanda, provocative, trying to unsettle me. She should have known I'd give as good as I got.

'Lap dancing? I don't fancy—'

'Who would? Better than shifts in a grotty pub, but it's still long hours.'

'So ... what do you do?'

'Escorting.'

For a moment, I must have looked shocked, because Amanda continued quickly.

'Don't worry, it's safe. I pick and choose, regular clients, when and where, how often.'

'But sex ...?'

'It doesn't have to be sex. Guys are lonely. With some you can just have a meal and chat. Of course, sex pays more and I'm in it for the money. If I fancy a guy, I'll go to his hotel room and stay for an all-nighter. Just one of those will pay for a week in the Maldives.'

'But, how did ... how do you ...?'

'Organize it? Online.' Amanda moved to her computer. 'Come, I'll show you my website. If you fancy it –' she smiled '– we could set one up for you.'

Amanda was right, sex paid more, and sometimes I enjoyed it. A couple of hours a week, on my terms, kept me out of debt and living the life I wanted. As a postgrad, I pulled all-nighters to pay off my student loan. When I qualified, I was debt-free. I carried on, wanting to build up some savings, but then I stopped and started applying for dental posts. It was a complete break; escorting had served its purpose and, without it, I felt clean. I resolved never to do it again. I joined Metcalffe and Metcalffe in Canterbury, determined to live within my means, content with annual salary increases and the prospect of considerably more money when I became a partner in the practice.

Life was good, but once again, it turned and bit me. I'll never forget it: the surprise holiday, escaping from Rachael's questions, and taking the stairs down to the front entrance. My eyes flicked to the brass plate by the door; it still read Metcalffe and Metcalffe, Dental Practice. Not for much longer. I wanted promotion and I was confident of success. Ever since taking the job in Canterbury I'd been working towards a partnership. Gradually, without confrontation, I engineered the introduction of new revenue-enhancing initiatives. In my hands, Rachael was easy meat.

At the ATM, I selected cash with receipt. It was just a matter of time. Soon, there'd be a new plate reading Metcalffe, Metcalffe and Hamilton. My thoughts were interrupted by bleeping from the machine. I shoved the cash, receipt and bank card into my purse and doubled back down Guildhall for the 15-minute walk home. On the way, I stopped at the Kingsmead supermarket to pick up a ready meal and a foil-sealed glass of white wine. At the checkout, I had to move smartly to avoid a beardie who wanted us to share our lonely meals for one. I thought I'd played it clever, but, now I know, unwittingly I'd played right into Colin's hands. If only I'd invited beardie back to mine, we would have confronted him together and none of this would have happened.

After uni I swore I'd never use sex as a means to an end again. I felt clean but you, Colin, you made me feel dirty, you made me use sex to escape with my life. No way can I forgive you, but don't worry, now it's my time, payback time, now I'm taking my revenge!

47

Ed and Jenny were drinking coffee when Anna came back to the interview room with Gina, who was wearing paper overalls and carrying a cup of tea.

'Thanks, Anna. I'll just step outside for a word before you leave. Gina, would you like a biscuit or something to go with that drink?'

'No, I'm good, the tea's fine,' said Gina casually, before adding in a weaker, small voice, 'Thank you.'

Ed nodded. 'Gina, this is my colleague, Detective Constable Jenny Eastham. She'll stay with you while I have a quick word with the Medical Officer, then we'll talk some more about what happened to you.'

In the corridor, Anna summarized what she'd found.

'All the signs are that she's been physically attacked and probably raped. I've bagged all her clothes and taken swabs. Before she cleaned herself up we got photographs. Aside from torn clothes the most obvious injuries are ligature marks around her neck and some light scratches on her back and breasts. There's bruising on her thighs, which would be consistent with forced penetration. All the samples and clothes are ready for forensics.'

'When I first started questioning her, she said he tried to strangle her with her bra,' said Ed.

'That's odd.'

'I'm afraid it happens quite a lot.'

Anna nodded. 'Yes. I didn't mean the strangulation. The marks on her neck could have been caused by a bra but there was no bra among her things.'

'Perhaps he took it as a trophy; that's not uncommon. I'll look into it. How about her, how is she?'

'Physically she's not seriously hurt.'

'Not even after being almost strangled to death?'

'Whatever happened, it didn't go that far. There were ligature marks round her neck, but they weren't as deep as I would have expected if he was really trying to kill her. I think her attacker found the act of strangulation stimulating. Maybe it gave him an added sense of power.'

Ed wanted the MO's opinion of Gina's state of mind but didn't want to ask directly.

'I spoke briefly with her before you arrived. She seemed hesitant but coherent.'

'Initial reactions vary. Some victims are hysterical, others are withdrawn, and some appear quite calm, repressing their feelings, hoping it will all go away, hoping to maintain control and not fall to pieces.'

Ed was annoyed that Anna should speak to her as if she were an inexperienced officer. 'I've seen all of those reactions when working in London. Do you think she's fighting to maintain control?'

'Yes, I do. When she was with me she was almost matter-of-fact, doing exactly what I asked and trying her best to help me do my job. From what I've seen of her, she's a classic case,

194

a victim of rape fighting to stay calm and repressing her emotions.'

'With me she spoke hesitantly, but I thought she was quite coherent. Of course, I haven't been with her for long.'

'When you question her further, I'm sure you'll see signs she's very disturbed. Treat her gently – she's vulnerable, and she's going to have difficulty coming to terms with what has happened to her.'

'I'll keep that in mind. Thanks for getting her a drink.'

'The least I could do after making her wait. I'll be off. Maybe see you later today when you've had a chance to question her further.'

'Give me a call when you're around.'

Back in the Interview Room, Gina was looking better for the cup of tea and clean clothes. Ed joined Jenny at the table.

'If you feel up to it, Gina, we'd like to hear your account of what happened. Is that okay with you?'

'Yes. I want to tell you. I want him caught.' Although she spoke without hesitating, her voice was once again weak, almost child-like.

'Right, I'll just switch this on to record what we say. First, we'll identify ourselves and then I'll ask you to tell us what happened.'

Gina nodded.

'Until we've assessed the evidence, I shall be referring to the incident as alleged rape. This is procedure; it doesn't mean I don't believe you. Do you understand?'

Again, Gina nodded.

'Fine.' Ed checked the tapes in the recorder and switched it on. 'It's 04.35, Wednesday the 10th of July. This is DI Ed

Ogborne and with me is DC Jenny Eastham. We're here to interview the victim of an alleged rape, Georgina Hamilton.'

'This is DC Jenny Eastham.'

Ed looked across the table at Gina. 'Please identify yourself.'

'Oh, sorry, I'm Gina ... err ... that is, Georgina, Georgina Hamilton.'

'And where do you live, Gina?'

'Apartment 32, Great Stour Court, Canterbury, CT2 7US.' The address tripped off Georgina's tongue with some pride.

'Thank you, Gina. Perhaps you could tell us what happened. Start at the beginning, tell us the time and where the incident occurred and then everything in the order it happened. Try to tell us everything you can remember, however small, however painful. The more you can tell us the greater the chance we'll have of catching your attacker.'

Gina began speaking. Once more her voice was weak but, from time to time it slipped briefly to a more normal register.

'I remember now, it was three o'clock. I know it was three. I'd just left work and—'

'Sorry to interrupt you, Gina, but why were you in work at that time of night?'

'Sometimes I wake up and can't get back to sleep.'

'And coming to work?'

'I found doing things in my apartment didn't help, but going into work for half an hour does.'

'Where exactly is work?'

'The dentist, Metcalffe and Metcalffe, in Sun Street, near the Buttermarket.'

'And tonight?'

'I'd just left the practice when he ... he grabbed me.' Gina drew in a sharp breath and her shoulders flinched. She wrapped her arms across her chest and hugged herself.

'You were on your way home?'

'Yes.'

Jenny caught Ed's eye and she nodded for her to speak.

'Excuse me, Gina, but if I were walking back to Stour Court from Metcalffe and Metcalffe, I'd have walked the other way, down Sun Street and out of the city centre via Palace Street.'

'Yes, that's my normal route, but –' Gina coughed '– on these night-time walks, I come in that way, via Palace Street, then walk home along Burgate and use the main roads.'

Jenny looked back at Ed who continued.

'You said he grabbed you and dragged you towards the pub.'

'I'd just started walking across the Buttermarket, towards Burgate. He grabbed me from behind, put his hand over my mouth and forced me across the square towards the pub in the corner. I think it's called The Old Buttermarket.'

'Did he say anything as he dragged you?'

'Well, it wasn't *dragged* exactly. More like he ... err ... pushed me. I was putting one foot in front of the other, trying to keep my balance.'

'And then what happened?' asked Ed.

'He ... he forced me to the ground, in the corner.'

'Did he say anything?'

'Keep quiet or he'd ... he'd really hurt me.'

'Did you cry out, Gina?'

'No ... No, I don't think so. I was too scared – petrified.'

'What happened next?'

'He ... he pulled up my skirt and ...' Gina paused as if the memory were too painful to put into words. 'He tore my ... my knickers ...' She gulped and put her hands to her mouth.

Her chest heaved as if she were about to be sick.

'Are you okay?' Ed leant forward as she felt Jenny getting to her feet. 'Gina, we can take a break if that would help?'

'No. I want to tell you. I want to get it over with, so you can arrest him.'

The two detectives relaxed as Gina reached for her tea and took a careful drink.

'Sorry.' Gina put down the cup. 'He tore my knickers off and then ... then he pushed himself into me.'

At this, Gina put her head in her hands, her face inches above the table. Ed and Jenny could only just hear what she was saying.

'I told myself it would soon be over. He pulled my T-shirt off, then my bra. I thought he wanted to see my breasts but he ... he tried ... tried to kill me.'

Gina was now sitting straight in her chair, rigid, staring across the table, eyes fixed on a point between the two detectives.

'Why do you say he tried to kill you?'

'He was strangling me – with my bra.'

'But you got away,' said Ed.

'Yes ... no ... I mean ...' Gina slumped forward, dropping her head into her hands. Her voice became a horrified whisper. 'I thought ... I thought I was going to die. I was choking. I couldn't breathe ... I couldn't cry out ... but suddenly he finished, got up and left me lying there.'

'The bra was still round your neck, still choking you?'

'Yes ...' Gina looked up, frowning, puzzled, thinking. 'Err ... no ... I'm not sure.'

'Where is it now?' asked Ed.

'Sorry ...?'

'The bra you were wearing, Gina. The one he strangled you with. Where is it now?'

'The doctor took all my clothes.'

'But not your bra. You didn't have it with you.'

'I didn't?' Gina's eyebrows creased in puzzlement. She turned her face to Ed. 'But ... my bra ... where is it then?'

'That's what we'd like to know. We want it for forensic testing. It appears you weren't wearing it when you arrived here, which isn't surprising given what happened.'

'After it happened I was ... dazed. I'm not sure what I did.' Gina frowned again. 'I don't remember picking it up. It must still be there ... on the ground somewhere.'

'We'll get people out to look for it. If you left it at the scene or dropped it on your way here, it's unlikely to have disappeared at this time of night.'

Ed glanced at Jenny and mouthed, 'Questions?' When the DC shook her head, Ed turned back to Gina and spoke reassuringly.

'Thank you, Gina. We know this is a very difficult time for you and we are here to support you in whatever way we can. Don't feel guilty. This is not your fault. Through doing what you're doing you are getting justice. You've been brave to take this step, now you must stay strong. You are a victim, but you can be a survivor, you will get closure, you are not in the wrong.'

The semblance of a smile flashed briefly on Gina's face. Quickly, she covered it with her hand and coughed.

'Thank you ... thank you for being so supportive and understanding.'

'We'll leave it there for now, Gina,' said Ed. She passed her a card. 'If you need anything, anything at all, ring this number day or night. Now, if we run you home, is there somebody we could call to stay with you?'

'No, not in ... no, not nearby.'

'DC Eastham, Jenny, will come with you to make sure you get home safely. Will you be all right?'

'Yes, thank you. I'm used to living on my own.'

'Jenny, get a squad car round to the front. Gina and I will meet you there.'

At the front of the building, Jenny was waiting with a rear door of the squad car open. She closed it behind Gina and was turning towards the door on the other side of the car when Ed touched her arm.

'Go into the flat with her and look round to make sure everything's okay. Don't make a thing about it, but do your best to judge if she's living alone.'

Jenny gave Ed a puzzled look.

'Okay. Will you still be here when I get back?'

'By then I hope to be checking the CCTV, but first I want the missing bra. I also want the Super to get a description of the attacker on local TV and radio. If we can't pull a good shot from the CCTV, we'll have to get Gina back to produce an e-fit. My guess is we're already too late to find him on the street, but maybe the appeal will turn up someone who knows the attacker.'

Jenny left with Gina in the car and Ed went back into the building. She organized a search for the missing bra and then went to the front desk.

'No sightings of our potential rapist?'

'Nothing yet.'

'It was always a long shot. After an attack like that, I'm

sure he went to ground as fast as his wiry little legs could carry him. What about the CCTV?'

'It's on its way.'

'Good. Let me know as soon as it arrives.'

Ed left the front desk and walked to the Evidence Room. She found Gina's clothes, which had been bagged for forensic examination, and checked through the items carefully. The outer garments were crumpled and dirty, consistent with Gina having been on the pavement. The T-shirt and knickers were torn and, as Anna had said, there was no bra. Things appeared to be consistent with Gina's story.

Ed took a closer look at each item of clothing. They were all rather old and the whites were a bit grey. Of course, it had been the middle of the night and Gina had said she couldn't sleep. Having decided to go for a walk it seemed reasonable she should throw on some old things. After all, at that time of night she wasn't going to meet anyone.

48

By the time Jenny returned from Stour Court, Ed was working through the CCTV tapes with an IT technician.

'Okay, Steve, that's the best shot. We'll use that one of his face for the patrols and the local TV appeal. It would be great if you could find and enhance any logos on his clothes and shoes.'

Ed turned to Jenny.

'How did you get on at Gina's?'

'I walked her to the door and offered to check inside. She wasn't very enthusiastic, but she thanked me and then never left my side as I went through all the rooms.'

'Any signs she wasn't living there alone?'

'None that I could see, but Gina stuck to me like glue. There was no way I could check drawers, wardrobe or the bathroom cabinet.'

'No matter, it was a long shot and it's probably not important.' Ed indicated the chair, which the technician had just vacated. 'Take a seat and have a look at this CCTV.'

Jenny sat beside her boss.

'Fortunately, the Buttermarket is well covered by CCTV cameras. Steve's edited the tapes to produce the best overview of the incident. It's pretty much as Gina said. The sequence starts with her stepping out into Sun Street from the dentist's where she works and turning towards the Buttermarket.' While speaking, Ed retuned to the beginning of the recording and hit play. 'It starts here at 02.59.'

Gina could be seen walking away from camera towards the Buttermarket. Then, the camera angle switched to a side view of Gina entering the open space. As she passed the Christchurch Gate entrance to the cathedral, what appeared to be a male figure, in dark clothes, stepped out of the shadows to follow a few yards behind her. He was wearing a hooded sweat shirt and sweat pants. The hood covered his head and hid his face. Gina didn't turn round, suggesting he was walking silently in rubber-soled trainers. As she passed the central War Memorial, the figure took four quick strides, threw his arms around Gina and bundled her towards a secluded corner by the pub. The view switched to a camera mounted on the wall of the pub. It should have provided a view of the attacker's face but he was hidden by Gina's head as he propelled her rapidly onto the pavement. Gina appeared to be resisting, but her efforts were unsuccessful.

The view switched to a reverse angle. Had they still been on the pavement the attacker and his victim would have been hidden by tables and chairs chained for the night outside the pub. However, Gina had staggered into a doorway where she finally fell to the ground. She was now on her back and, for the first time, her face was visible and her distress was unmistakable. She was no longer struggling, but from the movements of her lips, she appeared to be crying out. *No. No. Stop it. Let me go.*

Pinning her down, the attacker pulled up her skirt and tore at her underwear. What followed was the clearest evidence of rape either of the two detectives had ever seen. After a few moments the assailant paused and leant forward, his head now covering Gina's face. For a couple of seconds there was no movement, then he pulled off her T-shirt. He must have already unclipped her bra because he yanked it from her body and wrapped it around her neck.

Jenny was surprised and upset by the vigour with which he began to strangle his victim. Gina couldn't break free. Suddenly he arched his back and it was all over. He knelt over Gina's body for a few moments then stood, pulled up his sweat pants, and turned to walk away. At that moment, there was a brief but clear view of his face with blond hair visible beneath his hood. That was the shot Ed had asked the technician to use.

Gina didn't move. There was no sign of her bra. After a few seconds she sat up, retrieved her T-shirt and put it on. She appeared to make no attempt to find her bra. Instead she got to her feet, made a half-hearted attempt to straighten her clothing and walked out of the Buttermarket into Burgate. The screen showed the time as 03.13.

Ed hit pause and turned to Jenny. 'What do you make of that?'

'Assuming there was penetration, which looks likely, I've never seen such clear-cut evidence of rape. If we get a DNA match, we've got the bugger as soon as we pick him up.'

'I hope so.' Although she'd seen the images several times Ed still sounded as shocked as Jenny. 'It's horrendous. What a toxic experience. Those memories could be with her for ever, destroying her self-esteem.' Ed paused before adding, 'And the strangulation, what did you make of that?'

'It was so violent. I can't believe she wasn't hurt more than she appeared to be.'

'Exactly. Anna, the MO, said the same.'

Ed pushed back her chair and got up. 'Make sure the mugshot Steve pulled from the tape is made available to patrols and prepared for TV and newspaper appeals. Then try to get two or three hours' sleep. It looks like we've a long day ahead.'

Fifteen minutes later, as Ed was leaving the building, she was stopped by the Desk Sergeant.

'DI Ogborne! Have you got a minute?'

'I was just off for a couple of hours of sleep.'

'I thought you'd like to know. A bra's been found pushed deep into a litter bin by the car park at the end of Iron Bar Lane. It's bagged and in the Evidence Room.'

'Thanks. I'll take a look before it goes to forensics.'

49

By 08.50, Ed was back in the CID Room where Jenny was working through photographs.

'Hi, Jenny. Are they from the Buttermarket CCTV?'

'I'm looking at the attacker's clothing. There are some reasonable shots of logos on his tracksuit and shoes. We should get a match.'

'Excellent. There's also a good chance we've struck lucky with her missing bra. Last night, Uniform found one discarded not far from the Buttermarket.'

'There's often discarded underwear in quiet corners of the city centre. Where did they find it?'

'At a secluded spot by the car park at the end of Iron Bar Lane. It was pushed deep into a litter bin as if someone were trying to hide it so I think it could be Gina's. I checked it against the CCTV of the attack on Gina and it looks similar to the one round her neck. If we can get both Gina and her attacker's DNA on the bra, that'll be conclusive.'

'If her attacker was on his way home from the Buttermarket via Iron Bar Lane, that suggests he lives to the east or south of the city,' said Jenny.

'Or that he'd parked a car there. Get the CCTV and see what's happening around 03.15.'

* * *

By mid-morning there had been a few crank calls but no serious responses to the local radio and TV requests for the public to come forward. Ed was at her desk when the phone rang with an internal call.

'DI Ogborne.'

It was the Desk Sergeant, Barry Williams. 'The manager of a local store's just called. A skinny guy with blond hair and wearing running gear has just walked into his shop.'

'Get a patrol car to bring him in. If he makes a move to leave the shop, ask the manager to keep him talking.'

50

I wake late, drowsily aware of the sheet against my skin and an earthy animal odour which, in the right place at the right time, is arousing, but otherwise I find it faintly repulsive. With my eyes closed, time and place return as if I were still with Gina. I'm tired, but the memories of last night are pleasantly arousing. I reach for my mobile to intensify the moment.

Gina had been *so* up for it, totally absorbed in the role she'd devised. I still can't believe how perfectly my plan has succeeded. Like a punter who knows that one last bet will reverse his fortunes, I knew all I needed was sufficient time alone with a woman and she would come to know my worth. What happened with Gina could not have been bettered. She's perfect, a perfect match for the professional women who'd rejected me at Scotts. Gina's response to being alone with me has gone further than I could have imagined. Sometimes, like our time at the Palio in Siena and last night in the Buttermarket, her enthusiasm has been so great I've felt a touch uneasy. I wanted my chosen woman to want me as much as I wanted her. Now there are times when Gina wants me almost too much, times when her passion is scary.

Scary, yes, but it was the sort of scary I was beginning to relish. So it came completely out of the blue when Gina suggested we should see less of each other. After what we'd experienced, what we had, I couldn't believe it. How could she think we should see less of each other? This morning it's different. I've changed. Gina's right. Relaxed in my bed, I'm relishing being alone, thinking of her, and knowing we'll be getting together again soon.

On my back under the covers I plan a day of more indulgence. First breakfast, a leisurely fry-up; I can almost smell the bacon in the pan. The prospect overcomes my idle musing. I push the covers from my body, swing my legs from the bed, shower and pull on some clothes. A full English means a walk to the corner shop. Leaving the flat and stepping onto the street, I feel good.

Nodding to the manager of the local minimarket, I make my way around the aisles. It takes some time to find what I want. Hesitating over black pudding and sausages, I go for the bangers. All I need now is fruit juice. Walking to the cold shelves, I notice two police officers come into the shop. Ever since Dover I feel a stab of anxiety whenever I come face to face with the law. I've got to stop doing this, put it from my mind. The Dover flat's clean. I'd made certain there was nothing left that could be traced to me. Why am I still jumpy? What's there to worry about? The local paper said she died of natural causes. Forget it and enjoy life. I've got my life with Gina to look forward to. Dover is history, collateral damage. A pity she died, but it wasn't my fault. Heart attack. Natural causes.

I pick up a carton of fresh orange juice and move towards the counter. One of the police officers is blocking the aisle. As if I'd forgotten something, I turn back to find the older officer coming towards me.

'Excuse me, Sir, my colleague and I would like a word.'

My first instinct is to drop the basket and run. Crazy! I force myself to stand still, to speak calmly.

'I'm sorry, officer, how can I help?'

'I'm Sergeant Hadley and this is Police Constable Neave. We think you may be able to assist us with our inquiries. May I ask your name, Sir?'

My mind is racing. When planning and carrying out my project I'd used various false names, but I hadn't attempted to set up real aliases. If I lie, the police will soon discover my name. I try to breathe slowly. Why am I thinking like this? I'm being irrational. There's no way I can be linked with the death of Kay in Dover. With Gina I'm safe; we go well together. Gina will stand by me.

'Bradshaw, I'm Colin Bradshaw. May I ask what this is all about?'

'You happen to fit the description of a man who was involved in an incident last night. I'm sure that if you come to the Station with us now we can ask a few questions, run a few checks and the matter can quickly be resolved.'

Despite the logic of my thoughts I still felt an icy chill at the officer's words.

'I'll just go and pay for these things.'

'Better to leave them here, Sir. You can come back later, when we've finished at the Station.'

The other officer stepped forward. 'I'll take those and ask the manager to keep them safe for you.'

As the younger officer reached for my shopping, my mind became completely clear. Neave, Police Constable Neave, and his colleague is Hadley, Sergeant Hadley. It is the Sergeant who leads me to the patrol car parked at an angle to the kerb outside the shop.

51

'Mr Bradshaw, I'm DI Ed Ogborne. We're sorry to have kept you waiting.' Ed nodded to PC Neave. 'Thank you, Constable. DC Eastham and I will take it from here.'

The two detectives sat at the table, facing their suspect. Ed explained the need to record the interview, switched on the tape and identified herself together with the time and date, before looking at Jenny.

'I'm DC Jenny Eastham.'

'Err, Colin Bradshaw.'

'And where do you live, Mr Bradshaw?' asked Ed.

'At 7 King Street ... err, Flat C.'

'That's a rented flat. I understand you also have a home in Gravesend.'

'Yes. Can you tell me exactly why I'm here?'

'As Sergeant Hadley will have told you, your description matches that of a man who was involved in an incident that occurred last night.'

'So the Sergeant said, but what incident, when and where?'

'We'll get to the details in a moment, Sir. First, can you tell me where you were in the early hours of this morning between 2 a.m. and 4.30 a.m.?'

'I was asleep in my flat.'

'Can anybody confirm that?'

'No. I live alone.'

'You didn't go out at all last night?'

'No. I had a pizza with a can of lager and watched a film on TV.'

'Do you have the receipt?'

'Not on me. It's probably at my flat in the bin with the pizza box and empty can.'

Ed opened a file, took out some photographs, and placed them face down on the table. She took the first photograph, turned it over and placed it in front of Colin.

'This was taken just after three o'clock this morning. Please look at it closely and tell me if you recognize either of the people walking towards the Buttermarket.'

Although he tried to disguise it, Colin reacted with concern when Ed said "three o'clock" and "Buttermarket". His poorly suppressed anxiety increased when he saw the photograph.

'No ... how could I recognize them? They both have their backs to the camera.'

'Perhaps these will help.'

Ed set out three more photographs. The first showed the attacker bundling Gina towards the pub. The second showed Gina on the ground with her face visible over her attacker's shoulder, and the third showed the attacker turning to walk away, his face and blond hair clearly visible.

As Colin and the two detectives faced each other, no one was in any doubt that Colin was the man in the photograph.

'Oh, dear.' Colin paused and then, to the detectives' surprise, visibly relaxed. 'The young lady is not going to be very pleased. What do you call it, outraging public decency?'

Ed started to speak. 'If the act was consensual—'

Colin ignored her. 'Hang on! Those shots must be from street cameras. Surely not even bored police officers trawl through CCTV on the off-chance. Somebody must have tipped you off. Did someone see us?'

'The young lady brought it to our attention.'

Colin's jaw dropped. His face registered a flash of astonishment then, looking perplexed, his eyes moved from Ed to Jenny and back again. 'I don't believe you.'

'I assure you it's true. She is claiming you attacked and raped her.'

Surprise, fear, outrage and astonishment flashed across Colin's face before his shoulders sagged and he sat openmouthed, struggling to control his emotions.

'We're getting a warrant to search your flat. In the meantime, you'll be photographed and we'll take your fingerprints and a DNA sample.'

'Doesn't that require my consent?'

'Not since 2004. You're suspected of committing a recordable act.'

'But if I refuse?'

'We are allowed to use reasonable force.'

'Which means?'

'Well, for DNA we'll use hair follicles pulled from your head rather than a mouth swab.'

'Okay, I'll come quietly. When you've finished, can I go?'

'Given the clarity of the CCTV evidence, I'm afraid not.' Ed paused and glanced at Jenny before proceeding. 'Colin Bradshaw, I am arresting you on suspicion of raping Georgina Hamilton. You do not have to say anything, but it may harm your defence if you do not mention when questioned something that you later rely on in court. Anything you do say may be given in evidence.'

Colin's astonishment and perplexed disbelief at what was happening were now directed firmly at Ed, who continued to follow procedure.

'Do you understand the charge?'

'Yes.' Colin spoke weakly, clearly overcome by the speed with which his life had changed.

'Do you have anything further to say at this time?'

'No comment.'

His voice was firm, but the response was delivered automatically, without thought. In shock at the position in which he now found himself, Colin Bradshaw's mind was clearly racing.

52

Rape! What the fuck's going on? Arrested, fingerprinted, swabbed and now banged up in a police cell! And it's all down to Gina. It can't be right ... can it? Gina ...? What's the bitch playing at?

No comment. That was a reflex, sparked by watching too many TV cop shows, but back there, I needed time. I still do – time to think.

A deep breath and breathe out slowly ... Calm ... I've got to stay calm. Easily said, *stay calm*, I'm struggling here. Must keep a neutral expression for the cops, can't let them see how I'm feeling. It's all happening so fast.

I begin pacing the confines of my police cell, small, slow steps in time with my thoughts.

Everything was going so well. I woke this morning feeling great, taking a lie-in, thinking of Gina and the scenario she'd come up with for last night. Not just the sex. The sex was good, but I was thinking how well we get on, how good we are together, thinking we've really got something going. Gina was the sort of woman who'd always seemed out of reach, but my plan had worked. She was mine. I was successful.

Now this! How could it have gone so wrong? Gina ...? What made her ...? The bitch! How could she go to the police?

And rape!

I smash my fists against the wall of my cell and then sink onto the bed.

Rape ...? No! It's not possible ... it was her idea ... she suggested it. It was Gina who wanted to do it outside. I was cautious, but she was all for it. Talking about Siena and the Palio, planning where and when, talking about the thrill that somebody might see us, hinting what it would do for her and what that would mean for me. She was the one pushing for it.

She even came up with the bra idea. Said, now she knew me, she felt able to confide, to trust me with things you'd only tell someone you were close to. Now we were together, it would be a secret between us – she liked to be dominated, to feel forced. More than that – she liked to feel in danger of her life. Feeling close to death really turned her on.

When she was saying this, I could see what she meant. Each time she talked about it, she really turned me on. I told her I didn't want to hurt her, but she just smiled. *Don't worry, it'll be okay*.

How could I have been so naive? No need to ask where it went wrong. I can see that now – now it's too late. For Gina it's all been an act. The bitch has set me up.

She fooled me. Perhaps I'm not as smart as I thought. Perhaps I'm no match for the women I want. Maybe I'm not in the same league.

No way!

I spring to my feet and start pacing the cell again.

Gina didn't play fair – she double-crossed me. I had her, my plan worked perfectly, but then I was careless. Too full of my success, I took my eye off the ball. She turned the tables.

She didn't try to submit. She gained control and then showed she wanted me as much as I wanted her. She begged me to take her. From a position of strength, she begged – that was her masterstroke.

Wait. Let's get this in context. She planned her attack, she won a battle, but that's all it was, a battle. She hasn't won the war. I'm not done yet! I'll not be beaten so easily.

Georgina Hamilton, smug little Gina, I bet you're thinking you're so clever. You're thinking I'm down and out. You're wrong. I've got a comeback. I can prove it wasn't rape. I can prove it wasn't the first time you've had sex with me. Your claim of rape will blow up in your face. After what I can tell them in court, if it gets that far, no jury – not even the police – will believe you.

Okay, I've got a plan. My position isn't good, but when you've got a plan, things are always better.

I sit and lean back, stretching out on what passes for a bed in a police cell. With my eyes closed I start to develop a strategy. The trip to Italy, Siena for the Palio, taking an apartment together overlooking the Campo, you don't do that, spend that kind of money, unless you've got something good going. There's plenty of evidence, enough to convince a jury if it comes to that – isn't there?

With no one to bounce my thoughts off, I begin to have doubts. Have I got a good case? I wish I knew more about the law.

Where do I stand? What are my strengths? More to the point, what are my weaknesses? What exactly have the police got? CCTV of us in the Buttermarket. From the photos I appear to be forcing Gina to have sex. But that's what she wanted. She wanted me to strangle her with her bra. She wanted to be totally dominated – at least, that's what she said. Now the bitch is out to get me. She'll have given the police all the forensic evidence they need. They've taken my DNA. Soon they'll have confirmation that penetration occurred. And there's her bra. If they find that, can they get DNA from it?

I'll say we had sex earlier that evening. That would explain any DNA they find. My mind's racing. I'm not thinking straight. Get a grip. How would sex earlier in the evening get me out of the Buttermarket CCTV? Even if a jury could be persuaded to doubt it's me, there'll be no other male DNA. Everyone believes DNA. DNA doesn't lie. It has to be me attacking her, strangling her with her bra. A jury might accept we had sex earlier in the day, but when they see the CCTV, they'll be convinced I violated her in the Buttermarket.

God! What if the police can lip-read her saying *no*? Whatever she's said, I can show we've been together for some time. So what? That'll not help. Without her consent it'll be rape and the CCTV will back her story.

Maybe I could use the speed with which she jumped into bed to discredit her? It could make her appear less sympathetic in the eyes of the jury, but that's all. They'll be sure to argue that whatever the relationship, she can still say *no*, at any time. She's sure to claim it happened without her consent. She'll deny she suggested it. She'll even deny she agreed to outdoor sex. Gina will say I jumped her. She'll say she was scared. She'll say she said *no*, but I wouldn't stop. And the CCTV will support her.

But it wasn't like that. With Italy, Siena and the Palio, I can show it was part of an ongoing relationship. Her protests weren't for real. She was acting. It was a sex game. *Her* sex game, and for a sex game, saying *no* wouldn't work. For a sex game you have to have a safe word. Not that we had a safe word. Still, the jury won't know that. It'll be her word against mine. Not everybody will believe me, but it'll be enough to show I had reason to believe she wanted me to go ahead, to continue.

Suddenly I'm sitting bolt upright, eyes open. Sex games ... Dover ... Will I never get that woman out of my head? Dover was months ago. The paper said it was natural causes. Nothing more has happened. It's gone quiet. No! It's *been* quiet, but now things have changed. As of today, the police have got my fingerprints and my DNA. No matter. Whether they've got my DNA or not, Kayleigh's flat was clean. I can relax on that score.

Maybe it's too quiet. The police don't release everything they have to the press. The concealer on her wrists and ankles, that might have fooled them at the scene, but there would have been a post-mortem. I've seen it on TV. They wash the body. The pathologist would have found the marks on her skin from the cords I'd used to tie her to the bed. There'd be no evidence of burglary, so what would they think? They'd have to think it was a sex game gone wrong. If I mentioned sex games as a defence with Gina the police might start linking me to Kayleigh's death in Dover. What would that be? Manslaughter? Murder? I wish I knew more about the law.

Perhaps I'm being over-cautious, over-thinking the Dover episode. There are sex shops in every high street. Sex toys are big business. Half the couples in England must be at it. There can't be any reason to link Dover with me and Gina in Canterbury. The two towns have separate Police Forces. But, with computers and databases, they must share information.

Even if they do, so what? There can't be any reason to link me directly with the Dover flat. *Stop worrying, you're in the clear.*

I relax and lock my hands behind my head. There's nothing to stop me using sex games and Gina's failure to use our safe word as a defence. Of course, she'd deny it, deny we were playing sex games. She'll deny we had a safe word, say I've invented that, but I'm a plausible liar. What I say should be enough to sow seeds of reasonable doubt.

They'll be back, they'll question me again. I've got to play it cool, not appear too eager, let the police drag it out of me.

53

Back at her desk, Ed picked up the phone and dialled a local number. The line went to an answer phone.

She waited for the bleep before speaking.

'This is Detective Inspector Ed Ogborne, Canterbury CID. Ms Hamilton, if you are listening to this, will you please pick up. I need to speak to you urgently.'

There was a pause and then a tired-sounding voice came on the line.

'This is Gina Hamilton. I'm sorry, Inspector, I didn't feel up to taking any calls. How can I help?'

But you were monitoring your phone all the same, thought Ed.

'Gina, I'm sorry to bother you, but we need to speak. DC Jenny Eastham and I can be at your apartment in 15 minutes.'

'So soon?'

'There's been a development, one you should know about.'

'Can't you tell me over the phone?'

'We also need to review the transcript of your interview, prior to preparing your statement.'

'I'm really very tired. Perhaps—'

'That's understandable, Gina, but it won't take long and then we should be able to leave you in peace.'

'All right, Inspector, if you must. I'll be waiting for you.'

'Thank you, Gina.' Ed hung up and turned to DC Eastham. 'Jenny, get a copy of the Gina Hamilton transcript and meet me outside. I'll have my car at the main entrance.'

Ten minutes later, Ed parked at Great Stour Court. Gina, wearing a crumpled cotton dressing gown and pyjamas, met them at the door to her apartment. Her hair was uncombed and she looked exhausted.

'I really hope this won't take long.'

Her voice no longer had the child-like quality apparent during her interview at the Station, but she spoke as if every word were an effort.

'It's little more than nine hours since I was attacked and raped. I've tried to sleep, but I can't. The horror keeps replaying in my head.'

'We appreciate this is a very difficult time for you, Gina. A support officer will be in touch and you should consider contacting your GP for short-term help sleeping.'

Ed paused, waiting for Gina to invite them in, but she remained in the doorway, holding the frame for support.

'Perhaps we could ...'

'Oh ... sorry.'

Gina turned listlessly and led them through to her living room where she slumped onto a small sofa, leaving the two detectives to face her in dining chairs.

'You said there's been a development. Does this mean you've ...?' Gina's remaining breath escaped silently through slack lips. She stopped speaking, sinking deeper into the sofa, apparently too tired to name the possibilities.

'Yes, Gina. This morning we arrested a man who matches the description you gave us and the image on the CCTV.'

Gina visibly brightened.

'You've got the bastard! Do you know his name?'

'Colin Bradshaw.'

Ed noted the briefest of reactions to the name, surprise perhaps, and wondered if Gina knew the man. Maybe, but that was not something she wished to pursue here.

'What happens now?' asked Gina.

'Bradshaw's currently under arrest and he's assisting us with our inquiries.'

'Assisting? Surely there'll be a DNA match and he'll be convicted?'

'We're waiting on the results of forensic tests, but you're right, the presence of his DNA would provide strong evidence. In that regard, you'll be pleased to learn that we found a bra not far from the scene. It closely resembles the one visible in the CCTV images. The presence of his DNA and yours on that bra would also be powerful evidence.'

On mentioning the bra had been found, Ed thought she detected another brief reaction from Gina. This time she gently pursued the issue.

'I wonder, Gina, would you be able to describe the bra you were wearing last night?'

'Inspector!' Gina wearily levered herself into a more upright position on the sofa. Her tired eyes regarded Ed accusingly. 'It was the middle of the night. I pulled on whichever clothes came to hand. I was raped. I haven't slept. And you're asking me to describe my bra.'

'I'm sorry. It's a minor point. DNA will identify it as yours.' Ed's apologetic look reverted to one of sympathetic efficiency. 'I do have a more important request. We would like you to formally identify your attacker.'

'Would I have to meet him?'

'That wouldn't be necessary. We can use VIPER, a video identification procedure. Perhaps you could come to the Station tomorrow and sign your statement at the same time?'

Gina sighed but remained upright on the sofa. 'Yes ... I see that's important. I could come any time during the day.'

'Excellent. Thank you for being so cooperative. Now all we need to do is go over the transcript.' Ed stood and turned her chair to face the dining table. 'Perhaps you could come here, Gina, so Jenny and I can confirm what you told us yesterday and see if there are any additions or alterations you wish to make.'

Sitting at the table, Ed let Jenny take the lead. After a few minutes, when Jenny and Gina were well into the details, Ed interrupted to ask if she might use the loo.

'It's off the hall.'

While Jenny re-engaged Gina in reviewing the transcript, Ed closed and locked the bathroom door firmly behind her. After a count of ten she quietly unlocked the door and slipped into Gina's bedroom. All the furniture was new. Doors and drawers opened silently. Ed rapidly checked the contents and then returned to the bathroom, closing the door quietly. She flushed the loo, checked the bathroom cabinet, washed her hands and returned to the living room.

Five minutes later, they finished going over the transcript.

Ed thanked Gina for her help and they agreed she'd come to the Station at 11 the following morning.

Back at the car, Ed asked Jenny to call the dental practice and make an appointment to speak with the staff.

'Right.' Jenny nodded, partly lost in her own thoughts. 'How did you get on when you took a look around Gina's apartment?'

'Interesting ... but I found no signs at all that anybody else is living there, or even visiting on a regular basis.'

'What was interesting?'

'Just an idea I have. Once I've checked something else we'll discuss it.'

As Ed drove towards the city centre, Jenny called the dental practice.

'Rachael Metcalffe could see us now or at the end of the afternoon.'

'Say we'll be there in five minutes.'

54

I'd been expecting the call. They were bound to pick him up sooner rather than later. Colin doesn't plan meals ahead, he was sure to be out in town eating or shopping. I was expecting the call, but not what happened next. Two detectives turning up on my doorstep was something else.

They insisted they came immediately, but there was no need for me to feign tiredness. I haven't slept since they drove me back from the Police Station earlier this morning. That was another surprise: at the Station, they were much nicer to me than I'd expected. A woman reporting rape: from what you hear, I'd thought they'd not be sympathetic, maybe give me a hard time, but far from it. Having seen how supportive the police were, have I gone for the right option, made the right choice?

When I escaped from the apartment I felt triumphant. Having turned the tables I was more than happy to let him stew. It felt good to give him a taste of his own medicine, but the more I thought about it, the more I realized Colin was no longer my real problem. My real problem was Colin tied to the bed. If only I'd managed to get out when I returned from work and found him in my apartment. If I'd got out then, and reported him straight to the police, they would have believed me, but that isn't what happened. Once he'd over-powered me, there was only one way to escape and that's created my problem.

Outside the apartment, standing by the lift, I imagined coming back with the police. Who would believe my story? No one would ever accept I was able to overpower Colin and tie him to the bed against his will. '*But, officer, he broke in, held me prisoner. I had to escape.*' And the evidence? All gone. He'd fixed the phones, fixed the locks and repaired the wall. At the very least, the police would doubt me. They'd ask Colin for his version of what happened. I can see him now, all choirboy innocence. '*But, officer, you can see for yourself what a humiliating position I'm in. It's so embarrassing. I'm afraid it was a sex game gone wrong.*'

That morning, sitting in Deakin's eating breakfast, I remember looking at the other customers, all oblivious to the narrow line between their safe lives and unsought horror. Every one of us is vulnerable. Any one of us could make an everyday choice that invites horror into our homes, into our worlds. I pride myself on being careful. I'm smart and street-wise. If I could unwittingly invite evil into my life, none of us is safe.

Of course, that wasn't the full story. I might have made a bad choice ringing the decorators on Colin's fake junk mail flier, but I escaped. However, escaping hasn't turned out quite as I'd imagined. My initial rush of triumph, the exuberant joy, was short-lived. My freedom was tainted. Gaining the upper hand had allowed me to escape, but in escaping, I'd left my world behind. The bastard had not only conned me and held me prisoner, he'd taken over my life as well. No matter how I contrived to oust him, the imprint of his presence would remain like the sounds of breathing and the dry slithering that still lurked in the recesses of my mind.

Worst of all, Colin coerced me into sex. Had I met him in a bar, he'd have stood no chance. Sex, even a one-night stand, couldn't have been further from my mind. He forced me to use sex in order to escape. After my postgrad training, I vowed I'd leave the escort business behind – and I did. Because of Colin, I was forced back to using sex as a means to an end, something I'd promised myself I'd never do again. Once I'd decided to stop working as an escort, I'd felt clean, but Colin had made me dirty again. You bastard, Colin. You thought I was yours, you thought you'd achieved your goal. Have no doubt, I'll get my revenge.

It was difficult, but I've made the right choice; this will put Colin out of my life, I'm certain of that. But ... the thought lingers, perhaps I should have trusted the police. It's too late for that now. Push that thought aside, concentrate on getting rid of Colin. The detective said the potential evidence was powerful. Well, they'll certainly get the forensic evidence they need, the evidence to charge Colin with raping me. He'll be convicted, sentenced, out of my life.

I'm not happy they found the bra. That's men for you, bloody useless. I told Colin to lose it. What with the CCTV and the forensic evidence on me and my clothes we didn't need the bra. I'd rather the police didn't have it, but I can't see it being a major problem. I'm the victim, for fuck's sake. With CCTV and forensics, the police will look on the bra as just another piece of evidence against Colin, another nail in his coffin.

All told, I'm feeling good. My triumph is inevitable. I will come out on top.

Tucking my legs beneath me, I'm just getting comfortable on the sofa when a new thought strikes – I didn't tell the detectives I knew my attacker. They didn't ask, but I should have mentioned it. Colin's bound to raise it in his defence. If they search – they're bound to search – our names will be in the airline's records. I must tell the Inspector, what's her name? Osborne ...? Tomorrow, when I go to the Station to identify Colin, I'll admit my oversight. By next week, life will be back to normal. I've already called the practice to tell Rachael what happened and to say I'll be off work for a week. Better see my GP and make that official.

55

When Ed and Jenny arrived at the dental practice, Rachael Metcalffe showed them to a room at the back of the building.

'We'll not be disturbed here. Fortunately, the locum, who covered for Ms Hamilton when she was on holiday, was free. He and the hygienist are seeing patients at the moment, but I have a break. Would you like tea or coffee?'

'We're good, thank you.'

'What can I do to help, Inspector? Georgina's already called in to tell us the terrible news, and to say her GP recommended a week off work. Have you caught the culprit?'

'A man is in custody, but it would help us formulate a case if we can build a comprehensive background for both the victim and the perpetrator.'

'How so?'

Jenny gave Ed a sideways glance.

'There are a number of ways in which it might help. The man is not from Canterbury and he has the right to remain silent when questioned. If we are to trace his movements, to see if he's been in the vicinity of other such incidents in the past, it would help to have a profile of likely victims. The more we know about Gina, Ms Hamilton, the better we'll be able to construct that profile.'

'I see ...' Rachael faced Ed co-operatively. 'What would you like me to tell you?'

'Perhaps you could begin with your general impression of Ms Hamilton.'

Ed looked at Jenny, to check she was ready to take notes.

'Georgina's an excellent dentist. When we interviewed her, my father and I thought she had potential and I've not been disappointed. She immediately fitted in and is well liked. She's established a very successful professional relationship with our patients and she's suggested several innovations. I was wary at first, but she persuaded me to adopt them and every one of the changes she put forward has been good for the practice.'

'How do you find her as a person?'

'She's very much on top of things. Persuasive, as I've already said, and excellent with clients.'

'Is she an outgoing person? Does she have lots of friends?'

'We don't socialize or discuss our personal lives. Earlier this year she bought an apartment and I think she's been occupied getting that just the way she wants it.'

'You mentioned a holiday.'

'Yes.' Rachael paused and then added, 'That was a stroke of luck.' She paused again, as if there was no more to say.

'In what way was it lucky?' asked Ed.

'Well, what with buying the apartment and furnishing it, plus the work she's had done, I would imagine she's been living on a tight budget. Then, out of the blue, she won a competition. The prize was a fortnight in Italy. Georgina was delighted. It included a visit to Siena, something she'd always wanted to do. She was there for that horse race and, to judge from her photographs, she had a great time.'

'A horse race, was that the Palio?' asked Ed.

'Yes … She really wanted to see it. Actually, I thought it was odd.'

'Why should it be odd to want to see the Palio?'

'No, not wanting to see it, but her photographs. She had photographs taken from the stands. They appeared to be before and after the race, but none of the race itself. I asked her about it. She said the race was so exciting she forgot to take photographs.'

'Can you tell me the dates of this holiday?'

'Her last day at work was Friday the 21st of June and her flight was the following morning. I'm not sure when she flew back but it was a two-week holiday, a week in Orvieto and a week in Siena. She was certainly at work on Monday the 8th of July.'

'Thank you. Did she go by herself?'

'I'm afraid I can't say. Is there anything else? I have my next patient in a few minutes.'

'No, that's been very helpful. Thank you for your time.' Ed passed Rachael one of her cards. 'Please call this number if you think of anything more that might help us.'

Back at the Station, when Ed walked into the CID Room she found Jenny telling Mike and Nat about last night's incident. She seemed pleased at the speed with which the case had been resolved.

'Georgina Hamilton came in this morning around 03.20 claiming she'd been raped in the Buttermarket just after 03.00.

Ed and I interviewed her and already the man she accused is in the cells.'

'Do we know him?' asked Mike.

'Colin Bradshaw. He's not a local.'

'And he's confessed?'

'No, but we have the entire incident on CCTV. You can see her protesting.' As Jenny spoke, Ed thought she glanced meaningfully at Nat; he was silent and looking uncomfortable. 'When the attacker gets up and walks away, you can clearly see it's Bradshaw. His full face and distinctive blond hair are on camera.'

'And you've got forensic samples?'

'We got her clothes and swabs. He didn't want to give fingerprints and DNA but Ed arrested him and we took them anyway.'

'Sounds like you've got him.'

Finally, Nat spoke. 'He could plead she consented.'

'The CCTV clearly shows her protesting, no, no, no!'

'Maybe there's history and he can argue he thought he had consent,' said Mike, ever-cautious.

'Well, I've never seen CCTV footage like it. He stalks her, pushes her to the ground, rapes her and walks away.'

'What did he say when you questioned him?' asked Mike.

'No comment,' said Ed, who had made her way unseen to her desk.

'Nothing new there then,' said Mike as both men, who'd been standing when Ed entered, started making their way to the door.

'As soon as you get back from lunch, watch the Buttermarket CCTV and the video of Georgina Hamilton's questioning. Team meeting at 14.30 to discuss the case.'

When the men had left, Ed suggested she and Jenny get a coffee and walk across the road to The Mound in Dane John Gardens. They climbed the path to a bench looking back over the city wall towards the Police Station.

'I forgot to ask, did you have any luck with the CCTV of the Iron Bar Lane litter bin?'

'Sorry, I should have said.' Jenny joined Ed on the bench. 'The images are very clear. At 03.11, Colin Bradshaw, looking just as he does in the Buttermarket CCTV, appears at the car park and thrusts something white deep into the bin.'

'What did he do next?'

'He disappeared off the cameras.'

Ed shrugged. 'Never mind, the main thing is, it's looking certain the bra we've got is hers.'

The two women relaxed, drinking coffee and looking over the heavy traffic to the buildings on the other side of the inner ring road. It was Ed who broke the silence, turning questioningly to Jenny.

'Back at the Station, I got the impression you thought the Hamilton case was pretty much sewn up.'

From her face, it was clear Jenny sensed the potential disagreement in Ed's voice, but she stood her ground. 'Yes, I think so. Don't you?'

'Well ... Bradshaw hasn't confessed, he implied it was consensual, it could be his word against hers.'

'But we have the CCTV and the forensic evidence,' protested Jenny. 'We can identify him from his face and hair, which you can see on the tape, and DNA from her body and clothes will confirm it was him. Also, both their DNA should be on the white bra.'

234

'I don't doubt DNA will confirm it was Bradshaw and probably that penetration occurred.'

'And you can clearly see Gina saying, "No, no, no," on the tape.'

'True,' said Ed, 'but assuming he contests it, what do you think his defence will be?'

'I don't know. The evidence is so clear cut. Has he got one?'

'We didn't ask Gina if she recognized her attacker, but I thought she reacted when I mentioned his name. If they have any history at all, Mr Bradshaw would have support for a belief in consent.'

'But she was clearly protesting.'

'Right.' Ed finished her coffee and stood up. 'I'll need your help in 30 minutes or so.'

'Okay.'

Jenny followed her boss down the path. At the bottom, Ed turned towards the centre of town.

'I'll call your mobile when I get back to the Station. First, I have to buy a couple of bras.'

Too much information, thought Jenny as they parted.

56

'Hi, I'm almost back. Drop whatever you're doing and meet me at the front desk. I'll be there in three minutes.'

Once inside the Station, Ed led Jenny to the Incident Room, slipped off her jacket and stood by the table.

'I've got two new bras here,' said Ed, handing Jenny a shopping bag. 'I want you to take one and strangle me with it.'

'If we're re-enacting the rape, wouldn't it be better if we got Nat to do that?'

'I want a reconstruction, Jenny, not complete verisimilitude. And besides, if I'm going to look ridiculous, I'd like you to be the witness, rather than one of our male colleagues.'

'Okay ...' Jenny took the shopping bag, but didn't open it. 'Tell me, why exactly are we doing this?'

'Something I noticed that struck me as odd. I thought we should follow it up.'

Ed seemed intent on being mysterious. Jenny had noticed her do this in team meetings. When introducing a new idea, she would sometimes leave a crucial point unsaid. Jenny saw it as a test; how soon before the others would get the point. On those occasions, she'd always gone along with it, but this time was different. Jenny wasn't about to attack her DI with a bra without knowing why.

'What was it, what was odd?'

'When Gina came to report rape, all the clothes she was wearing were well worn. Her knickers and T-shirt were obviously originally white, but had become a touch grey. In contrast, the bra retrieved from the litter bin looked brand new. Apart from obvious signs of mishandling, it was pristine white.'

'So she bought a new bra,' said Jenny, as if, for her, that was the end of the matter.

'Yes ... but why wear a new bra last night? Gina's told us she pulled on whichever clothes came to hand. All the other items were old, but the bra was new. However, when I asked, she couldn't, or wouldn't, describe the bra.'

'Are you thinking she didn't want us to pay attention to the new bra?'

'It's possible ... but, nine times out of ten, Jenny, why do rapists take items from their victims?'

'As trophies.'

'Exactly, so why did Colin take the bra only to hide it in the bottom of a litter bin 200 yards away?'

'Perhaps, walking away, he thought better of it,' said Jenny, rather lamely.

'Or perhaps Gina put him up to it.'

'Why would she do that?'

'Maybe she didn't want us to see the bra?'

'But why?'

'Let's do the reconstruction first.' Ed put out a hand to locate her position beside the table. 'I'm closing my eyes because I don't want to see or touch the bras. Take one from the bag and put it on me over the top of my shirt.'

When the bra was in place, Ed swung her legs up onto the conference table and lay on her back.

'Right, Jenny, get on top of me, take off the bra and strangle me with it.'

'Perhaps I should lock the door first?'

'I locked it as we came in.'

Jenny climbed onto the table with her knees either side of Ed's body and leant forwards, passing her arms around Ed's torso to undo the bra.

'There's one more thing. If I tap the table three times like this –' Ed rapped the table top with her knuckles '– stop strangling me and get the bra off as fast as you can.'

'Understood.'

Bent low, with her face close to Ed's, Jenny released the clip, pulled off the bra and looped it around Ed's neck. As soon as she pulled it tight, Ed started to choke and vigorously tapped the table. It took Jenny longer than either of them liked to loosen the bra from Ed's neck.

'Right, let's go with the other one. Don't be concerned if I struggle, but remember to get it off fast if I tap the table.'

With the second bra in place Jenny asked Ed if she was okay.

'Go for it!'

Jenny removed the bra and pulled it tight round Ed's neck. This time her boss didn't choke. Instead she fought back, trying to push Jenny away. Finally, after 20 or 30 seconds, Ed casually tapped the table.

'That'll do, you can take it off now.'

Jenny removed the bra and climbed from the table, allowing Ed to sit up.

'I guess that looked as clear to you as it felt to me. We can check, but I reckon my neck's about the same size as Gina's. Had we kept them on longer, the second bra would have left some ligature marks, but I would have survived; the first bra would have killed me. Which was which?'

'The second bra was padded and underwired,' said Jenny. 'The first wasn't.'

Ed smiled. 'Just as I thought. The second was a 34D and the same type as the bra found in the bin. It looks exactly like the one Gina was wearing in the CCTV.'

'I guess she was lucky she chose to wear that one.'

'More like careful planning if you ask me,' said Ed.

Jenny reacted with surprise. 'What do you mean?'

'This morning, while you were keeping Gina busy going over the transcript of her interview, I had a look round the apartment.'

'You were checking for signs someone had been living with her and didn't find any.'

'Right, but I also checked her underwear drawer. All of Gina's bras are wire-free, unpadded, soft cup size 34C, similar to the first bra we tried. I didn't find any like the one she's wearing in the CCTV.

'Anna Masood said the ligature marks on Gina's neck were consistent with attempted strangulation with a bra, but they were not as severe as she would have expected. Now we know why. Just now when we tried it, you couldn't get the 34D underwired padded bra tight enough to kill me. The padded cups and underwiring jammed together round my neck. That bra was tight, but I could still breathe. On the other hand, the soft cup bra, which doesn't have that extra support, acted like a stocking and would have choked me to death had we continued.'

'You think Gina knew what was going to happen?'

'She's a bright woman.' Ed moved towards the door. 'I think we should see what Mike and Nat make of it.'

57

Mike Potts mumbled an apology as he pulled out a chair and joined his three colleagues at the Incident Room table. Ed opened the meeting.

'Eleven hours ago, Georgina Hamilton – she prefers Gina – walked into the Station and alleged she'd been attacked and raped in the Buttermarket. CCTV fixes the start of the attack as 03.02 this morning. Nat and Mike, you've had a chance to watch three tapes: the initial VIs with Gina and with her attacker and we've all seen the Buttermarket CCTV. The attacker was recognized by a shopkeeper from a TV appeal and a car patrol brought him in.'

Ed paused briefly and Nat interrupted.

'Have we got a name?'

'It's the next point I intend to make, Nat, although you should have picked that up from the VI. The attacker's name is Colin Bradshaw. He has a house in Gravesend, but is currently renting a flat at 7 King Street in Canterbury. He didn't deny being the man in the CCTV, but he implied the act was consensual and was disinclined to give bio-samples.'

Mike roused himself. 'From the tape, we saw you arrested him on suspicion and I assume DNA and fingerprints were taken. After that, did he offer any more information?'

'No. He refused to answer further questions. He's now in the cells and we expect his DNA sample to confirm Gina's story. Before I hear your views, let's take another look at the Buttermarket CCTV.'

Ed played the edited tape and they watched in silence. The sequence ended with Gina trying to straighten her clothes before walking away via Burgate. Ed hit pause.

'I spent a few minutes with Gina soon after she arrived at the Station. She gave a brief description of her attacker, which I had circulated to patrols. Gina was examined by Anna Masood. I'll tell you what Anna found and then we'll run her interview tape.'

Mike interrupted. 'What was your initial impression of Gina during those first few minutes before the MO arrived?'

'I want to hear everybody's impressions of Gina Hamilton's behaviour, so let's leave my views until we've watched the tape.'

'Okay,' Mike agreed.

'Anna's physical examination revealed Gina had been attacked and probably raped. Her clothes were torn, there was bruising on her thighs, light scratches on her back and breasts, and ligature marks around her neck. Fortunately, Gina was not seriously injured. Anna stressed victims' initial reactions vary. Some are hysterical, others withdrawn, and some appear calm and in control of themselves. Anna thought Gina was a classic case, calm, but in reality, fighting to maintain control, suppressing her emotions and trying not to go to pieces.'

Ed looked round the group. 'Any questions?' No one spoke. 'Okay, let's run the VI.'

The team watched the interview in silence. Ed stopped the

242

tape and turned to the team. 'Right, what do you make of Gina Hamilton's behaviour? Nat, perhaps you'd kick off.'

The young DC looked surprised and a little uncomfortable at being chosen to go first, but he soon got into his stride.

'Well ... from the CCTV it's clear who the guy is. He certainly grabs her and appears to push her to the ground. It looks as though he has sex with her, but what did she think she was doing, out by herself, dressed like that, in the deserted city centre at that time of night? I just don't buy her story about not being able to sleep and walking to work for—'

During Nat's contribution, Jenny's anger visibly increased to the point where, out of character, she interrupted him.

'Nat! You can't say that. It's like saying if a woman is drunk or wearing sexy clothes then she's asking for it. The CCTV shows him forcing her to have sex, something forensics will confirm. The tape also shows Gina is protesting, saying *no*. We're living in the twenty-first century. Everyone should know that *no* is *no* and a woman can say it *at any time*.'

Nat looked uncomfortable under Jenny's verbal attack and didn't reply. Ed stepped in to move the discussion to the topic she'd raised.

'We can come back to the points you've made. What I want us to discuss is Gina's behaviour during the interview. Mike, what did you make of her in the VI?'

'Much the same as the MO. To me it looks like a classic case, a victim of rape fighting to stay calm.'

'Thanks, Mike. Jenny, from what you said to me earlier, I think you agree with Mike and Anna.'

'Assuming the DNA confirms penetration by Colin Bradshaw, yes. You can clearly see her saying *no*. A lip reader could confirm that.'

'Nat, anything to add?' asked Ed.

'Well ... in the VI she's speaking hesitantly, using an unnaturally small voice, sometimes drying up completely but she doesn't lose it, she doesn't break down ...'

Looking increasingly exasperated, Jenny glared angrily at Nat and interrupted him a second time.

'Exactly, Gina's just been attacked and raped. She's completely stressed out, but she's fighting to stay in control.' Jenny turned to Ed for confirmation. 'In the interview she was fighting to keep her self-esteem.'

'That's what it looks like,' said Nat, 'and that's what it sounds like but ...' He was directing his comments to Ed and avoiding looking at Jenny.

'But what?' asked Ed.

'When running the VI, I put aside Gina's behaviour and concentrated on the content of what she said. As I see it, she gives a very complete account. It's as if she knows exactly what she wants to say and she says it – all of it. I haven't much experience of rape cases, but for someone who was stressed, I would have expected a more jumbled account with pieces missing from the story.'

As Nat spoke, Jenny's eyes widened incredulously. She was now staring at him furiously, but she held herself in check, waiting for him to finish before exploding.

'I can't believe that. A woman's been raped and you're saying she's acting!'

Nat began to reply with his eyes still fixed on Ed.

'Well ... I think the small voice and hesitations ... we should ask—'

Ed raised her hand, palm out, and stopped Nat in mid-sentence before addressing the entire group.

'What is coping if it's not behaving in a way that doesn't match how we feel?'

No one responded. There was silence and Ed moved the discussion on.

'What will Colin say in his defence?'

'What they all say,' said Jenny, her voice still tight with anger. 'Short skirt, tight top, she was gagging for it.'

Ed had already turned to her DS.

'Mike, what do you think?'

'We don't know enough about either of them for me to form an opinion. You said Colin implied the act was consensual. Does this mean Colin and Gina know each other? Are they in a relationship?'

'Valid questions, Mike. In normal circumstances, I'd agree with Jenny, *no* is *no* and a woman can say *no*, at any time. However—'

'Exactly!' said Jenny, glancing appreciatively at Ed. 'When a woman says *no*, the man should respect her decision.' Jenny's eyes flicked to Nat and back to Ed. 'No matter what might have happened up to that point, a woman can still say *no*!'

'Right, Jenny,' said Ed, 'I agree completely that it's a woman's right to say *no* at any time, and that all men should respect her wishes, but –' Ed paused to ensure she had everyone's attention '– as I was about to say, that applies under normal circumstances. I also—'

'What possible circumstances would justify a man not stopping, not respecting a woman's wishes? Consent is consent. No means *stop what you're doing*!'

'Consent is crucial, Jenny, but *no* doesn't always mean *stop what you're doing*. I agree with Mike that we need to know more about Gina Hamilton and Colin Bradshaw. In particular, we need to know if Gina and Colin were in, or had been in, a relationship and, if so, what was the nature of that relationship.'

'But why?' asked Jenny. 'You've said that *no* is *no* and a woman's wishes should be respected at any time!'

'Yes, Jenny, but I said I believe that to be true *in normal circumstances*. By that I mean in all but one situation.'

'What possible situation could be different?'

'As you've said, Jenny, consent is crucial. However, a consenting couple could agree times when *no* didn't mean *stop*.'

Ed's colleagues looked at her in surprise. Jenny, sounding puzzled, was the first to speak. 'What do you mean?'

'If a couple have both freely consented to engage in a sex game, resisting and saying *no* is likely to be part of the game. *No, stop,* could mean *yes, go on*. If a couple had agreed to indulge in rough sex, they would normally agree a safe word.'

'A safe word?' asked Jenny.

'It comes from the world of S&M, sadism and masochism. Before starting, a couple would choose a word or phrase totally unrelated to the proposed activity, "East Thanet" for example. Then, if one should ever say the safe word, the other should stop immediately.'

From the corner of her eye Ed saw Nat raise his eyebrows. He appeared to be seeing her in a new light. Jenny and Mike were certainly looking at her with renewed attention.

'If Gina and Colin were indulging in a rape fantasy, then protests on her part, cries of *no* and *stop* et cetera, would be stimulating. If things got out of hand and Gina wanted to stop, such protestations wouldn't work.'

'Exactly,' said Nat without convincing anyone he knew

246

much about the world of bondage. 'Gina could have been directing things from the start.'

Jenny glanced at Ed who simply nodded in her direction.

'There's no evidence it was a sex game. If they were playing sex games, Gina must have known Colin well. She didn't tell us that when Ed and I questioned her. She could barely describe her attacker.'

Ed coughed. 'That's true, Jenny. She didn't volunteer the information, but I didn't directly ask that question.'

'She's not going to say they were old friends if she's out for revenge,' said Mike. 'Remember how much she emphasized she wanted the bastard in jail.'

'And then there's the question of the bras.' Ed dropped the statement into the exchange almost as if she were musing to herself.

'Bras?' exclaimed Nat 'You mean there was more than one?'

'She wasn't wearing any when she arrived at the Station,' said Ed, 'but Uniform found a bra, just like the one you can see on the CCTV, dumped in a waste bin nearby. We're waiting on DNA to show it was Gina's and that Colin handled it.'

'Right ... but why bras?' persisted Nat.

'The one found is a 34D, underwired and padded. None of the bras at Gina's apartment are like that. They're all 34C soft cup, no underwire and no padding.'

'Why would a woman have a bra that's too big for her?' asked Mike.

'Why have it and why wear it when you go out in the middle of the night?' Nat looked steadfastly at Ed. 'Would you?'

'I probably would if I thought somebody was going to strangle me with it.'

Jenny gasped and turned to her boss with a look of angry surprise.

'That's speculation!' Jenny paused, seeking to justify the force of her statement. 'How would she know somebody was going to strangle her with her bra?'

'If she'd arranged it,' suggested Nat. He continued to avoid Jenny's eyes, but he couldn't avoid her comment.

'Nat! That's the bane of our society, people not believing women who report rape. You must have been taught during training to guard against the belief that women reporting rape were either asking for it or lying.'

Now both Nat and Mike looked uncomfortable.

'Jenny's right, but that doesn't mean all claims of rape are true.'

Jenny looked sharply at Ed, but didn't interrupt.

'We should approach all cases with an open mind. We should always behave sympathetically and be ready to believe the claim. However, we should also be prepared to consider any indication that the claim may not be true.'

Mike mumbled agreement and Ed continued.

'I've had wide experience of rape cases and seen all the typical responses at first hand, including a determination to maintain control. With Gina, I had doubts, especially during the first few minutes I spent with her. Despite her weak voice, hesitations and pauses, what she said appeared to be seamlessly constructed. It was as if she had thought carefully in advance about exactly what she was going to say.'

'Exactly,' said Nat, but Jenny objected strongly.

'Of course! A professional woman who was determined to maintain control would have thought about what she was going to say.'

'The main issue,' said Mike, 'is not how Gina spoke during her interview, but that Colin is denying that he raped her.'

'Exactly, which brings us to our reconstruction.'

'Reconstruction?' said Nat, looking questioningly at Ed.

'Jenny and I tried reconstructing what it would be like to be strangled with the two types of bra. My neck's a similar size to Gina's. A size 34C soft cup could have killed me. On the other hand, a 34D bra, like the one she was wearing, with padding and underwiring, was tight enough to leave ligature marks, especially if I'd struggled violently as Gina did, but it would have been very hard, probably impossible for it to have strangled me. Using the 34D, the underwire and padded cups jammed together, making it impossible to pull the bra tight enough round my neck.'

'So you're saying ...?' asked Jenny.

'That Colin was set up. Gina wanted solid evidence of aggravated rape, but she didn't want to be badly hurt, still less killed. So she bought a padded, underwired 34D bra and wore it last night in place of her usual soft cup 34C. Clearly, Gina's a bright woman. She must have realized there was a good chance the bra being different from her normal size and type might give her away, so she got Colin to dump it.'

Mike attempted to sum up and move the discussion on. 'Okay. We've CCTV evidence that appears to support Gina's allegation of rape and we think forensics will confirm her claim. But against that clear picture, her subsequent behaviour and the oversized bra she was wearing point to the possibility that Gina had planned the whole event. Why she should do so, I've no idea.' Mike looked at Ed. 'What do you propose we do?'

'It's my decision, but I appreciate the team's contributions. Let me hear what you'd do. Nat?'

Once again, the young DC hesitated for a moment, but then, with his eyes moving from Ed to Mike and back again, he replied, 'From what I've seen and heard, it looks as though sex occurred. However, there seem to be reasonable grounds to believe Gina set it up. I'd question Colin again and try to persuade him that it's in his best interest to give us his side of the story.'

Jenny looked at Nat in exasperation, but he didn't meet her eye. Ed assumed he knew what was coming. When Jenny spoke, her voice betrayed an anger that went beyond a typical difference of opinion in a team meeting.

'Even if the whole thing was Gina's idea and she encouraged him to simulate rape, she can still say *no* – at any time!' Jenny's eyes flicked to Nat and back to Ed. 'The CCTV shows clearly that she is protesting, telling him to stop.'

'But the safe word—' began Mike, before Ed spoke over him.

'Okay, we've kicked this around enough for now. With no evidence of sex games, we must remember that *no* is *no* and a woman's decision should be respected. However, there are a number of questions we need answered. On the basis of what we've seen and heard it would be possible to build a case for questioning Gina's claim. On the other hand, if Colin has effectively admitted it's him in the CCTV attack, why should he refuse to answer our questions? Mike and Nat, I want you to question Colin and stress it would be in his interest to cooperate. We'll leave Gina alone for today.'

'Shouldn't we ask Gina again about Colin? You've just said that we didn't ask her specifically if she knew him.'

'Yes, Jenny, but she's coming here tomorrow, we'll ask her then.'

'What about her colleagues at the dental practice?'

'Been there, done that.'

The moment she said it, Ed knew it sounded like a putdown. She turned and nodded appreciatively in Nat's direction.

'You're right, Nat, they're the only people in Canterbury we know who knew Gina. Jenny and I spoke with Gina's boss, Rachael Metcalffe. She said they're good professional colleagues, but they don't socialize and they know little of each other's personal lives.'

'Rachael mentioned Gina had recently been on holiday to Italy. Said she won it as a competition prize.' Despite her previous anger, Jenny was quickly back to efficient police officer mode. 'She was in Orvieto and then Siena for the Palio.'

'What's the Palio?' asked Mike.

'A bareback horse race,' said Ed, before turning to her young DC. 'Jenny, it's likely that prize was a place on an organized tour. Check with tour operators and airline passenger lists. Check the dates Rachael gave us, and if Gina was alone or with someone.'

Jenny nodded and Ed turned to her number two.

'Mike, as I said, I'd like you and Nat to question Colin, but first, get onto Gravesend and see what they can give us asap on Colin Bradshaw. Wait until you've got a preliminary from Gravesend before you interview him.'

Ed glanced at each of her colleagues. 'If there's nothing else, let's get to it.'

Mike and Nat moved towards the door of the Incident Room, but Jenny hung back and signalled Ed to do the same.

'What is it?' asked Ed as the door closed behind the male detectives.

'Do you think Gina does know Colin?'

'That's what I've asked you to find out. Get on to the tour operators and airlines. Before we see Gina tomorrow we need to know more about her holiday in Italy.'

58

'You're a man of leisure, Mr Bradshaw.' Mike Potts was sitting upright in his chair opposite Colin at the table in Interview Room 2. Nat Borrowdale sat to one side with a notebook and pen.

'What do you mean?'

'You resigned from your job at Scotts and haven't worked since.'

'I came into an inheritance from—'

'Bullshit!'

Mike opened a folder, but didn't take his eyes from Colin's face.

'Inheritance my arse, it's a bloody lie.' Mike ran his finger down a page in the file and then looked back at Colin. 'Do you often tell lies, Mr Bradshaw?'

'No.'

'And the trip to, where was it, Australia, New Zealand?' Mike paused, his eyes still on Colin's face. 'More lies, Mr Bradshaw?'

Colin was silent.

'Yes, more lies, Mr Bradshaw. You're not on the other side of the world, you've taken a flat in King Street, right here in Canterbury.'

Colin sighed. 'Okay ... you're right. I wanted time to myself. I had a big win on the football pools. If the word gets out, winners can be hounded to an early grave. The inheritance, Australia and New Zealand were to put people off, cut myself some slack.'

'You're charged with rape, Colin.' Nat had spoken quietly, without raising his eyes from his notebook. As Colin turned to look at the DC, Nat met his gaze and added, 'You've told us about the pools win. It would be in your best interests to tell us everything.'

Mike coughed, drawing Colin's attention back across the table. 'Tell us about Georgina Hamilton. You know her well, don't you, Mr Bradshaw?'

Colin didn't answer.

Nat tapped his pen against the pages of his notebook. 'What did you say, Colin? *Outraging public decency, the young lady's not going to be pleased.* It seems you know Gina very well.'

There was another cough. 'We're waiting, Mr Bradshaw.' Mike leant back in his chair, inviting a response.

'I want a lawyer.'

'That's your right, Mr Bradshaw.' Mike's hand moved to switch off the recorder. 'Interview suspended until the arrival of the duty solicitor.'

An hour later, questioning recommenced in Interview Room 2. As soon as the preliminaries were over, Colin addressed Nat.

'Is Gina really claiming I raped her?'

Mike replied. 'That's what she's told us, Mr Bradshaw, more than once. She says you attacked her, tried to strangle her and raped her. The whole incident is on CCTV, your face as clear as a full moon in a cloudless sky.'

Colin had a brief whispered exchange with the solicitor and then turned to face the two detectives.

'It was her idea, the simulated rape. She suggested it, all of it.'

'You've just arrived in Canterbury and a young woman asks you to strangle and rape her?'

'No, of course not. Gina and I have known each other for some time.'

'How did you meet her, Colin?' Nat was leaning forward, his notebook and elbows on the table.

'In a bar, I can't remember which one.'

'And you and Gina had sex, did you, Colin?'

'Not straightaway. It wasn't like that, but after a while, yes.'

'Kinky sex?' asked Mike.

'Not at first. It was later she suggested spicing it up. She wanted to do it where someone might see us.'

'Bondage?' asked Nat.

Colin shifted in his seat, crossed and uncrossed his legs, trying to get comfortable.

'No, no, nothing like that.'

'So it was your idea to put the bra round her neck,' said Mike.

'No, no. That was Gina. It was the first time we'd done anything like that. I didn't like the idea, but she kept on at me; she really wanted it. She said it turned her on to be dominated and forced to do it where somebody might see.'

'And so you did it in the Buttermarket,' said Nat.

'Yes, but I asked her to stop me, the moment it started to hurt.'

'And she did say stop, didn't she, Mr Bradshaw? We've all seen it on the CCTV,' said Mike.

'That's what she wanted. She wanted to struggle, to say *no* and *stop*. That's why we came up with the safe word, but ... she didn't say it.'

'What was your safe word?' asked Mike.

'Palio.' Colin pressed on earnestly, seeming not to notice the two detectives exchange glances at the word. 'It's a horse race. She'd didn't say the word, so I assumed she wanted to go on.'

'One final question,' said Mike. 'Did you meet any of her friends?'

'No. Whenever we met, it was always just the two of us.'

Back in his cell, Colin went over the questioning in his mind. He'd played it cool. He'd let them draw him out about sex with Gina, but not said anything too specific. He'd stressed she was the one who wanted kinky sex, particularly doing it where someone might see them, and that she wanted to be dominated. He'd got that in, but steered well clear of bondage. The last thing he wanted was to let something slip out about intrusion and tying Gina to the bed. Kayleigh was still at the back of his mind. He was relieved there'd not been another word about Dover.

Things had got tricky when they asked how he met Gina, but he'd given that question some thought. If asked, he was sure Gina would go for the mundane, meeting in a bar, something impossible to check. With no hesitation, he'd said the same, but claimed he couldn't remember which bar.

All told, he thought he'd handled it well.

59

'What have you got for us, Mike? How did it go with
Colin Bradshaw?' Coffee in hand, Ed joined her team,
who were back at the Incident Room table.

'Just like Priestfield.'

Ed valued Mike for his extensive local knowledge, but she
found his inability to get straight to the point exasperating.
Thinking Priestfield must be a Canterbury case from before
her time, Ed put her drink down rather more forcefully than
she intended and looked at Mike with ill-concealed annoyance.

'Priestfield?'

'The Gills ground.'

Exasperated, Ed was close to saying something she might
regret when Nat stepped in.

'Gillingham FC, the only Kent club in the Football League.'

Mike continued as if nothing had happened. 'Our questioning of Colin Bradshaw was a game of two halves.'

Ed held back her frustration to give her DS one more chance
to answer her question. 'I'm not a great fan of football, Mike.
Exactly what do you mean?'

'He behaved like two different people. When we started
asking about the alleged rape, he stonewalled all our questions.'

'No comment, no comment, no comment,' said Nat by way of illustration.

'And then ...?'

'We switched tack to how he came into money. He said it was a win on the pools. Once he'd admitted that, Nat, who's more his age, pushed the line that it would be better for him to give us his account of events and he opened up.'

'Not just like that,' said Nat, annoyed Mike was underplaying his work. 'It took time. I had to work on him.'

'True, but then it was just as if the whistle had blown for the second half. He stopped stonewalling and asked for a brief. We had to wait for the duty solicitor to come in and then give them time together before we could continue.'

Ed resisted looking at her watch and tried to move things along.

'Good, Mike, give us a brief outline of what you got from Gravesend and then we'll go back to your questioning of Colin.'

Mike turned to Nat.

'You took notes.'

For once Nat had seen this coming so he'd committed the information to memory in order not to be outshone by Jenny.

'Colin David Bradshaw, born 29th February 1984 in Gravesend, left secondary modern at 16 and studied computing and general electronics at North Medway College. He then worked in electronics at a local firm, Scotts. He appears to have been valued by his employers.'

'Evidence?' asked Ed, but Nat wasn't thrown by the interruption.

'At one point they sent him, all expenses paid, on an Outward Bound course in the Lake District.'

'Right. What else have you got?'

'He inherited the family home when his father died. The mother had passed away three years earlier. Bradshaw continued living in the house alone for a while, but he's not been seen there for some time. The word was he got an inheritance and went travelling, but we now know it was a football pools win and he's here in Canterbury renting a flat at 7 King Street. There's no record of any criminal convictions.'

'Thanks, Nat.' Ed smiled her appreciation of his concise summary and looked at her DS. 'So, Mike, what happened when you continued the questioning?'

'He was stunned that Gina had accused him of rape. Claimed they'd been lovers for a while. He said *she* was the one into kinky sex. Said she particularly wanted to do it where someone might see them. He was adamant that the whole scenario in the Buttermarket was Gina's idea, including strangulation with her bra.'

'He said she liked to be dominated, to be forced,' added Nat.

Jenny, her face registering total disbelief, protested. 'No woman wants to be forced. Strangulation with the bra can't have been Gina's idea. He must have lost his head, got carried away with feelings of control and domination.'

'Not according to Colin.' Mike continued to speak in level tones. 'He insisted it was all Gina's idea. In fact, he said he wasn't keen on the strangulation, but Gina wouldn't let it drop 'til he agreed.'

'He's lying,' Jenny insisted. 'On the CCTV you can see she looks terrified and that she's clearly asking him to stop.'

Nat could barely wait to get in.

'She didn't use their safe word!' He paused to let his

information sink in. 'Colin said when they planned the strangulation they agreed a safe word, *Palio*, but Gina didn't use it, so she must have been okay with what he was doing.'

Ed put her pen on the table with a sharp click and looked up from the notes she'd been taking.

'Palio! That's a coincidence. We know from her boss that Gina was fascinated by the Palio. She went to Siena to see it. Jenny, you were looking into that holiday. What have you got for us?'

'I've found the probable package holiday, but I'm still waiting for the tour company to get back to me.'

'Get onto them now. We need to know more before we see Gina tomorrow.'

60

I must get to the Police Station early today, tell them about me and Colin. Keep it simple. I'd known him for a few weeks. We had a relationship. I broke it off. Not a word about how he got into my home. Steer well clear of that – it won't sit well with my claim he raped me. Just stick to the short-term relationship. It didn't work for me. I broke it off. He was devastated. Angry. He retaliated, waylaid me and raped me.

I mustn't let them catch me out. Get my story in quickly, as soon as I meet the detectives. Apologize. Confess I knew my attacker. *I'm sorry, with the horror of the rape … my head was all over the place. It slipped my mind.* I must tell them immediately, before the identification procedure, put a gap between my admission and any further questioning.

That's not the only thing. I could have done without them finding the bra. Bloody Colin, why couldn't he have done what I asked and got rid of it properly? That detective, the older one, Osborne, she's sharp. And she's my build. She's likely to guess the bra they found, the one I was wearing, is not my type and not my size. I must buy another one, wear it when I go in this morning, with clothes like the ones I was wearing Wednesday, when it happened.

One last thing, forget make-up, look wan; I'm still stressed by the horrendous thing he did to me.

261

61

Sergeant Barry Williams looked up and beckoned to Ed. 'I thought you should know, Georgina Hamilton's here. I've put her in Interview Room 1.'

'She's early. We agreed 11.00. Ms Hamilton can wait 'til I've finished my breakfast.'

When Ed reached the CID Room, Mike and Jenny were working on items recovered from the recent spate of burglaries. Mike was on the phone, but Jenny turned to greet her.

'I've finally got details of Gina's holiday. The dates don't match those the dentist, Rachael Metcalffe, gave us.'

'That's interesting. What have you got?'

'A Ms Georgina Hamilton was booked on a Tuscan Sun Tours package to Orvieto and Siena, leaving Gatwick on Saturday the 22nd of June and returning a fortnight later.'

'Isn't that what Rachael told us? Gina was back at work on Monday the 8th of July.'

'Yes, but that holiday was cancelled at the last minute by her brother, Colin Hamilton—'

'A brother!' Ed walked over to Jenny's desk, her breakfast croissant forgotten. 'I thought Gina was an only child. No one's ever mentioned a brother.'

'Exactly, but a Colin Hamilton booked the holiday and then cancelled, saying his sister Georgina was too ill to travel.'

'Did they give you a description of this ... brother?'

'No. It was all done by telephone and post.'

'If the holiday was cancelled and she didn't go to Italy, what about the photographs Rachael saw?'

'I checked airlines with flights to Tuscany over the next few days. British Airways came up trumps.' Jenny was looking very pleased with herself. 'Six days after Gina was supposed to go to Italy, a Mr Colin Bradshaw and a Ms Georgina Hamilton took return flights, Gatwick to Pisa, on Friday the 28th of June. They came back on Friday the 5th of July; that was the day Gina was originally booked to return from her two-week trip.'

Jenny pulled some notes from a file and passed them to Ed. 'Here's the details.'

'Two Colins is a bit of a coincidence. Did you check out Colin Hamilton?'

'As I said, the Colin calling himself Hamilton, who booked and then cancelled Gina's holiday, did everything by telephone and post. He even paid by postal order. So –' Jenny smiled '– I checked with Gina's mother. You're right, she *is* an only child.'

'Good work, Jenny. Gina's already waiting in Interview Room 1. We need her to formally identify her attacker. Run the Colin Bradshaw VIPER with her and I'll join you as soon as I've finished my breakfast. We've got some interesting questions for Ms Georgina Hamilton to answer.'

62

'Good morning, Gina. We did say eleven, but it's good you're early. We'll have time to get the identification out of the way before DI Ogborne joins us.' Jenny stood in the entrance to Interview Room 1, holding the door open for Gina to follow.

'Before we do that, I need to tell you something I omitted to say yesterday.'

'That can wait until DI Ogborne gets here.'

'No.' Gina remained standing in the room. 'I feel bad about it.'

'Okay. What is it you want to tell me?'

'I should have told you yesterday. I know the man who raped me. Before, I was so upset it didn't occur to me to mention it. I was so stressed, it just didn't enter my head.' Gina smiled apologetically. 'I'm sorry. I hope this hasn't had a bad effect on your investigation.'

'Don't worry, Gina. Forgetting to tell us yesterday is perfectly understandable. The other night, you endured a horrendous experience. However, the fact that you knew your attacker could influence the way we pursue this case, so it's good you've told me now. You'll be able to tell me, and DI Ogborne, more, after we've completed the identification.'

Jenny stepped into the corridor and waited for Gina to join her.

'What will happen?'

'I'll take you to the VIPER Suite where two independent officers, not connected with this case, will take you through the identification process. You'll be shown video images of nine people and asked to identify the man who attacked you.'

Later, back in Interview Room 1, Jenny and Gina were joined by Ed.

'Good morning, Gina, thank you for coming in to see us and for identifying your attacker on VIPER. I'm sorry if this all seems overly formal, but it's essential we follow procedure.'

'Of course, I understand and want to do everything I can to help.'

'I'll just start the recording and, like last time, we'll introduce ourselves for the tape.' Ed reached to switch on the machine and, after stating the date and time, added, 'Second interview with Georgina Hamilton concerning an alleged rape in the Buttermarket. This is DI Ed Ogborne, present with DC Eastham and Ms Hamilton.'

'DC Jenny Eastham, Canterbury CID.'

'Gina – Georgina Hamilton of Great Stour Court, Canterbury.'

'Thank you, Gina. Jenny says there's something you neglected to tell us yesterday.'

'Yes. When we spoke before I was under a lot of stress. It had happened so quickly and I was so frightened that I'd barely registered the man himself. It was as if a thing, an animal, was overpowering me. I was aware of what he was doing to my body, but not of him as a person. My head was filled with the horror, not who was doing it, but what was happening to *me*, me as a *person*. So, it wasn't until much later, at home this morning, I remembered I hadn't told you, I know the man.'

Gina looked at the faces of the two detectives, apparently trying to judge their reactions to her confession. As trained interrogators, neither revealed any sign of their thoughts. Both remained professionally calm.

'You know him,' said Ed with a barely rising inflection. 'What's his name?'

'Colin Bradshaw. I should have said when you came to see me yesterday. I think you mentioned his name, but my head was all over the place.'

'How did you meet, how did you come to know him?'

'In a bar ... that is, we met in a bar. It was some time back. I got talking to Colin while I was waiting to buy drinks. He gave me his mobile number and later, at a loose end, I called him.'

Ed ignored the vague timetable. She was more interested in the relationship. 'How well did you get to know him?'

Gina looked down at her hands, clasped in her lap. 'We were ... it became ... physical.'

Ed placed her fists on the table and looked at Gina. 'That's a very different picture from the one you painted yesterday. Let me get this straight. You're now saying that the man you claim raped you in the centre of Canterbury at 3 a.m. yesterday was your lover!'

'No!' Gina looked at Ed with a mixture of embarrassment and defiance. 'Yes ... no ... he was ... err ... had been. It wasn't working for me, so ... I'd ended it.'

'Was that before or after your holiday in Italy?'

'What!' Gina looked genuinely startled by the question. 'Who—'

'—told us about your trip to Orvieto and Siena?' Ed turned over a page in her file. 'You'll appreciate, Gina, that I'm not at liberty to say.'

Slowly, Ed leant forward across the table, holding Gina's gaze.

'When did you end your relationship with Colin, before or after your trip?'

'I'd already decided to end it when, out of the blue, Colin surprised me with the holiday. I thought it would be ungrateful not to go.'

Ed coughed. 'We've been given to understand that you particularly wanted to see the Palio?'

Gina pulled a tissue from her bag and dabbed at her nose. To Jenny and Ed, it appeared she was trying to distract from the questioning look that had appeared in her eyes and from the pause as her mind raced through the possibilities.

'Err ... that too. Some time ago, I'd mentioned to Colin that I wanted to see the horse race in Siena. Out of the blue, he arranged the holiday as a surprise. As I've already said, I'd decided to end our relationship, but hadn't yet told him. When he was so nice about the holiday, I couldn't bring myself to turn him down.'

'You're saying the holiday was a gift, from Colin to you.' Ed paused, then added, 'We've been told you won the holiday as a prize, a package holiday with Tuscan Sun Tours starting Saturday, 22 June.'

Gina looked accusingly from Ed to Jenny and then back again. 'You've been talking to my colleagues at work!'

'It's our job, Gina. We need to build a broad background,

the big picture, corroborate statements – we'd be failing in our duty if we didn't conduct a thorough investigation.'

'It's complicated. I should have been completely open with you from the start but—'

'That's always a good idea when serious accusations are being made.'

'Yes, but there wasn't ... wasn't an opportunity.'

Ed looked steadily across the table at Gina. 'How many opportunities do you need? Here at the Station when you reported being attacked? Yesterday, when we came to your home?'

'When I reported the attack, I was completely stressed out. At home, when we were going over my statement, my head was still all over the place.' Gina looked accusingly at Ed. 'You could have asked me then, but you didn't.'

'Okay. I'm asking you now.'

'Well, it's no great mystery. My work is my work, Inspector. I don't mix my work with my social life. I expect the same is true of you and your colleagues. I had to mention the holiday at work because it was a surprise and I had to take time off at short notice. I said the holiday was a prize because I didn't want to reveal it was a present from Colin, especially because I was about to end that relationship.'

'But the package holiday was cancelled by somebody pretending to be your brother.'

'Oh dear. It's all *sooo* complicated, Inspector. That was Colin. He thought it would be easier to book the holiday for me if he said he was my brother.'

'So, Colin, pretending to be your brother, booked the holiday for you and then cancelled it the day before you were due to leave. Why would Colin do that when, a few days later, the two of you were happy to enjoy a holiday together at his expense?'

Gina straightened in her chair.

'Inspector, you're making me sound very mercenary.' Looking frankly into Ed's eyes, Gina continued. 'As I said, it's complicated.'

'Perhaps you could explain.'

'I don't deny that I've always wanted to go to Siena for the Palio. At first, I was pleased when Colin booked the package holiday for me, but then, having decided I was going to end our relationship, I couldn't accept the present of a holiday. I didn't want to hurt his feelings, so I said I didn't want to travel on a package tour with people I didn't know. He understood and cancelled it.'

'And then you dumped him?'

'No ... not at that point.'

'What then?'

Ed was firing her questions rapidly, but Gina was responding slowly, clearly thinking carefully while she was speaking.

'He ... surprised me ... with the private holiday, for the two of us.'

'And you still hadn't told him it was over?'

'No ... I thought the trip, spending time together, would demonstrate it wasn't working between us.'

'So you managed to enjoyed your holiday and the Palio after all?'

'I enjoyed going to Italy and seeing the horse race but, having already decided our relationship wasn't working, I didn't enjoy spending more time with Colin.'

'Are you saying your relationship had become more distant?'

'Yes ... somewhat more distant.' Gina looked Ed and spoke openly. 'As a woman, Inspector, you'll understand. I was trying to let him down gently.'

Ed leant back in her chair, keeping her pen poised over her notebook. 'And when did you finally tell Colin it was over?'

'A few days after we returned from Italy, Sunday –' Gina hesitated '– no, it was Monday.'

'Two days before the attack?'

Gina moved her fingers as if counting and agreed, 'Yes, just over two days.' Suddenly, her eyes widened. 'Do you think he was taking revenge?'

'I really can't speculate.'

Ed turned to a new page in her file.

'There have been two developments since you reported the alleged rape. As you know, we are holding Colin Bradshaw in custody, and we have found a bra similar to the one in the CCTV. We expect DNA evidence to confirm it's the bra you were wearing at the time of the attack, the one he put round your neck.'

With no discernible reaction to Ed's revelation, Gina asked, 'What has he said, the man you've arrested, Colin Bradshaw?'

'He admits it's him in the Buttermarket CCTV but, in other respects, his account differs from yours.'

'In what way?'

'He says it was all your idea. That you're into kinky sex and that you persuaded him to role-play the open-air sex, domination and strangulation.'

'That's a lie!' Gina looked shocked. For a moment she didn't move, but then she pulled herself upright in her chair and glared at Ed. 'He's lying!' Gina's gaze switched questioningly between Ed and Jenny. 'You can't possibly believe I'd do something like that!'

'We're not here to make judgements, Gina.' Ed spoke calmly. 'Our job is to collect and assess the evidence, which brings me back to the bra we found. We're sure the presence of DNA from both you and Colin, plus the Buttermarket CCTV images, will confirm the bra is the one you were wearing. What puzzles us is the size. You're a similar build to me so I'd say you were a 34C. The bra we found was a 34D. Can you explain that?'

To Ed and Jenny's surprise, rather than being wrong-footed by the question, Gina smiled and answered immediately.

'No problem. You're right, I am a 34C, but when I'm chilling, I prefer a looser fit. Today, I'm off work, spending most of my time lounging around at home, so I'm wearing a 34D. Look!'

Gina lifted her T-shirt, reached back and pulled the label from behind her bra strap while turning to show the detectives. She was wearing a bra identical to the one the police had found in the waste bin, a pristine underwired, padded 34D.

In the silence that followed, Gina straightened her clothing and turned back to face the table.

'Please don't be distracted by my bras. It's a habit of mine.' Gina glanced at Jenny and then looked seriously at Ed. 'Inspector, the issue here is rape. Colin Bradshaw attacked me, he raped me, he nearly killed me. He's a psychopath out for revenge. For my sake, and for the sake of other women, you must put him behind bars.'

Back in the CID Room, Ed handed Jenny the bag with the two bras. 'I want to know when Gina bought the padded 34D. I think she got one during the week since she's been back from Italy and a second one yesterday or this morning. I got these from Little Pretty Things in Whitefriars. Start there but, if they have no record of her purchase, check all other possible outlets in Canterbury.'

63

I wish I could have seen the looks on their faces. Unfortunately, I had my back to them when I showed the label in my bra. Still, I can imagine their expressions – that move stopped them dead in their tracks. We'll not hear any more about my choice of underwear.

The questions about my relationship with Colin got a bit tricky but, all told, I handled it well. He's the last person who's going to tell them how we really met. Like me, he'll say something vague. Meeting in a bar was the obvious thing to go for – I didn't even say a pub, so I've left it as wide open as possible.

Colin, you chose the wrong woman, when you chose me. The forensic evidence will be solid. My stone to your scissors; my scissors to your paper; my paper to your stone. To mix metaphors: game, set and match!

64

'Come!'

The command carried clearly through the substantial door of Chief Superintendent Karen Addler's corner office. From others, the word would have been a simple invitation, but the Super imbued it with an unambiguous message: enter at your peril should I judge you to be wasting my time.

Ed took the visitor's chair, which Addler, with an inclination of her head, had indicted as she replaced the cap on her fat fountain pen.

'DI Ogborne, you wished to discuss the current rape case. Is there a problem?'

'Thank you, Ma'am. Not a problem as such, but at present there is a difference of opinion among the CID team concerning the interpretation of the evidence.'

'You surprise me, Ogborne. I thought it was an open and shut case. You have CCTV and DNA evidence that Colin Bradshaw attacked and raped Georgina Hamilton in the Buttermarket in the early hours of last Wednesday, July the 10th. Not only did he rape her, but CCTV and DNA show he attempted to strangle Miss Hamilton with her own brassière. As if that were not enough, the man has confessed.'

'What you say is correct, Ma'am, but there are reasons for

thinking aggravated rape may not be the true interpretation of those events.'

'Interpretation? Those are the facts.' Addler tapped her notepad with her fountain pen in time with her last four words. 'I've taken the trouble to review the CCTV myself. There is no doubt that Bradshaw attacks her. Miss Hamilton is terrified and clearly protesting. You have Bradshaw's DNA confirming penetration. You have DNA from both of them on the brassière with which he can be seen trying to strangle her. What possible other interpretation can there be but aggravated rape?'

'Colin Bradshaw claims Georgina Hamilton derives pleasure from bizarre sexual acts and that she instigated and encouraged him to role-play rape with strangulation in a public place.'

'He's lying. Rapists do it all the time.'

'There are some reasons to believe that Ms Hamilton may not be telling the truth.'

'And those reasons are?' The Superintendent began to mark the notepad with her pen and her intonation implied Ed was stretching her patience and coming close to wasting her time.

'At her first interview Gina neglected to tell us that Colin Bradshaw was, or had been until recently, her lover. In fact, she had just accompanied Bradshaw on an expensive holiday to Italy for which he'd paid as a gift. The brassière in question was a larger size, and a different style, from the ones she normally wears and, when placed tightly around her neck, it was guaranteed to mark but not kill her. Her reason for being out on the street in central Canterbury at 03.00 was weak. Her behaviour throughout—'

'Enough, enough.' The Super held up her hand. 'Miss

Hamilton is a woman with integrity and she has provided explanations for all of these issues.'

'But Ma'am, her explanations themselves are weak. And DC Eastham has just ascertained that two brassières of the type in question were purchased during the last few days, Tuesday the 9th, the day before the alleged rape, and early on Thursday the 11th, less than an hour before Ms Hamilton came for a VIPER and we questioned her about her underwear.'

'Coincidence, coincidence. This discussion has gone far enough, DI Ogborne. Frankly, I'm surprised that you, a female officer, should entertain such doubts. The attitude of the Force to women reporting rape has changed, but more change is necessary. The Chief Constable and I are at one on this. Every member of the Force must rigorously adhere to the recommended changes to the way in which we handle allegations of sexual assault. In the light of recent directives, it's imperative we are seen to pursue allegations of rape with the utmost vigour.'

Ed believed she was doing just that, exactly what a police officer is trained to do: pursue the evidence without prejudice. Unfortunately, it seemed she was going to find it difficult to obtain the support of her superiors for such an approach.

'I agree, Ma'am, but in this case, I believe there are reasons to doubt Ms Hamilton and that further investigation might show she is attempting to pervert the course of justice.'

'Miss Hamilton is an educated young woman and a well-regarded local professional. We see no reason to justify the expense of further investigation. Let me have a draft report for the CPS by the end of this week.'

Addler pushed her notepad aside and reached for a file.

'That will be all, DI Ogborne.'

When Ed returned to the CID Room, Jenny asked how things had gone with the Super. Mike and Nat looked up from their work to listen.

'Addler's been talking to the Chief Constable. Neither of them wants to be seen dragging their feet over an allegation of rape from a professional woman, especially when there is so much CCTV and forensic evidence supporting her claim. They won't fund further inquiries and Addler wants a report for the CPS this week.'

'And you disagree?'

Ed knew Jenny's implied question was: *How can you possibly disagree?*

'We've been over this. You know that Colin Bradshaw claims it was Gina Hamilton's idea. And—'

'That's what they all say,' Jenny replied quickly, glancing at Nat, who avoided her gaze.

'And ... as I was about to say –' Ed paused for emphasis '– there is some evidence that would be consistent with that view.'

Mike grunted. 'If it comes to court, it'll be his word against hers.'

'And much good it will do him,' said Jenny, sarcastically.

'Not if, but when, Mike. With the CCTV and the forensic evidence we've gathered, the CPS will certainly prosecute Bradshaw for rape even if there are some questions concerning Gina's behaviour.'

Nobody spoke. Mike seemed to have lost interest, Nat too, while Jenny's face registered complete satisfaction. Each, at their own pace, turned back to their work.

65

Ed was just about to call it a day when her telephone rang. It was Baines from forensics.

'You just caught me, Bill, what's new?'

'We've got a match for the DNA from the print on the split-button flush in Dover.'

'Why didn't we get that sooner?'

'We've had a break. It's a new profile, only just uploaded to NDNAD.'

'Great!' At Ed's exclamation, her colleagues looked up from their desks. She smiled and gave them a thumbs-up before turning back to the telephone. 'Who is the bastard?'

'Colin Bradshaw.'

Ed's lips parted in amazement. 'Are you certain?'

'It's an exact match. Not only that, it's his DNA in the smudged palm print on the door to the flat.'

'So he was outside the door and inside the flat. Thanks, Bill.' Ed ended the call and swivelled to face the room. 'We've got a breakthrough in the Kayleigh Robson case. There's a new DNA profile on the National Database. It's an exact match with the DNA recovered from the partial fingerprint and smudged palm print found at her flat.'

'You sounded particularly pleased,' said Mike. 'Is it someone you know?'

'It's someone we all know, someone we have in the cells.'

'Bradshaw!' cried Jenny. 'Now we'll get the bastard for manslaughter as well as for Gina's rape.'

'Let's not get ahead of ourselves, Jenny. It's the break we've been waiting for, but we'll need more than Bradshaw's DNA to tie him to manslaughter in Dover. The DNA match simply tells us he was in Kayleigh's flat, it doesn't tell us when. He could have left that print long before she died.'

Seizing his chance to score a point, Nat nodded. 'On that evidence alone, a defence lawyer would pull the case apart in no time.'

Aware of the tension between her DCs, Ed did her best to keep the discussion neutral. 'For a strong case we'll need more. We particularly need evidence linking Bradshaw to the time and manner of Kayleigh's death.'

'All of our inquiries on that score have led to nothing.' The euphoria sparked by the DNA match had left Nat's face. 'Nobody remembers seeing anybody with Kayleigh and nobody has been seen going into her building. Her mobile's missing and the two potential dating app hook-ups I identi-fied from her phone records, C6 and C7, both stood her up and there was no way we could identify them.'

'That *was* true,' said Jenny, 'but things have changed.' She looked at Ed, who smiled encouragingly. 'Before, we were asking about strangers and looking for a stranger. Now we have a face. We can show images. We know who we're looking for.'

'We certainly do! Bradshaw's photograph may jog some

memories.' Buoyed by the breakthrough and the enthusiasm shown by Jenny, Ed turned to her DS.

'Mike, get on to Sergeant Burstford in Dover and get Bradshaw's mugshot over there. Have them re-question all the witnesses. Tell Burstford we'll scour the CCTV we've already got, but if any more CCTV becomes relevant, ask him to send it across.'

Mike pulled a notebook and from his jacket pocket. 'Same route and dates as before?'

'It's possible C6 and C7 were both Colin: C6 on Monday the 3rd of June and C7 on Thursday June the 13th. We can check that immediately on the tapes we've got. If it is, he may be surreptitiously observing her on the days between those two dates. Of course, on seeing his image, witnesses may come up with other sightings elsewhere, so we'd need extra CCTV to cover any new locations.'

As Mike continued to make notes, Jenny spoke. 'If it was Colin in the flat when Kayleigh died and he did the extensive cleaning, he probably had to go out to buy bleach and other stuff.'

'The precise constituents of bleaches tend to differ,' said Nat. 'If forensics could identify the brand we might locate stores and get him on security cameras buying the stuff.'

'Good thinking!' Ed smiled at her two DCs, but they continued to avoid looking directly at each other.

'If Colin is C6 and C7, which he could well be by using different phones or SIM cards, and we see him in the vicinity of Kayleigh on both the 3rd and 13th, then we'll have ...' Mike paused.

Jenny took over. 'Fourteen days of CCTV from multiple locations and cameras to search.'

'I'll get the Super to authorize Uniform to help,' said Ed.

'Bradshaw doesn't have a car, so he probably took public transport from Canterbury to Dover,' mused Mike, almost to himself.

'He was C7 on the train at Aylesham,' said Jenny.

Ed nodded. 'We'll need to find him on camera – for example, buying train tickets from Canterbury to Dover. When Uniform have indexed relevant sightings, I want us to build a complete picture of Kayleigh's movements, and Colin's too. First, Mike and Jenny, check the tapes we've already got for Monday the 3rd and Thursday the 13th of June. Look for Colin and see if he was at The Three Horseshoes both evenings. If he turns out to be both C6 and C7, this will extend our searches.'

Nat, looking disgruntled, started to speak. 'What about—'

'Patience, Nat, I want you with me when we search Colin's flat at 7 King Street a second time. This time we'll be looking for anything that could link him to Kayleigh and Dover.'

Ed pushed back her chair, intending to see Superintendent Addler if she was still in her office. 'Good work, everyone. The DNA match was the breakthrough we needed.'

As she left the room, Ed turned back to her team and said, 'Let's get on top of this. It's up to us to get justice for Kayleigh and her parents.'

66

Monday morning, feeling good but tired after a weekend with Daniel, Ed was at her desk by 09.00. Just after ten, her phone rang with an internal call. It was the Chief Super.

'Ogborne, Bradshaw's DNA at the flat in Dover was a lucky break. Now the CPS want solid evidence tying him to that young woman's death.'

'We're on it, Ma'am. Getting good evidence will take a massive CCTV search, but that's underway. My team are collaborating with Dover and you've authorized help from Uniform. Even so, it will take time.'

'Quite.' The Super paused before changing tack. 'With the emergence of a potential manslaughter charge the CPS will be taking time to consider carefully how to proceed with the rape case.'

Ed was surprised. 'We've gathered very strong CCTV and forensic evidence. I thought they'd be bound to prosecute.'

'Oh, they'll prosecute, but they'd like to go for joinder, prosecute for rape and manslaughter in a single trial, save time and money. Sensible decision, I could see it coming.'

'Ma'am—'

'It's a complex issue – they want to get it right. It's imperative you get the manslaughter charge sewn up pronto!'

'Yes, Ma'am, as I say—'

'You've got extra resources, Ogborne, make it happen! Get the evidence to the CPS asap. That's your job!'

'Yes, Ma'am.' Ed continued quickly, before Addler could terminate their exchange. 'If I may go back to Ms Hamilton for a moment. With the CPS going for a joint trial it's going to take longer for her allegation of rape to come to court than she might have expected. Should I inform her, or will you?'

'Leave it with me, Ogborne. My interviews with the media have gone well and we are securing good PR from our progress with the Dover case. It's been all over the press. Ms Hamilton cannot be unaware of Bradshaw's implication in the death of Kayleigh Robson. Consequently, I've instructed the Family Liaison Officer to arrange for her to see me so that I can explain the repercussions of this development. You do your job, Ogborne. Get the evidence to nail Bradshaw for Dover and leave the potentially delicate matter of Ms Hamilton to me.'

With that, the line went dead.

Once again, Ed was left resenting the way her superior treated staff. It wasn't being told that Ms Hamilton should be seen by a senior officer, but the implication that that she, Detective Inspector Ed Ogborne, was incapable of doing the job properly.

When Gina arrived at the Police Station she was immediately directed to Chief Superintendent Karen Addler's office. As she approached, the door opened and the Superintendent ushered Gina to a seat at the small conference table where coffee, tea and bottled water waited.

'Ms Hamilton, as a busy young professional, I'm pleased

you were able to find time to come in. The Chief Constable and I are aware that you have made significant contributions to the Metcalffe Practice since your arrival and I wanted, personally, to keep you abreast of recent developments.'

Addler paused and indicated the refreshments.

'May I offer you a biscuit and something to drink?'

'I'd rather hear what's happening. When's he going to court?'

'Yes, of course. This has been a very trying time for you.'

Addler turned so she was directly facing Gina across the corner of the table.

'Let me begin by explaining the stages through which a case such as yours progresses. In that way you will be able to understand fully the point we have reached.'

A look of concern crossed Gina's face. She made to speak, but Addler pressed on.

'In England and Wales, the full process of the law involves three agencies: the police, who investigate the incident, the CPS – Crown Prosecution Service – responsible for the preparation and presentation of criminal prosecutions to the Courts, and the Courts, where guilt or innocence is decided.'

'Yes, yes, I understand, but what I want to know is, when will my attacker go on trial?'

'I'm coming to that, Ms Hamilton.' Addler's expression softened. 'There is no doubt that you were the subject of a violent sexual attack, which was graphically recorded on CCTV and supported by abundant forensic evidence confirming Colin Bradshaw was the perpetrator.'

'You've known this for some time. I want to see him convicted for what he did to me. When will he go on trial?'

'Ms Hamilton, sensitive cases such as this involve complex

issues. The CPS are responsible for the optimal use of judicial resources.'

Gina's face registered concern at the direction in which the conversation was going. Her voice rose in pitch as she replied. 'But you've seen what he did to me and you have the forensic evidence to prove—'

'The strength of your case is not the issue. We, the police, investigate the incident, collect relevant evidence and then present the case to the CPS for forward action.'

'Yes, but why the delay?' Gina was struggling to control her voice, to speak forcefully.

'Ms Hamilton, we and the CPS are of the same mind. It is in the public interest for the two indictments facing Mr Colin Bradshaw to be joined in a single trial. Therefore, it will take longer to bring the cases to the Crown Court. Inevitably, as far as the alleged rape is concerned, there will be a delay.'

'And should you have problems building the case for manslaughter, are you implying Bradshaw will not stand trial?'

'That is not what I'm saying, Ms Hamilton. Rest assured, we shall keep you informed of developments.'

Addler pushed back her chair, preparing to stand.

'I'm not happy with what you've told me.'

'I am sorry you feel that way. Unfortunately, as I've said, the matter is out of our hands. Decisions as to when and how to prosecute rest with the CPS.'

285

67

All the way home from the Police Station, thoughts were raging in Gina's head. She stormed into her apartment and switched on her laptop.

Where's the justice? The CCTV and forensic evidence are over-whelming – I made sure of that. It all went so well, just as I'd planned: Colin arrested and charged with rape. He should stand trial – the jury's bound to find him guilty – but now the Crown Prosecution Service are delaying my triumph. Some official has decided it's not in the public interest to proceed with a trial at this time. Not in the public interest! The CCTV shows him raping me in a particularly violent way – it even looks as if he might kill me – and yet it's not in the public interest? I'm sure there are thousands of women out there who'd disagree!

It may be worse. We all know how badly women reporting sexual assault can be treated by the authorities. Perhaps that senior policewoman, Addler, was giving me the run-around. Maybe it's more than the CPS dragging their heels; perhaps they're kicking it into the long grass. If so, they've picked the wrong woman! I'm Georgina Hamilton, raised by my mother, willing to use people for my own ends *and* very skilled at doing so. I always come out on top!

Getting Colin convicted and jailed was to be my revenge. I wanted him out of my life. With him behind bars, I'd feel free from his encroachment into my life, his presence in my home. I can't live with the thought that the CPS won't bring a public prosecution.

Agitated, Gina began browsing the internet.

Right, I can bring a private prosecution, but it costs. By rights, I should be able to turn to my parents for help, but that option's been taken from me. That pitiful old man, my father, squandered my inheritance. Men, they always let you down. The money I saved from my time at uni, that's all gone on this apartment, but why not? It was my money, money I'd earnt before putting the escort life behind me. One thing's for sure, I'll not return to escorting so how else can I raise money for a private prosecution?

Where do people turn in times of need? Charities: there must be one that would finance me. I've found nothing suitable on the internet, but I did come across something interesting – crowdfunding. Until now, it's been used by businesses to raise capital, but why shouldn't it work for an individual? I've used people to get what I want; with crowdfunding I could use the power of the internet to approach thousands – tens of thousands – of women. Women out there who'll agree with me – the man who raped me must be punished. He must be prosecuted, found guilty and sent to prison. Rapists must pay for their crimes.

I've no time to get on top of the law, nor the technology, but I can get help for that. My part will be to write the pitch and that's not a problem. I'll not be speaking to thousands of people in some great hall, I'll be speaking directly to each person who visits the website. It's in my head already. I'll tell the story – *my version of the story* – tap into the sisterhood, draw on their sympathy and support. How could any woman not be moved when they read of my rape and near death in the centre of Canterbury? Stand together, contribute what you can, help to fund my legal costs, help to bring a private prosecution, help to ensure my attacker gets his just deserts.

I know just the person who can help. Amanda, the only person I've ever been close to – we understand each other completely. If necessary, she'd use me and I'd use her. We keep in touch infrequently, birthdays mainly, even though I know she's got my date wrong and I'm not sure about hers. Amanda's working in PR for a London art dealer; modest salary, not that that bothers her. She hardly ever spends time at her own place, not Amanda. She's in her element meeting loads of generous men who are only too willing to loan her their homes now and then in exchange for her particular favours. Unlike me, Amanda never really put the escort life behind her, although now it's even more discreet, with payment in kind, not cash. I know it's months since we last spoke, but when she hears my story, she'll rally round.

Of course, it will be *my story* that I'll tell – not the truth. I've gone over and over this in my head ever since I escaped Colin's clutches. Doing what I'm doing sickens me but I had no other choice. No one – the public, the police, a judge, a jury – would ever believe the truth.

68

I'm in London, walking to a restaurant in a back street, east of Covent Garden. When I called her, Amanda was appropriately sympathetic – *just*. But, being the woman she is – we're so alike – she immediately got down to practicalities.

'First off, you need legal advice. I know just the man, he's a top criminal barrister. I'll arrange lunch, for the three of us, at his favourite restaurant. He's really into game – and *games* too for that matter.'

'Isn't legal advice expensive?'

'Darling, this will be a favour to me.' I heard Amanda take a short breath. 'Of course, it'll still cost. He'll expect a free lunch and a fuck.'

'I ...'

'Don't worry, you pick up the tab and I'll take care of the fuck. I know what he likes and, anyway, I owe him one, although I doubt he'll remember that. It's one of the advantages of old men, give them what they want from time to time and they tend not to remember how much they've done for you.'

Amanda's barrister friend certainly liked his claret. He commandeered the bottle, which Amanda had chosen, and was well into a second glass before we'd finished our starters. It was only when she whispered something in his ear about *afters* that he began drinking the mineral water and addressing my predicament.

'*Prosecution of Offences Act, 1985*, Section 6.1,' he said, leaning forwards, his face inches from mine. 'That's your lifeline, Gina.'

I began taking notes.

'Provision 6.1 gives you a statutory power to bring a private prosecution against a fellow citizen.' He leant towards me again, but this time he put a large hand firmly on my thigh, and sniggered. 'Though from what Mandy tells me, fellow citizen is probably not your preferred term for your attacker.'

'Whoa there! Hands over here or Mandy's going to get jealous.'

'Hmmff!' he snorted, with a look conveying his opinion that we all knew it was a game. However, he did remove his hand, like a naughty schoolboy, and continued, averting his eyes from Amanda. 'I gather they've not declined to prosecute, but they're taking their time about it.' He drank some mineral water, followed by a sip of wine. 'Of course, the CPS is not flawless, far from it. That said, you have to feel some sympathy for the underfunded buggers – and the police too.' He swirled his wine glass and took another sip of the claret. 'No matter, you're right to be prepared and a private prosecution is your way forward.'

'How should I go about that?'

'I'll get one of my juniors to advise you.' He pulled out a phone, hit speed dial, barked a time and cut the call before there was any sound of a reply. His hand returned to his pocket and he handed me a discreet but thickly embossed business card. 'Abi will see you at three-thirty.'

'Thank you. I—'

'A pleasure, my dear.'

Once more he leant towards me, but this time his lips were almost touching my ear.

'Now you've got my number, give me a call whenever you're in town.'

Unfortunately, the sentence came out like a stage whisper. This didn't worry me, but Amanda reacted quickly. There was a barely perceptible note of displeasure in her voice, but I could tell immediately that she was annoyed.

'Now, now, it's time for *afters*.'

Pushing aside his main course, which had been reduced to a pile of bones on the plate, plus a few drops of sauce on his tie, and with his hand still hovering just above my thigh, Amanda's over-friendly barrister said, 'My dear, I'm afraid Amanda and I haven't time for pudding.' At this, he stood and elaborately helped Amanda from her seat. 'However, don't let us prevent you. I can vouch for the satisfaction one gets from their jam roly-poly.'

Amanda, her hand on his arm, rolled her eyes, but allowed herself to be slowly escorted from the restaurant, leaving me to pick up the tab.

Using my mobile's maps, I arrived at the stone steps of the address on the barrister's card a little before half past three and asked for Abi. The immaculate receptionist, trapped in the narrow hallway between a high counter and a wall of pigeonholes, smiled sympathetically. 'You mean Mr Abayomi. Christopher's expecting you.' She picked up a phone, pressed a button and said, 'Ms Georgina Hamilton is here to see you,' then lowered the handset to its cradle. 'He's coming down.'

Christopher Abayomi appeared at the top of the carpeted stairs. 'Ms Hamilton, delighted to see you. If you'd follow me, we can talk through what you need to know.'

He led me up three flights of stairs and into the smallest of rooms, which was equipped with a small table, two hard-backed chairs, a carafe of water and glasses on an ageing lace doily. If the receptionist was immaculate, Christopher was a male model – a dark suit hung flawlessly on his slim, and undoubtedly toned, body. From a distance on the stairs, it was his dramatically high cheekbones, gently softened by the deep black of his skin, that caught my eye. Now, sitting almost knee to knee, I could see he had a complexion to die for.

'Ms Hamilton, may I offer you some water?'

'Gina, please, and, no, thank you, I'm good.'

'I understand you are contemplating bringing a private prosecution and you need to know what that would entail.'

'Yes, the CPS are dragging their feet over prosecuting a man who attacked me. Should they kick it into the long grass, I want to be prepared.'

'In that case the *Prosecution of Offences Act, 1985*, section 6.1 gives you statutory power to bring a private prosecution.'

'So I've been told, but what would that entail?'

'First, you would have to waive your statutory right to anonymity.'

'That wouldn't concern me. I intend to come out on top.'

Christopher looked serious, but continued speaking in a calm, reassuring voice. 'Here I should warn you, Ms Ham ... Gina, there can be no guarantee that your private prosecution would be successful. In fact, there are a number of hurdles in your path.'

'Hurdles? I thought this was my statutory right.'

'Indeed, but there are checks and requirements. There's no guarantee you and your legal team will be able to get access to evidence collected by the state. Of course, you would be able to employ private investigators, but they don't have the legal powers of the police. In addition, your team would have a duty to disclose material that you have to the defence.'

'What sort of material?'

'Anything that might assist the defence and/or weaken your prosecution case.'

'Surely this stacks the odds against me?'

'It's no more than a state prosecutor has a duty to do. And that's not all. The head of the CPS, the Director of Public Prosecutions, can take over a private prosecution—'

'You mean they'd do it for me?'

'Possibly, but the DPP could withdraw your prosecution. Indeed, the defendant has a right to ask the DPP to take over the case and stop it.'

By this time, I wasn't listening to Christopher's litany of problems. I wanted revenge and, ultimately, I was determined to come out on top. I always did. 'If the reluctance of the CPS forces me to act, I'm sure that won't happen. The evidence against my attacker is so strong. How much money will I need to raise in order to bring this prosecution?'

'Realistically, you should have one hundred thousand.'

Christopher escorted me back down the carpeted staircase to the main entrance where, as we said our goodbyes, he gave me his personal card. I promised to be in touch and then hurried to rejoin Amanda. We'd arranged to set up my crowd-funding appeal this evening.

* * * *

When I arrived at her flat, Amanda was in an asymmetrical off-the-shoulder top and harem pants.

'On seeing you leave for *afters* with your barrister friend, I wasn't sure you'd be back.'

'Another advantage of older men, their fantasies are bigger than their stamina. I'm back, showered, changed, on my computer and on top of crowdfunding. All we need is the text of your appeal.'

'No prob. It's been in my head for days.'

Twenty minutes later, after several tweaks to the text I'd dictated, Amanda swivelled her laptop towards me. 'What do you think?'

My words looked more powerful on the screen than they'd sounded in my head.

ALL RAPISTS SHOULD BE PUNISHED
HELP ME PROSECUTE MY ATTACKER

Walking from my work to my home, I was violently attacked in the centre of Canterbury. There was no one nearby when my attacker struck, pushing me to the pavement, tearing my knickers off and forcing himself into me. My protests were useless. He was stronger and determined. Then, not content with raping me, he tore off my bra and began to strangle me. I thought I was going to die! He left me humiliated, traumatized and cold in the gutter. As soon as I had collected my wits, I staggered to the Police Station and reported the rape and the strangulation. The authorities have overwhelming evidence, both forensic and CCTV, but the Crown Prosecution Service are reluctant to put my attacker on trial. He says the incident was my idea, some rough sex in public, which he claims I enjoy. He's lying!

The CPS have said it's not in the public interest to pros-
ecute at this time. Not in the public interest? Sisters, I'm
sure you disagree. Join with me, donate whatever money
you can, small or large, so that we can ensure this evil
predator is put behind bars where he belongs. Help me
protect other women. We are all vulnerable to men like
him. Together we must set an example. Enough is enough.
Donate and let us tell the world: all rapists will be punished.

'What do you think?' I asked Amanda.

'It's good, a strong message but—'

'But what?'

'In the big wide world, you're an unknown and this is the first crowdfunding appeal of its kind. Businessmen have a relevant CV to back their appeals. Chefs can cite experience in other restaurants.'

'Okay, but I'm appealing to the sisterhood, surely women will rally round?'

'You're not a celebrity.'

'There's nothing I can do about that.'

'But there is. Publicity! One of my friends is the editor of a national tabloid. Here's his number. Ring him now, give him an exclusive and he'll splash your story and your crowd-funding appeal.'

69

Ed was interrupted by her desk phone ringing with an internal call. It was Chief Superintendent Karen Addler. 'My office, now.'

Following a barked order to enter, Ed was faced by the Super waving a tabloid newspaper. 'The Chief Constable has just been on the phone. This is bad publicity, Ogborne, damn bad publicity!' Addler pointed to the visitor's chair and tossed the offending paper across her desk.

Ed straightened the paper, glanced at the headline and read the first two lines.

'I THOUGHT I WOULD DIE'
YOUNG WOMAN 'STRANGLED AND RAPED'
Georgina Hamilton waives anonymity to crowdfund a private prosecution. 'He left me humiliated, traumatized and cold in the gutter,' says Gina, but the CPS will not set a trial date.

'What does she think she's doing?' Addler sounded simultaneously bemused and indignant.

'Exercising her statutory right—' began Ed, but the Super wasn't listening.

'Waiving her right to anonymity, broadcasting her identity alongside such—'

'But, Ma'am, it's her right to—'

'To be foolhardy, yes, but to use the tabloid press in an attempt to pressurize the Director of Public Prosecutions. It makes us look as if we're dragging our feet. Why can't the woman be patient? I told her, it's a complex issue, the CPS have a difficult decision, but there's never been any doubt the case would come to trial.' As was her wont when taking time to think or preparing to terminate a conversation, Addler reached for her fat fountain pen. 'That will be all, Ogborne.'

Back at her desk, Ed wondered if Gina was being poorly advised. She had her suspicions that Gina might have set Bradshaw up, but why would she have done that? No matter, the prosecution could easily finesse the issue; no evidence Ed and her team had collected would stand in the way of a guilty verdict. Her bizarre visits to the dental practice in the early hours of the morning and recent purchase of bras that were different from the ones she normally wore could be shrugged off as coincidence.

70

'Hi, Amanda. Hope I'm not interrupting anything intimate.' There was no immediate reply, so Gina continued. 'This could wait. Just say, I can call back tomorrow.'

'No probs. David's in Gloucestershire with his family. He's given me the run of his place in Chelsea for the entire weekend.'

'Nice.' Gina knew such an event was far from unusual in Amanda's London existence and assumed David must be another of her many friends.

'It's been a mega week, a new exhibition at the gallery, then David every evening, dinner out and no sleep 'til the early hours. A girl can have too much of a good thing. Can you believe it, he didn't leave for the country until eight-thirty last night.'

'You must be exhausted.'

'Too right! I'm chilling with a box set and takeaways, but so bloody knackered, I haven't the energy to invite the delivery boys in for a quickie.'

'Poor you.'

'How are things with you, Gina? How's the crowdfunding going?'

'That's why I'm calling. It's really slow.'

'Slow? I'd stake my life what you'd written and the publicity you've got in the papers would generate thousands of hits.'

'Don't get me wrong, there's been a deluge of responses, but they're small donations, a fiver, ten, almost all are less than twenty pounds.'

'Your target was a hundred k, what have you got so far?'

'Just over six grand, but I think the frequency of donations has peaked. From now on, I imagine they'll start to decline. At this rate it could take years for me to raise the money I need.'

'It's an unusual use of crowdfunding, Gina. You're an unknown woman and your cause doesn't involve a sick child or the mistreatment of animals.'

'That's not my only problem. Even if I raise the money, I've discovered there'll be another legal hoop to jump through before I can get the case in front of a jury.'

'Surely, if you're funding a private prosecution that's down to you.'

'Apparently not. Unless we can convince a magistrate and then a Crown Court judge, my case won't get as far as a trial.'

'How can that be fair? It's your money.'

'To get my private prosecution to court, we'd need new evidence. If there was sufficient new evidence, the CPS would be obliged to bring a public prosecution.'

'Not all doom and gloom then.'

'Will I never get Colin out of my life?'

'Don't be so hard on yourself. Something will turn up, it always does.'

'It had better.'

'Look, Gina, David's away all weekend. Come up to London and keep me company. We'll forget your troubles with a night on the town.'

71

'Ms Hamilton, Gina, please, come in, take a seat.' Chief Superintendent Karen Addler ushered Gina to a seat at the small conference table. 'Coffee?'

'The Family Liaison Officer said there'd been a development I should know about.'

'Yes. Thank you for coming in to see me. I wanted you to hear it from us. Are you sure you wouldn't like some refreshment?'

'Give me the news first.'

'Yes. Yes, of course. As I told you on a less propitious occasion, it was in the public interest for the CPS to seek a joinder for the two indictments faced by Mr Colin Bradshaw. However, for a date to be set for the double trial, it was necessary for the police to present the CPS with solid evidence for the manslaughter—'

'So Bradshaw *will* stand trial for raping me?'

'Please!' Addler didn't like being interrupted, but the word came out sharper than she'd intended. She gave Gina a placatory look and continued in a controlled voice. 'It is essential that I present you with the full picture. Assembling that evidence has required an immense collaborative effort by our team and the team in Dover. Naturally, I have commended the officers personally for their painstaking work.' Addler paused, as if expecting equivalent praise from Gina.

'And ...?'

'To cut to the chase, the Director of Public Prosecutions has assessed the evidence against Mr Bradshaw in the manslaughter case and is convinced it will lead to a conviction. She has authorized the CPS to set a date for the joint trial.'

'Why has it taken so long?' Thoughts were whirling in Gina's head. *Two months! If they'd got the bastard when it happened, when he killed the girl in Dover, none of this would have happened to me!*

'As I've said, it was a complex case; appropriate evidence was difficult to acquire.'

'What does this mean for me, for what he did to me?'

'In tandem with the manslaughter charge, Colin Bradshaw will be tried for aggravated rape in the early hours of Wednesday, the 10th of July, in central Canterbury.'

'But when?'

'As soon as a definitive date is set, you will be informed immediately.'

Gina was still angry at the delay but, for the first time in weeks, she relaxed. She'd won. Colin would be tried for rape. With all the evidence stacked against him, no jury could fail to find him guilty.

'Thank you. I'll have that coffee now, if I may.'

As soon as she left the Police Station Gina called Amanda and was unable to keep the excitement from her voice. 'Hi! Guess what? You were right. The CPS are going to prosecute the bastard for raping me!'

'Woohoo!'

'If you're still on for tomorrow, we can make our girls' night out a celebration!'

'Why wait until tomorrow?' For once, Amanda seemed as excited as Gina felt. 'Pack a bag, catch the next high-speed train, text me your ETA and I'll meet you at St Pancras.'

'You're on!'

'Great! We'll have our first glass of bubbly at the champagne bar!'

While Gina was arranging her trip to London, Ed returned to the CID Room. 'I've just seen the Super for an update.'

'Bradshaw and Dover?' asked Mike.

'Bradshaw, Dover *and* the rape of Gina Hamilton, I hope,' said Jenny.

'Right. I've just been told the CPS will seek a joint trial for the aggravated burglary and manslaughter of Kayleigh Robson and the aggravated rape of Georgina Hamilton. Incidentally, on my way to see the Super, I passed Gina coming from Addler's office. She blanked me, but didn't wipe the smile from her face fast enough for me not to notice.'

'What about the evidence that Gina might have set Colin up?'

'It's all there Nat, and will be available to his defence. Frankly, I think it will be rendered moot.' Ed shrugged her shoulders. 'Gina's recent late-night trips to work and her new bra will be put down to coincidence. Faced with the solid CCTV and forensic evidence, no jury will give much credence to a suggestion that there might be another side to Gina's story.'

'Which means the bastard will get what he deserves.' As she spoke, Jenny glanced at Nat.

The weekend was approaching and Ed had promised herself a break, a short but real change of scene. Ever since the times she sat with her grandfather looking at his books of Egon Schiele's painting she'd wanted to see the originals. Last year it had almost happened but a change of circumstances prevented the trip. Suddenly she was fired with the idea of making it happen. After a rapid search of the internet Ed took her personal mobile and walked to the far side of the Police Station car park.

'Hi, Daniel. We've got a result. The CPS are seeking a joint trial of Bradshaw for manslaughter and rape. With that dusted, I feel like a proper break. Will you indulge me with a change of plan for this weekend?'

'What are you thinking of?'

'I'm feeling extravagant. Can you pack a weekend bag and meet me tonight at six, Gatwick North Terminal Departures? And bring your passport.'

'I can ... Where will we be going?'

'To Vienna, returning Sunday evening.'

'Vienna!'

'It's a long story. I'll explain on the flight – the tickets and hotel are on me. Will you come?'

'I'll be carrying my sports bag and will have an inquisitive look on my face.'

Ed smiled into her phone. 'See you at Gatwick.'

'So this guy was your dad's favourite artist?' Daniel was staring at a self-portrait by Schiele, apparently bemused by the angular, distorted, emaciated figure. Having experienced his less than enthusiastic response to the stunning Secession Building, Ed had eased him gently into the Leopold via a cold beer and a sandwich on the terrace.

'No, he was my *grandfather's* favourite. Just imagine, he was only 28 when he died from Spanish flu in 1918.'

'Your grandfather?'

'No!' Ed gave Daniel a puzzled look. 'Egon!' Ed's eyes softened as she turned back to the self-portrait. 'I remember my grandfather showing me books of Schiele's work and saying—'

A startled stranger standing nearby coughed and looked at Ed with a questioning frown. Daniel had already walked into the next room.

Ed's embarrassment was spared by the vibration of her work mobile. She took the call in an empty corridor and then went in search of Daniel.

'Sorry, the CPS have got their skates on. I'll be a principal witness and they want to start going over the evidence first thing tomorrow. We'll have to fly back tonight. I'll sort the tickets.'

Daniel didn't look too upset at the prospect of an early return.

The optimism Ed encountered in her meetings with the CPS was dashed at the preliminary hearings for the trial. The Crown argued that the manslaughter and rape indictments should be joined, but the judge rejected joinder for two reasons: prejudice in the rape trial and the lack of a sufficient factual nexus.

Ed agreed with the ruling. A single trial would be cheaper and save time, but it wouldn't be fair to the defendant for the same jury to consider a verdict for rape alongside one for manslaughter in which a young woman died. As for a factual overlap between the two charges, other than both involving

Bradshaw, there was none. Consequently, she was pleased that the judge had gone for fair play but knew the decision wouldn't please everyone, especially Georgina Hamilton. From the evidence her team had uncovered, Ed questioned whether Gina was telling the complete truth about the Buttermarket incident, nonetheless, she felt a twinge of sympathy for the young woman who would now be facing a long wait and a trip away from Canterbury before her day in court.

Part Three:
THE TRIALS

72

Gina was incandescent – outraged by what she perceived as unwarranted delays.

A few moments earlier, her Family Liaison Officer had called at Great Stour Court with an update regarding developments. Now, despite her repeated attempts to explain, and offerings of commiseration, Gina refused to be placated. FLOs often received flak for decisions made by others – that came with the job – but this time the young officer could do nothing to calm the situation. She was barely out of the door before Gina was on the phone to Amanda.

'Hi Gina, how's—'

'The bastards!'

'What's hap—'

'The bloody CPS. They're not doing what they promised.'

'How come? I thought it was all settled.'

'Me too!' Gina began taking deep breaths, trying to control her anger.

'You told me Bradshaw would be prosecuted for both offences – rape and manslaughter.'

'That's what Chief Superintendent bloody Addler told me, but there's been a change of plan.'

'How? What?'

'The judge ruled there was insufficient overlap between the two cases.'

'Well, other than Colin being responsible for both, I suppose—'

'That's not all. Apparently, it wouldn't be fair for Colin to be tried for rape and manslaughter by the same jury. There's going to be two trials.'

'Have they set dates?'

'Too bloody right.' Gina paused for more deep breaths before continuing. 'I'm not bothered about there being two trials but the manslaughter's set for October in Canterbury.'

While Gina took another deep breath, Amanda asked, 'And his trial for raping you?'

'That's why I'm so bloody angry. April! Next year! Eight fucking months before I get the chance to skewer the bastard in court. What's fair about that? Colin's the bloody criminal! What about fairness for me? I'm the victim. I want closure.'

'And you should get it.' Amanda's voice softened. 'Poor you. Such a long wait—'

'It's not just the wait. The rape hearing has been switched from Canterbury to Southwark. Not only do I have to wait months for justice, I've got to travel to London to get it!'

'I feel for you, babe, but look on the bright side.'

'What bright side?'

'You told me the evidence against him is overwhelming and now you've got what you want. The bastard Bradshaw *is* going to be tried for raping you. You may have to wait a bit longer for your day in court but that day *will* come and it'll be a *triumph*!'

Gina's anger was subsiding. 'I suppose so ...'

310

'And, every cloud as they say. With the switch to Southwark, you can stay at mine. I can take care of you during the trial. Then, when it's over and the bastard's been found guilty, we can really celebrate.'

73

Two months passed and Ed was due to appear at Canterbury Crown Court the following morning. She'd been called to give evidence in the trial of Colin Bradshaw for the aggravated burglary, false imprisonment and manslaughter of Kayleigh Robson at her flat in Maxton House. The evidence her team – with the help of Dover – had amassed was overwhelming. It was so strong that Ed thought Colin would be advised to plead guilty in order to receive a reduced sentence. Certainly, the CPS had been convinced the jury would find him guilty beyond reasonable doubt. Nevertheless, as a principal witness for the prosecution, Ed had to be prepared for every eventuality.

A specialist from forensics would be the expert witness regarding the prints from Kayleigh's flat and the DNA extracted from them. In the investigation, which Ed had led, hours of CCTV had built a complete chronological picture of Bradshaw's movements. The officers involved had been exhausted but elated. It would be Ed's job in the witness box to present the facts clearly and confidently.

In the fading warmth of an autumn sunset Ed sat on her balcony with a glass of sparkling water to review the evidence in detail. The CCTV had been organized to provide a chronological record from Colin buying train tickets at Canterbury

East Railway station, through his repeated stalking of Kayleigh, culminating with him rapidly closing the gap between them as they disappeared down the side street towards Maxton House. More damning was his subsequent reappearance, 22 minutes later, sitting in a pizzeria checking Kayleigh's mobile, copying writing from a notebook and then the signature from her bank card. Equally telling were security camera images at a 24/7 store showing Colin buying multiple bottles of the bleach of the type which forensics would show was used to clean her flat. A painstaking search of the railway track between Dover and Canterbury had recovered three empty bleach bottles still bearing recently printed price tags from the convenience store in Dover. Although Kayleigh's mobile and notebook were never recovered, Ed was confident their evidence, plus the corroborating forensics, would lead to a conviction.

It was ten-thirty when she put her notes aside, heartened by the prospect of nailing this evil man in court the next day.

Ed had invited Jenny to watch her giving evidence at Bradshaw's trial. When the day's proceedings came to an end, Jenny, thinking they would walk back to the Police Station together, was waiting for her boss at the entrance to Canterbury Crown Court.

'Sorry, Jenny, I've just arranged to meet a friend at Deakin's to unwind with a coffee. If you've anything you want to ask me, I'll see you at work tomorrow.'

For Jenny, it wasn't something she wished to ask her boss, but something she was wondering if she should tell her. By the time she got back to the CID Room, Jenny had decided to mention the incident to Mike and Nat.

'How did it go?' asked Mike, as soon as Jenny entered the room.

'Ed was brilliant: very clear and precise. She didn't let the defence barrister bully or confuse her. The jury hung on her every word.'

'The evidence we gathered was pretty compelling,' said Nat.

'Totally,' said Jenny, 'but there was one nasty moment. Ed didn't see it and I've been wondering if I should tell her.'

'What happened?' asked Mike and Nat, almost in unison, but with Mike half a second behind.

'Cross-questioning was coming to an end and Ed's evidence had been damning, complete and clearly delivered. She'd kept her eyes fixed on the jury throughout and was still looking at them when the barrister announced, "No further questions." Then, because Ed wasn't looking at the dock, she didn't see what Bradshaw did.'

'What?' said Nat and Mike together.

'He gave Ed a death stare. Bradshaw put fingers to his eyes, then pointed to Ed and drew two fingers across his throat.' Jenny paused, looking at Mike. 'Should I tell her?'

This time, Nat was silent, but Mike spoke reassuringly. 'Let's keep it to ourselves. No need to alarm Ed unnecessarily. It was probably an empty gesture. Even if it wasn't, Colin Bradshaw is likely to be found guilty on all three charges. With the evidence stacked against him, he would have been advised to plead guilty for a lower sentence. Why he didn't, I can't imagine. Arrogance, I suppose. Sentences for manslaughter have gone up. My bet is the judge will go for the maximum tariff and Bradshaw will be banged up for the best part of twenty years.'

Jenny still looked uncomfortable about not telling Ed, but she agreed. 'You're probably right. She has a lot on her plate at the moment. We can always tell her later should anything happen.'

When the verdict came through, Mike had been right. Colin Bradshaw was sentenced to 22 years, 16 for manslaughter and 6 for aggravated burglary, to run consecutively. He also got 4 years for false imprisonment, but they were to run concurrently. Jenny thought the sentences for manslaughter and aggravated burglary would normally be longer, so she consulted Ed.

'You're right, Jenny. These days manslaughter would be likely to attract 20 years and aggravated burglary 10, but the two offences overlapped substantially. Bradshaw got a lower sentence for each but they're to be served consecutively, so the total sentence is greater than for manslaughter alone.'

'The main thing is that the bastard has been put away for a long time. And Bradshaw still has to face trial for raping Gina.'

Ed left Jenny's last comment unanswered. Despite the CCTV and forensic evidence, Ed was less certain than her young colleague that Colin Bradshaw was guilty of the alleged rape.

74

Gina wasn't nervous; rather, as the date for Colin's trial approached, she was growing increasingly excited. At last, she was going to see the bastard in the dock and the evidence against him would be damning. By half past five on the Friday before the week of the trial, Gina finished with her last patient and went to collect her things from the room at the back of the dental practice. Buoyed by the prospect of staying at Amanda's flat, she was anxious to get away, but her colleagues had lined up to wish her well. Gina didn't begrudge the delay. Everyone had been so supportive and, anyway, she was in good time for her train to London.

Later, on the high-speed train from Canterbury West to St Pancras, Gina recalled her last meeting with the Family Liaison Officer. Once again it had been negative news.

'As you know, the CPS were planning to present Mr Bradshaw's conviction for manslaughter as evidence of bad—'

'Of course, it shows the evil shit had a thing against women.' Gina knew the evidence for rape was solid, but she wanted to throw everything at the bastard.

Familiar with Gina's outbursts, the FLO spoke carefully.

'Yes ... well ... I'm afraid the judge has ruled against it being presented at his trial for rape.'

'But why? He did it. It shows his attitude to women. It should be part of the evidence against him.'

'I sympathize with what you're saying, Gina. It's a complex judicial issue but the CPS and Counsel for the Crown are not worried about the judge's decision. They're in agreement that Bradshaw's conviction for manslaughter in Dover has no direct bearing on your allegation of rape in Canterbury.'

If only you knew, thought Gina, *that's exactly why I've accused him of rape. Colin Bradshaw conned his way into my home, tied me to my bed and, if I hadn't used sex to escape, eventually he would have killed me. There's only one difference: with Kayleigh Robson it was manslaughter, with me it would have been murder.*

Three hours before Gina boarded her high-speed train to London, Ed had gone to the CPS for a final pre-trial meeting with Zoë DuCairne, Counsel for the Crown. The moment Ed entered the room, Zoë took charge.

'Good afternoon, Inspector. Coffee?'

'I'm good thanks.' Ed took a seat among the CPS staff at the conference table. She poured herself some water and waited for Zoë to begin.

'Right. I'll start with the only negative. In the scheme of things, it's a minor issue – Bradshaw's conviction for aggravated burglary, false imprisonment and manslaughter in Dover. The judge acknowledged that the defendant's conviction for the incident had probative value as evidence of bad character but, on balance, ruled against its admittance at his trial for rape.'

317

There was some muttering from the CPS people but Ed spoke clearly to the whole table. 'As I see it, the manslaughter conviction has no direct bearing on the rape allegation.'

'No direct bearing,' sniffed Counsel for the Crown, 'but it would have been useful.'

'Rhys ... Rhys Hughes.' From the speaker's youthful appearance, Ed assumed he was the youngest member of the CPS team. With his hand half raised, Rhys was looking at Ed, but he waited to get everyone's attention. '*Criminal Justice Act 2003*, Section 101, subsection 3; the judge ruled against admittance on the grounds that it would have an unwarrantedly adverse effect on the fairness of proceedings at the trial for alleged rape.'

'Quite,' retorted Zoë. 'As I was saying, a minor issue, a non-problem for us. The evidence against Bradshaw is overwhelming. If I were his barrister, I would have advised him to plead guilty, knock a third off his sentence.'

'It *is* the defendant's right to ask for the case against him to be proved.' It was Rhys Hughes again. Zoë gave him a withering look before turning to Ed.

'We've already been through the CCTV and forensic material. Excellent work, Inspector, you've built an overwhelmingly solid case. You and your team are to be congratulated. Have you anything to add?'

Ed replied without opening the file she had with her. 'When questioned, Ms Hamilton said she often visited her workplace in the early hours of the morning because it helped with her insomnia. Does the CCTV data cover the surprisingly sparse evidence for such visits prior to the incident in the Buttermarket?'

A look of concern passed across Zoë DuCairne's face and

the Counsel for the Crown began turning pages in her ring binder.

Ed coughed. 'Also the nature of the bra Ms Hamilton was wearing on the night of the incident compared with the other bras she owns?'

Zoë looked up from her file and shot a steely look at one of the older CPS staff. 'John, have you—'

'There's the unused material ...' Rhys Hughes was interrupting Zoë for a third time, but he left this interjection hanging. The guy was really pushing his luck. Ed wondered what was going on.

'What unused material?' snapped the Counsel for the Crown. 'John, why haven't I been shown this?'

'Not for the first time, we received the unused material at the last minute,' said Rhys Hughes quickly.

At the same time, but in his more measured tones, John, the older member of the CPS staff, said, 'It arrived just after lunch today.'

Zoë looked accusingly at Ed. 'Inspector, I assume this unused material is evidence the police have collected that doesn't support the prosecution case. By law, such material must be made available and disclosed to the defence. What's going on?'

'That's what I'd like to know,' said Ed. 'I prepared that evidence for the CPS months ago, along with all the CCTV and forensic material you've seen. As soon as I get back to my desk, I'll find out—'

'No need, Inspector.' It was John, again. 'The unused material was hand delivered to us by a PC. It came with an apology from a senior police officer saying there had been an administrative oversight.'

'Scandalous!' muttered Rhys Hughes, while Zoë DuCairne spoke over him. 'Has this material been sent to the defence?'

John smiled weakly towards the Counsel for the Crown. 'Upon its arrival, I made that our immediate priority.'

'Good.' Zoë turned to Ed. 'Inspector, perhaps you could help by briefly summarizing what I've yet to see?'

Again, Ed responded while leaving her file closed. 'First, at the time of the incident, we found no evidence that late-night visits to the dental practice were an established behaviour. Extensive searches of relevant CCTV, revealed Ms Hamilton made just one such visit prior to the night of the alleged rape, although she made several more after the incident. Second, the bra she was wearing on the night of the alleged attack was padded and underwired, quite unlike the bras she habitually wore. My team discovered she purchased two of the new style bras, one the day before the alleged attack and one the day after. I thought it worth noting that, while at the station to identify the man she claimed attacked her, Ms Hamilton made a point of drawing our attention to the fact that she was wearing the padded bra.'

'And you questioned her about these issues?'

Ed nodded toward the Counsel for the Crown. 'Essentially, Ms Hamilton claimed it was coincidental that these changes in her behaviour occurred at that time.'

'Exactly, coincidence. I'm sure she'll say the same should Counsel for the Defence ask those questions.' Zoë DuCairne turned to the CPS staff. 'What line do the defence intend to take?'

'From the defence statement ...' This time, having started to speak, Rhys Hughes thought better of it.

John, the older member of the team, replied, 'As you might

expect, they will say there was no rape because the act was consensual. In addition, they plan to argue that the complainant is an experienced sexual fantasist.'

'Sexual fantasist,' Zoë raised her eyebrows dramatically, 'at least it's a variant on the usual.' With that remark, she closed her ring binder as if the defence's intentions were of no consequence, but then added, 'As Counsel for the Crown I shall allude to these points in my opening speech and give Ms Hamilton every opportunity to deny during her evidence in chief.'

Ed left the meeting incensed that someone in the Force had probably delayed disclosing the material until just before the start of a trial. Such failures to pass on unused material to the defence team were not unknown. Sometimes by accident but sometimes by unscrupulous officers playing on the fact that defence teams – their resources stretched thin – would have little time to process new evidence that ran counter to the prosecution case. Ed would have liked to expose whoever had been responsible but she knew, if she went to the Super, she'd get the same reply she got on a previous occasion: 'Admin error, nothing more, the officer responsible has been reprimanded.'

75

Colin Bradshaw's trial for raping Georgina Hamilton began the following week. After the expert forensic and CCTV evidence had been presented to the court, Gina was called to the witness box. It was then that she saw Colin for the first time since their encounter in the Buttermarket. His once bleached-white hair had been cut to a mousy stubble, but he wore a well-cut suit, sombre tie and white shirt. Gina assumed his shoes, hidden by the dock, were black and highly polished. Their eyes locked across the court room and neither looked away until the court usher coughed, handed Gina a card and indicated she should take the oath. Gina took the card but spoke from memory as she looked back across the court, fixing her eyes on Colin.

'I do solemnly, sincerely and truly declare and affirm that the evidence I shall give shall be the truth, the whole truth and nothing but the truth.'

As Gina handed the card back to the usher, Counsel for the Crown, Ms Zoë DuCairne, stood and asked her to state her name.

'Georgina Hamilton.'

Gently and respectfully, Ms DuCairne took Gina through her account of what had happened when she'd left work in the early hours of Wednesday the 10th of July the previous year. With the evidence in chief completed, Counsel for the Crown changed her tack.

'One more thing, Ms Hamilton, before I conclude my questioning. The defence will say that you consented to the act that occurred in the Buttermarket. Is that true?'

'No! He attacked me and raped me. I struggled and asked him to stop. At no time did I give my consent.'

'The defence will argue that not only was the act consensual but that it was your idea – that you suggested it. Was it your idea to indulge in some rough sex, Ms Hamilton?'

'Certainly not! I believe that physical relationships between partners should be loving and conducted in private. The very thought of engaging in such behaviour in public is abhorrent to me.'

'Thank you, Ms Hamilton, I have no further questions.'

As Ms DuCairne, Counsel for the Crown, regained her seat, Mr Jameson, Counsel for the Defence, rose to his feet.

'Ms Hamilton, so that we all can be perfectly clear of what you have just stated under oath, would you be so kind as to answer for me questions similar to those to which you have just responded for the Crown?'

Gina nodded.

The judge intervened. 'Ms Hamilton, please state your replies aloud, both for my benefit and for that of the jury. Will you answer Mr Jameson's questions?'

'Yes.'

'Thank you,' Jameson said quietly. He paused and then continued in a tone which, although neutral and pitched at a conversational level, nonetheless carried to all corners of the court room. 'First, I'll remind you that you are under oath,

Ms Hamilton. Now, please tell the court, did you or did you not consent to the sexual activity that occurred between you and the defendant, Mr Colin Bradshaw, in the centre of Canterbury during the early hours of Wednesday the 10th of July, last year?'

'No. That is, no, I did not consent.'

'Mr Bradshaw claims, and we shall attempt to demonstrate, that not only did you consent to the activity that occurred but to do so was your idea. You planned the event and encouraged Mr Bradshaw to participate. Is not this the true account of what happened?'

'No. No! Who could believe such a thing?'

'Let us be clear, Ms Hamilton, are you saying that role-playing rape with strangulation was not your idea, that it was not an act you encouraged the defendant to perform in public?'

'No. Err ... you're confusing me. I mean yes. Sex in public was not my idea and I certainly didn't encourage it. Physical relationships between consenting adults should occur in a loving private environment. Colin Bradshaw forced—'

'Thank you, Ms Hamilton. To be clear, it is not your wish and has never been your wish to engage in sexual acts in locations where you might be seen by members of the public going about their daily lives?'

'It is not my wish, it has never been my wish and I have never voluntarily had sex in a public place. It has always been my belief that sexual relationships should occur between loving partners in private.'

'Do you not love Mr Bradshaw?'

'No!'

'Were the two of you not in an intimate relationship?'

Gina reached out to rest her hands on the front of the

witness box, bowing her head momentarily before raising it defiantly. 'Yes, briefly. But I ended our relationship because it wasn't working for me.'

'Indeed, that statement is true, Ms Hamilton. You did end your relationship with the defendant, but not before you enjoyed a holiday in Italy at Colin Bradshaw's expense.'

'The timing was unfortunate. When I decided our relationship was over, I wanted to let him down gently. And then ... then he did this, he attacked me.'

The judge stirred, as if to intervene, but Counsel for the Defence continued quickly.

'Ah, yes ... timing.' Jameson paused and consulted his notes. 'You have said, under oath, that the incident in the Buttermarket wasn't your idea, wasn't something you had planned and encouraged the defendant to perform. If that is true, how do you explain that the brassière you were wearing that night was brand new, of a size and style that was guaranteed not to strangle you, and, moreover, it was purchased by you just a day before the event?'

Gina almost smiled. 'I like to relax in something different from my day-to-day underwear. Many women do. I've tried a number of different styles and just happened to be trying that bra at that time.'

'So, coincidence?'

'Yes, coincidence.'

'Was it also coincidence that you first began going to work in the early hours of the morning just one day before the alleged attack?'

'Yes. I avoid taking drugs and at that time I was working through a number of activities in an attempt to overcome my insomnia.'

'So, coincidence again?'

'I know it seems unlikely but coincidences do happen.'

'When I call him to the witness box, Mr Bradshaw will attest that he was surprised how knowledgeable you were sexually and that you enjoyed what some might refer to as kinky sex.'

'If he says that he'll be lying.'

'When you say that, Ms Hamilton, would it surprise you to learn that information has come into our possession that supports his claim. Indeed, we shall be calling a witness from your days at university.'

With a look of alarm, Gina turned towards Counsel for the Crown, but Mr Jameson continued speaking.

'I should add that, during your university days, our witness knew you by a different name.'

Gina went white and clung to the witness box for support.

'The witness in question will testify that you, Ms Hamilton, ran an online website offering your services as an escort under the assumed name of Juliette. Those services included sado-masochistic acts including mock rape and strangulation.'

The judge, who had been poised to speak, finally did so. 'Mr Jameson, do you have a question for the witness?'

'My Lady – Ms Hamilton, is it true that you engaged in the activities I have this moment described?'

With her eyes closed, Gina spoke in short bursts. 'That was a long time ago. I was a different person. It was a different life. I've put all that behind me. I don't do those things anymore.'

'In that case, would you be so kind as to comment on a short video clip which we are about to show? This video was downloaded from YouTube and is clearly recorded from the central piazza of Siena during the famous local horse race.'

Gina stood ashen-faced as the entire court watched the video on strategically placed screens. The camera swept across the crowds in the centre of the Piazza del Campo to bareback Palio riders and their horses jostling for position at the starting rope. A blue-clad rider waited at a distance behind the others. Suddenly, the blue jockey urged his horse forward, the rope dropped and the race began. The camera followed the head-long charge but, as horses and riders turned the first corner, a hand appeared before the lens and pointed upwards. The camera swung unsteadily up the face of the buildings and came to rest on an upstairs window where it refocused and remained until sometime after an explosion had signalled the end of the race. There were gasps from the public gallery at the sight of a naked Gina having sex with Colin in the window of the apartment overlooking the Palio crowds in the Piazza del Campo below.

'Ms Hamilton, would you kindly identify the two people seen in the window?'

With her head lowered, Gina could barely be heard as she replied.

'I'm sorry to push you, Ms Hamilton.' It was the judge speaking. 'If you need to take a break, I can adjourn the hearing. However, when you reply to questions you must speak in a way that enables the court to hear what you are saying.'

With her head still lowered Gina spoke more clearly. 'It's me and Colin Bradshaw.'

Counsel for the Defence responded without triumph. 'Exactly, it is you, Georgina Hamilton, with the defendant, Mr Colin Bradshaw, in Siena at the Palio on Tuesday the 2nd of

July last year.' Mr Jameson paused and then continued to speak gently. 'And now, Ms Hamilton, would you kindly explain what you and Mr Bradshaw are doing and why?'

'It ... it was before we split up. I was trying to let him down gently.'

There was a guffaw from the public gallery, which the judge stifled with a cold stare.

'So, you are not averse to sex in public?'

'I ... I ...'

'Thank you, Ms Hamilton. Finally, I should like you to comment on this audio tape, which the defendant recorded on one of his mobile phones. This evidence was obtained from unused material the police confiscated from his rented home in Canterbury.

Gina leant against the side of the witness box with her hands covering her face as the court listened to the recording. The voices were clear. Gina's voice suggesting and encouraging Colin to role-play strangling her with her bra while having sex late at night in the Buttermarket. Colin's voice expressing reservations about the strangulation but, with growing excitement, eventually agreeing to Gina's wishes.

When the recording stopped, the silence was broken by a whispered conversation between Counsel for the Crown and her associates. The discussion was short and ended with Zoë DuCairne rising to her feet and addressing the judge.

'My Lady, the Crown requests leave to withdraw this prosecution.'

There was noise from the galleries – journalists rushing to leave and the hushed voices of the public exclaiming at the unexpected outcome. The commotion was brief, silenced by the stern eye of the judge who then acted on the Crown's request and brought the proceedings to a formal close.

Gina heard none of this. She hung her head, dejected, unable to comprehend that she had lost. Colin had won. Her triumph been snatched from her and she'd been humiliated in the process. Gina was summoned to appear in court the following day.

That evening, there was no celebration and little support – consolation wasn't Amanda's strong suit.

76

Perjury! The bastards! It was going to be my ultimate victory, my final revenge on Colin Bradshaw. I should be free and he should be back behind bars with an extra sentence for raping me. Instead, he's acquitted and I've got 12 months for perjury. The bastards!

I'm furious! My anger is threatening to consume me. Deep breaths. I've got to think clearly – face the facts. Colin's the biggest bastard with his secret bloody recordings, but the disaster was started by that bitch the Inspector, DI Ed Ogborne. It was her, nosing around my bras, that raised the first doubt. Her preoccupation with my new bra, that's what led to the police to checking out other aspects of what happened. My revenge on Colin would have gone smoothly had it not been for Ogborne getting suspicious and sticking her nose in. It may be water under the bridge, but it's not forgotten.

I'm not done yet. I will be revenged! They may have sentenced me to a year but I'll be out in six months. I'll be on licence, may not be able to work, but there's still the money I got from crowdfunding. When I'm out, I'll have my final say. I'll need to tread carefully, keep to my supervision requirements, but I am Georgina Hamilton; I will come out on top!

77

Four months after Georgina Hamilton was released from prison, Ed and Jenny were working at their desks in the CID Room. Suddenly, the door burst open. An anxious-looking Mike Potts strode across the room and switched on the wall-mounted television.

'What up, Mike?'

'Disturbing news, Ed. Colin Bradshaw's escaped from prison.'

The voice of a newsreader filled the room.

'—back to our local reporter Megan Turner, who's outside the prison on the Isle of Sheppey. Megan, what more can you tell us about this amazing escape?'

'Julie, at five past nine this morning, a helicopter landed in a small courtyard immediately behind the main gates to the prison that you can see behind me.'

'Surely, these days, with the increased use of drones to access prison areas, open spaces within the walls are protected by anti-aircraft netting?'

'Quite, but it is my understanding that this small courtyard is used only by people entering and leaving the prison and, as such, it's the only open area without netting.'

'Megan, I'm going to interrupt you there. Please stand by.

We'll return to you shortly. Now, we have our Chief Crime Editor, Damian Wheeler, on the line.'

By this time, Ed and Jenny had joined Mike in front of the television screen, on which the crime journalist appeared behind the newsreader.

'Damian, what can you tell us about Colin Bradshaw?'

'In the spring of last year, Bradshaw was sentenced to a total of 22 years for the manslaughter of Kayleigh Robson in Dover. By all accounts he's been a model prisoner. However, he appeared in court again some 10 months ago, charged with the alleged rape of a dentist, Georgina Hamilton. In a sensational trial he was eventually acquitted and the purported victim, Gina Hamilton, was sentenced to 12 months for perjury. I understand she was released a few months back. Now Bradshaw has absconded from prison in this dramatic fashion.'

'Thank you, Damian. We'll now return to our local reporter Megan Turner, outside the prison. Megan, what have you got for us?'

'Julie, the Prison Governor has just issued a statement. The abandoned helicopter has been found burning on a remote part of the island close to a beach. The traumatized, but otherwise unharmed, pilot was handcuffed to a mooring ring on a nearby jetty.'

'Do we know how this audacious escape was carried out?'

'The escape is still ongoing. Within minutes of the helicopter leaving the prison, the bridge connecting the island to the mainland was cordoned off by police. However, the pilot of the helicopter has now said that Bradshaw and the men who helped him escape didn't travel by road. Instead, they transferred to a high-speed powerboat and have already disappeared.'

The live news updates, streaming across the bottom of the television screen began to read:

Bradshaw prison escape: Police tweet—

The camera switched to Julie Howes-Kilfoy, the newsreader, who announced, 'The police have just tweeted that a burning motorboat has been spotted in the Thames Estuary on a deserted stretch of coastline near Shoeburyness in Essex. Bradshaw and his accomplices are believed to have transferred to a vehicle. Members of the public are warned not to approach the men, who are armed and dangerous. Anything suspicious should be immediately reported to the authorities. Now, back to our local reporter at the prison on the Isle of Sheppey – Megan.'

'As I was saying, the statement released by the Prison Governor said that, at five past nine this morning, the helicopter landed in the small courtyard that lies behind the gates you can see over my shoulder. It had been highjacked from a local flying school by three heavily armed men who operated like a commando unit. Here, in the prison, one guarded the pilot and the helicopter while the two others used angle grinders to break into the visitors' centre where Bradshaw was talking to his lawyer. Prison staff and the lawyer were threatened, but nobody was hurt.'

'Do we know any more about the men involved?'

'They were masked and the raid was over very quickly. However, the helicopter pilot has said the one who guarded him spoke English with a heavy accent, and among themselves he thought the three men were speaking Italian.'

Jenny gasped. 'Bradshaw and Hamilton were in Italy for the Palio. We know he has money. I wonder if he was able to contact Italian criminals after he was sentenced?'

'Whatever,' said Ed, 'there'll be a massive manhunt. They'll track him down. He'll not be on the run for long.'

Jenny looked at her colleagues. 'Perhaps we should tell ...' Jenny's voice trailed away as she glanced at Mike for confirmation.

'Tell who what?' asked Ed.

'Something happened at Colin's trial for manslaughter. You didn't see it.'

'See what?'

'What I saw. We discussed it, Mike, Nat and I.'

'What did you see, what did you discuss, why didn't you tell me?' Ed was showing signs of exasperation. Had Jenny now caught Mike's inability to get straight to the point?

Jenny looked at Mike, who nodded.

'We didn't want to worry you.'

'You're worrying me now, Jenny. Get to the point.'

'At the manslaughter trial, when you finished giving your evidence against Bradshaw, he stared at you, put two fingers to his eyes, then pointed at you and drew his hand across his throat.'

'I think you should be careful, Ed.' Mike faced her, looking concerned. 'He'd probably been told by his brief that the evidence against him was overwhelming, told to plead guilty for a lower sentence. So Bradshaw knew he had nothing to lose by doing something like that in court. Of course, such a gesture might just be bravado, but it could be serious, an indication he's thinking of taking revenge.'

'I've seen criminals in the dock make gestures like that before. From my experience, they tend to be empty threats, but thanks for the warning.'

334

Part Four:
SEEKING REVENGE

78

The pensioners, Fred and Milly Rowcastle, were your point of entry. Originally, you'd planned to send them a letter, one that appeared to have been sent to all the residents, informing them of an imminent maintenance check by the company responsible for security at the apartment block. Forging the letter and a suitable ID were not a problem, but you realized there were too many risks. The old couple might have been cautious and rung the company or mentioned the letter to other residents. Even if they did nothing, they would still have seen you. Perhaps not face to face, but at least via the video entry system when you arrived at the building. The last thing you wanted was to be identified. You needed to enter unobserved and that required a change of plan.

After studying the layout of the block, you watched the residents' comings and goings, logging their routines. Most left in the morning and returned in the evening. The Rowcastles were different; they were retired. On Wednesday afternoons they went by car to shop at the supermarket. On getting back they drove onto the entry ramp, through the automatic garage door and straight to their parking bay at the back of the building. If the road were clear as they disappeared inside, you would have just enough time to roll under the closing grill. This plan was virtually risk-free, but you would need practice and equipment. No matter, in two weeks you'd be back.

79

Today is a Wednesday, two weeks have passed, and everything appears to be going to plan. You drop to the ground and roll under the descending grill, pulling your bag in after you just before the garage door clunks into its housing and locks in place. You move swiftly down the ramp to squeeze behind a pillar. With a dull click the lamps around you go out. There are voices and you look towards the sounds. Light spills from the rear of the underground garage where the Rowcastles are unloading their supermarket shopping. Moments later there's the thump of a closing tailgate and a bleep as the car locks. The lights in the far end of the garage go out and there's a low-pitched curse followed by a woman's voice. 'I've got them!' The lights come back on. There are no further sounds until the lift doors open and close. You wait until the entire garage is dark and silent.

After several minutes without a sound, you pick up your bag, walk past the line of residents' cars and take the stairs. You reach the top unobserved. The latched door opens readily from the inside and you step onto the roof. With no further use for the stairs you let the door swing shut and lock.

A double guard-rail encircles the flat roof. Walking to the rear of the building you cautiously check the drop to her balcony. No problem, your telescopic ladder will reach. Crossing to the street side you recheck your escape route. First, a thirty-foot abseil to the roof of the bin store, which is partially covered by the dense foliage of a nearby tree, and then your ladder for the ten-foot drop to the street. You attach your ropes to the guard-rail and lower them silently down the side of the building; their colour blends with the brickwork and an adjacent rainwater downpipe. Taking your harness and unicender from your bag, you place them ready at the top of the ropes. Then you change into your climbing shoes and return to watch the balcony with the ladder at your side and the cords in your pockets. Inevitably there'll be a long wait. You can't do anything until she's asleep. Fortunately, it's dry and the air is still warm. You relax and wait, satisfied that all is in place.

It has been an hour since the sky glowed pink and then orange with the setting sun. You continue to wait. From time to time, you stretch your arms and legs. Occasionally you arch your back. Small movements to keep flexible. Just after eight-thirty, the lights go on in the flat. Five minutes later, the doors to the balcony open. Although she's unlikely to look up, you withdraw your head and listen. First there is her voice saying something with a rising inflection: a question? Then a second voice joins hers on the balcony, a man's voice. There's the scrape of chairs and the sound of a bottle and glasses placed on the table. Easing yourself forward, you risk peeping over the edge. She's been joined by a guy. Even from above you recognize him as a man you've seen her with in Maidstone. You tune out their conversation and settle again to wait.

Another hour passes before there are more sounds of the chairs, glasses and bottle being moved. Peering over the edge of the roof, you see the man follow her back inside leaving the balcony doors ajar. It's a warm night. Apart from distant street sounds, all is quiet. Gradually, you become aware of a slowly building crescendo from within the apartment. The cries climax and silence returns. With decreasing hope, you wait until midnight, but the man from Maidstone doesn't leave. You'd anticipated setbacks, but that doesn't lessen your disappointment. There's no way you can act while he's with her, but the bitch will pay; if not tonight, tomorrow, or as soon as the time is right.

You stand, collapse your ladder and return it to the bag. Then you walk to your ropes and lower the bag to the roof of the bin shelter. You step into your harness, attach the unicender to the ropes and drop swiftly down the side of the building. With the harness and unicender back in your bag, you change your shoes and check the street is empty. As you lower your ladder into place you narrowly miss a large refuse bin that has been wheeled out for collection. On the pavement, you pack the ladder into your bag and cross the road to look at the side of the building. As you anticipated, your fixed ropes are hidden by the rainwater downpipe. With a quick glance left and right, you check the street is still deserted and take the shorter route to the city centre, hoping things will go better tomorrow.

80

It's Thursday and well after sunset before you make your way back to her apartment. Less than 20 yards from the building, two women are talking at neighbouring front doors. Rather than lingering with your bag in your hand, you continue walking and circle the block. By the time you return, the women have disappeared and the street is deserted. Extending your ladder, you reach the roof of the bin shelter, pull the ladder up behind you and collapse it into your bag. You change shoes and, with the harness and unicender, climb easily to the roof of the main building.

From this height, reflections from the River Stour glint through the trees to the left, while the rooftops of the city stretch away to your right. Directly below, Detective Inspector Ed Ogborne is sitting alone on her balcony with a bottle of white wine. Time passes slowly. The darkness deepens, but still she doesn't move. Occasionally the neck of the bottle catches the rim of her glass and the clink is followed by the gentle sound of pouring wine. It seems that any desire she might have for sleep is countered by a lethargy that permits no greater movement than that required to finish the bottle. You resign yourself to another long wait. Nothing can be done until well after she's gone to bed.

Despite flexing your muscles, you begin to stiffen. Just as you contemplate getting to your feet for some more vigorous stretching, there is a scraping sound as Ogborne pushes back her chair. You ease forward to look. With the empty bottle in one hand and glass in the other she disappears from the balcony, leaving the sliding door half open. Like yesterday, the night is warm and no burglar is going to climb to a fourth-floor balcony. There is the distant sound of a bottle being dropped into a bin and a glass placed on a stone worktop. Then, no more discernible sounds until the lights are switched off and the apartment is in darkness.

Two hours later, you lower the ladder and climb quietly down to the balcony. On your rubber-soled shoes, you move silently to the open door of her bedroom. It's dark, but you can just make out Ogborne, on her back, breathing deeply. The duvet has slipped or been pushed to the floor and her oversized T-shirt has ridden up around her waist. You don't give the detective a second glance – your mind is set on revenge. Avoiding the fallen duvet, you loop cords round her right wrist and ankle. Oh, so gently, you pull each cord until it is fully extended, allowing you to tie them to the head and foot of the bed. Stepping carefully, you move to the other side, loop a third cord round her left wrist, pass it round the head of the bed and pull slowly, gently extending her arm upwards. She stirs in her sleep. You pause and brace your foot against the side of the bed. Just one strong heave, a quick knot, and you'll have her spread-eagled with all but her left leg tied to the bed.

Out of the darkness there's blinding pain. You lose control and feel yourself falling to the floor as the world turns black.

* * *

Ed's left hand had been beside her hip. The movement of her arm disturbed her sleep. Without opening her eyes, she gently resisted the movement, giving herself time to assess the situation. Ever since the news of Colin Bradshaw's escape had come through, she'd thought there was a remote chance she might be attacked, but she hadn't expected it to happen in her own home. Ed could feel cords round her right wrist and ankle but neither was yet tight. From the cord around her left wrist and the direction in which it was pulling her arm, she judged her attacker must be standing on her left near the head of the bed. Still with her eyes closed, Ed stirred as if in sleep, turning her head to face the point where she judged her attacker to be crouching over the bed. There was a pause in the gentle movement of the cord and her arm. In that moment, Ed opened her eyes, located the figure by the bed and swung her right foot hard at its head. Her instep contacted what felt like the nose. With a cry of pain, the figure dropped the cord and fell out of sight beside the bed.

With her left arm freed, Ed rolled to her right and dropped to the floor, putting the bed between herself and her attacker. The movement loosened the looped cords on her right wrist and ankle. She slipped the bonds off and stood to face her opponent across the bed. Without shifting her gaze, Ed bent sideways and switched on the bedside light.

'Gina!'

'I'm glad I got here in time.'

'Gina?'

For a moment Ed was puzzled but then she took control. 'Stay where you are.'

Ed looked searchingly at her attacker. Something glinted in Gina's right hand. It must be a weapon.

'Drop that weapon on the bed.'

'Of course.'

Ed watched as Gina tossed the weapon onto the bed. It was a gun. Ed looked back at Gina, puzzled. A gun! Why bother with the ropes if she had a gun and intended to use it? She stared across the bed at Gina, who stood relaxed and motionless.

Ed thought rapidly. She'd felt the cords around her wrist. She'd felt Gina pulling the cords to stretch her out on the bed. At the last moment she'd kicked out and escaped. Ed had felt her foot contact her attacker's face. Ed looked at Gina, who was showing no obvious effects of that powerful blow. Ed couldn't make sense of the situation. She was still struggling to understand what was happening when there was a groan from the floor on the far side of the bed.

'What the ...!'

Another figure was rising to its feet in front of Gina. Blood oozed from a wounded nose and a hand clasped the back of its neck.

Gina remained motionless but called to Ed, 'You'd better arrest this man. He's out to kill you!'

The figure attempted to look at Gina, but appeared unable to turn. It raised its head and through puffy eyes tried, without success, to focus on Ed.

It was Colin Bradshaw.

Ed's eyes flicked from Colin to Gina and back in amazement. Gina seemed very relaxed, almost happy, but Colin was in a bad way. Although he had gained his feet, he was extremely disorientated. Suddenly he appeared to stagger. With a groan he dropped to his knees, putting his arms on the bed for support.

Alarm bells rang in Ed's head. The weapon Gina had tossed nonchalantly onto the bed – as a police officer she should have taken control of it immediately. Desperately, Ed launched herself forwards to secure the firearm before Colin could grab it. Her hand closed over the weapon and she regained her feet, ready to defend herself against an attack from Colin. She need not have worried. His apparent collapse onto the bed had not been a feint. He was uttering muffled groans as his muscles twitched uncontrollably. Colin was in a worse state than Ed had imagined. He was clearly in pain, still disorientated and oblivious to what was happening. Surely that couldn't have been caused by the blow she'd delivered to his nose?

Ed turned her attention to the weapon in her hand. It wasn't a firearm – it was a stun gun. She looked from the gun to Gina.

'Is this yours?'

Gina nodded.

'You know stun guns are illegal in the UK? It's an offence for a member of the public to possess or use such a weapon.'

Standing behind Colin, who was still slumped on the bed, Gina nodded again.

'What's going on, Gina?'

'It's a long story ...'

'We'll go into that later, at the Station.'

Ed took her mobile from the bedside table and called for back-up.

'There'll be no need to break down the doors. Tell them to ring and I'll buzz them in.'

Colin was now sitting on the floor with his back against the bed. Gina had barely moved throughout the whole episode.

Ed went to put her mobile in a pocket and realized she was still wearing nothing but an oversized T-shirt. She didn't embarrass easily, certainly not in a situation such as this. From a chair on which yesterday's clothes were scattered, Ed faced her two intruders and pulled on a pair of jeans. With the side of her foot, she flicked her discarded underwear and top out of sight behind the chair.

At that moment the doorbell rang. Ed glanced at Colin. He was still out of it.

'Stay where you are, Gina.'

'Of course.'

With a final glance at Colin, Ed walked to the door and buzzed her colleagues into the building.

81

Colin Bradshaw was in the cells waiting to be transported back to prison. Ed was in Interview Room 3, talking with Gina, when her mobile rang. It was Daniel.

Ed got to her feet. 'Sorry, Gina, I've got to take this. Give me one minute.' Ed stepped out into the corridor. 'Hi, Daniel, can I call you back?'

'I've just heard. Are you okay?'

'I'm fine. Just interviewing the woman who saved me.'

'I thought you'd not fancy going back to your place tonight. Shall I drive over, pick you up and take you back to mine?'

'Drive over, but we'll spend the night here, at mine. Meet me there in 45 minutes.'

'I'll be there. See you—'

'Looking forward to it. Must get back. Bye.'

Back in the Interview Room, Ed took her place at the table again. 'As I was saying, Gina, this is an informal chat. You committed an offence by having that stun gun, but you saved me from what could have been something very nasty. Your actions also resulted in Colin Bradshaw being recaptured and he will soon be returned to prison.'

'What will happen about the stun gun?'

'In the circumstances, you'll get a caution. Tomorrow, we'll need a formal statement. Tonight, I'll get a squad car to run you home, but first, how come I was so lucky to have you in my bedroom when Bradshaw attacked me?'

'Are you recording this?'

'No, but we can go somewhere else if you prefer.'

'I can trust you?'

'After what you did for me this evening, what do you think?' Ed looked directly into Gina's eyes. 'Yes, you can trust me.'

'You'll get a different story in my formal statement tomorrow.'

'Okay. This is just between ourselves.'

'I was in prison myself—'

'The perjury. What you did has been messing with my head, Gina. I can't understand why you set Colin up and accused him of rape? What was going on between the two of you?'

'You're not recording this?'

'I've already said so, but you don't have to tell me if you don't want to.'

'I'm ashamed. No one else knows. I've not told anybody but I'd like to tell you.'

'I'd like to know. And believe me, whatever you tell me will stay with me – I'll not repeat it to anyone.' Ed leant back in her chair, ready to listen.

'On Friday the 21st of June last year, Colin Bradshaw tricked his way into my home, tied me to my bed and, if I hadn't used sex to escape, I was convinced he would kill me.'

'Gina!' There was shock in Ed's voice and on her face as she leant forward in the chair. 'Why didn't you come straight to us as soon as you escaped?'

'I wish I had, but you read stories of how women reporting sexual harassment are treated by the police and—'

'Things are changing for the better.'

'I know. When I came in to say I'd been raped, you and your colleagues, the doctor, Anna, were so nice to me. I thought then that I should have come straight to you.'

Ed looked concerned. 'Why didn't you come immediately after you'd escaped from Colin?'

'I was worried about the way the police would react to the scene in my apartment. I escaped by using sex to trick Colin and I left him tied to my bed. Obviously, when the police arrived, he would say it was a sex game gone wrong. I was sure the police would believe him. No one would think that I could have escaped from my bonds and tied somebody like Colin to the bed in my place. If only you'd identified Bradshaw as the man who'd tied that poor girl to her bed in Dover sooner, I could have come to you. By the time that happened it was far too late. I'd taken the other route.'

The was no anger in Gina's voice. She sounded resigned and Ed felt bad for her.

'I'm sorry. It was only after we'd arrested Bradshaw for rape that we were able to link him to the manslaughter in Dover.'

Gina sighed. 'What's happened, has happened.' She looked at Ed and smiled. 'Don't they say, what goes around, comes around? If I hadn't gone to prison I wouldn't have been there to protect you this evening.'

'How come?'

'I wasn't inside for long, but almost immediately I fell foul of the prison bully.'

'It happens.'

'Yeah, but I was lucky. Donna, the oldest woman in there and hard as nails, took me under her wing. Nobody crossed Donna. She was tough, but she was kind and generous. They

350

all knew about the manslaughter and rape trials and they were sympathetic. Donna in particular thought I'd been hard done by, shouldn't have been banged up. The point is, after I was released, Donna got a message to me. She'd learnt Colin had used the promise of big money to set up an escape.'

'Why tell you?'

'Apparently, although he was polite and helpful to fellow inmates and screws alike, he'd got a reputation for ranting under his breath about getting even with the bitch. Donna was concerned he would attack me, perhaps kill me, in revenge for my accusation of rape. She warned me to be on my guard.'

'How did that lead you to my bedroom?'

'She told me the day Colin would be sprung from jail by some European gangsters who would then hand him over to British crooks in a supermarket car park on the outskirts of Southend. In turn, the British guys would drive Colin to a hideout. I had people stake out the car park and, when the handover occurred, my people followed the car with Colin in it.'

'That sort of surveillance would have taken money – your parents?'

'Don't ask.' Gina rolled her eyes. 'When the CPS seemed to be dragging their feet over prosecuting Colin for rape, I raised some cash, hoping to bring a private prosecution. The sisterhood rallied round. I got a sizable sum, but nowhere near enough for my prosecution. Then, as you know, the CPS changed their mind and I didn't need to fund the trial myself.'

'Knowing the whereabouts of an escaped prisoner and failing to report it to the authorities is—'

'An offence.' Gina looked unblinkingly into Ed's eyes. 'I was in fear of my life and, ultimately, I saved yours.'

Ed nodded, but said nothing.

'Donna put me in touch with the right people. Sufficient folding money buys the best and buys their silence.'

'Go on.'

'Colin was followed from the supermarket car park in Southend to the hideout in Kent. The next day, he was driven to a disued building where he was seen rope climbing and abseiling. As a precaution, I started taking intensive lessons myself. The rest was easy.'

'You were tipped off he was casing my apartment block?'

'And I was told he was showing no interest in me. He got me convicted for perjury, perhaps that was revenge enough. If the bitch wasn't me, I assumed it was you.'

'You decided to protect me?'

'I can't say you're my best friend, but I've a much bigger grudge against Colin.' Gina smiled weakly at Ed. 'Anyway, I want to turn my life around. Perhaps some of Donna's good-natured generosity rubbed off on me. I decided to prevent Colin from doing whatever he intended.'

'Thank you.' It was Ed's turn to smile. 'But tomorrow, in your formal statement, how much of this are you going to say?'

'Nothing about Colin getting into my home and holding me captive. As for everything else, I'll say the whole thing occurred by chance. I just happened to be walking by and came across Colin scaling the side of your building. Knowing how you put him away for the manslaughter in Dover, I assumed you were in danger.'

'And, by chance, you had the skill and equipment to climb up after him? And the abseiling?'

'I'd already started intensive training, which I've continued as a hobby. It passes the time, clears my head, and I'm meeting new people. As I said, I aim to put my past behind me and turn my life around.'

'Good luck with that, Gina. And thanks for this evening. I'm fit and I'm fast. I'm confident I would have got the better of Colin, but you made that a whole lot easier.' Ed stood. 'Come, let's get a squad car to take you home. Be back here tomorrow at eleven to give your formal statement. Ask for DS Mike Potts or DC Jenny Eastham.'

When Ed got back home, Daniel was across the road from her entrance, leaning against his car. He wrapped his arms around her in an enthusiastic hug.

'Are you okay?'

'I'm fine, but nothing that clean sheets, a glass of wine and you can't improve.'

Later, with Daniel snoring gently beside her, Ed leant back against two pillows and linked her fingers behind her head. She was drained but content. This was where she wanted to be, looking through her bedroom window at the moon-silvered towers of Canterbury Cathedral. This was her home; no deluded, vengeful man would take it from her.

82

The following day, Daniel was off playing rugby. Ed called the Metcalffe dental practice and asked to speak with Rachael, only to be told she was in surgery. 'Perhaps you could get her to call me back?'

'I'm afraid Saturday is a busy time for us.'

'It will be a very quick call. I'll give you my mobile number. Please ask her to ring me during her lunch break.'

When Rachael called, Ed asked if she would be able to meet her briefly after work. 'It's not a police matter, I'd like to speak to you in a private capacity. Perhaps we could see each other over a coffee across the street from your practice?' They agreed on ten past six in Deakin's.

Ed was sitting at a window table. Across the street she could see that Georgina Hamilton's name had been removed from the brass plate at the entrance to the dental practice. Ed watched as the receptionist and then a man she didn't know – presumably a new dentist – left the building and walked away. Rachael was the last to appear. When she'd locked the door and turned towards Deakin's, Ed tapped on the glass and waved for Rachael to join her.

'You said you wanted to see me privately. How can I help?'

'You've probably seen that Colin Bradshaw was apprehended yesterday.'

'Yes, I heard on the radio. Apparently, he was found in Canterbury. Odd that he should come back here.'

Ed nodded. 'I can't go into details and what I'm about to say won't appear in the media.'

'This all seems very mysterious.'

'Not really.' Ed stirred her sugarless coffee. 'Georgina Hamilton was instrumental in Bradshaw's recapture. I spent a long time talking with her yesterday. She doesn't want her name associated with the event and we shall respect her wishes.'

'What has this to do with me?'

'Gina has behaved foolishly – very foolishly. There were reasons she did what she did but she understands that she behaved unwisely. Now, having had time to think, I'm sure she's a changed person, determined to turn her life around.'

'And so ...'

'You told me that when Gina joined your practice she suggested a number of innovations that have proved profitable.'

'Yes, very profitable. We're getting more and more clients and are planning to expand the practice early in the new year.'

'That's what I heard and it's why I asked to see you.'

'What did you have in mind?' Rachael's expression had changed. She spoke guardedly.

'As I said, I'm convinced Gina is a changed person, desperate to turn her life around. When you expand, I assume you'll be taking on new staff. I wanted to ask if you would consider offering Gina her old job.'

'That's a big ask. All the publicity that surrounded the

rape trial. Her perjury. Her past as an escort. That's not something we could have associated with our dental practice. This is a small town with, unfortunately, many small-minded people.'

'Gina's sentence for perjury is spent. She's hardly been mentioned in the media in relation to Bradshaw's escape and recapture. She's a good dentist, you said so yourself, and I believe she deserves another chance.'

'I liked Gina and, until the horrible business with Bradshaw blew up, she was a good colleague.' Rachael paused, thinking. Ed remained silent.

'I'm sympathetic to what you say.' Rachael paused again and then said, 'I'll discuss what you've suggested with my father. It's not going to be an easy decision and I certainly can't promise a favourable outcome.'

'Thank you for listening and thank you for agreeing to consider it. If you would let me know what you and your father decide, I'd be grateful.'

'Of course.'

A month later, Ed received a call and immediately recognized Gina's voice. She sounded very excited.

'Hi, it's Georgina Hamilton, but not for much longer. The Metcalffes have been amazingly good to me. I've agreed to change my name by deed poll and they'll take me back into the practice when their expansion is completed early next year.'

'That's great news, Gina.'

'It will soon be Vicky, Victoria Harrison.'

'Congratulations, Vicky.'

'Of course, they'll not be taking me back as a partner.' Gina was silent, and then added, 'My life is getting better and I'm optimistic, and you never know, in time, a partnership could be on the cards.'

Ed smiled. Georgina Hamilton had changed in many ways, and soon she would change her name, but one aspect of her character was still in place, one Ed was sure Victoria Harrison would keep. It was a characteristic that Ed admired – her self-belief and determination to succeed.

'Gina, Vicky, I wish you well.'

Ed ended the call and, in pensive mood, began to consider her own life. She wasn't into new year resolutions but from time to time she did take stock. In her professional life she was decisive and successful. The same couldn't be said of her private life, especially her choice of men. When starting a new relationship, Ed liked to think she was decisive, but others – even Ed herself on occasion – regarded her behaviour as impetuous. When it came to ending a relationship, even Ed knew she was often slow to act – sometimes far too slow.

Daniel came to mind in thoughts she'd been having with increasing regularity. He was fit and caring, a desirable combination and one not frequently found in men, but ... but ... he lacked humour. No, that was unfair – to the extent Daniel had a sense of humour, it didn't match her own. And? And ... he didn't like Schiele's paintings, images she adored. Actually, it was more than not liking, he was uninterested, possibly even believed the drawings with their startling touches of red gouache were obscene. In her eyes, he was a bit prissy about such things. Ed sighed. Daniel was so *wholesome*. The moment the word came into her head Ed knew it would never go away.

Past lovers, those who stayed in her mind, all had an element of danger. Was it that she was missing?

Ed didn't want to go there. What she needed now was a glass of cold white wine and a relaxed chat with a female friend. She'd never been one for besties; in fact, all the women in her life had been acquaintances rather than friends. That changed when she arrived in Canterbury. Ed reached for her phone. The first number she tried went to voicemail. She dialled an alternative.

'*Canterbury Chronicle*, Verity Shaw, editor, speaking.'

Ed imagined her friend's impeccably cut steel-grey hair and her habitual half-smile.

'Hi, Verity, it's Ed.'

'Long time no see.'

It had been a while. Ed wondered, was Verity smiling now or she was miffed?

'Sorry, it's been busy.'

'Dangerous too, from what I've heard.'

Now there was a hint of playfulness in Verity's voice, something Ed loved.

'I feel like a night out. Do you fancy a meal at Gino's?'

There was a pause and Ed hoped the half-smile was in place.

'Give me an hour. I'll see you at Deakin's for a glass of white before we move on to the Italian.'

'Great, see you there.'

Ed walked into her bedroom to select clothes for the evening. Through the window dusk was descending on the great west towers of the cathedral. When the moon came out, the towers would shimmer silver against the night sky. Ed loved this view.

Despite herself, she returned to reflecting on her life. Almost three years had passed since she'd been transferred from London to Canterbury. To her surprise, it was probably as many months since she'd last thought about returning to the Met.

Acknowledgements

Initially, *The Victim*, my second DI Edina Ogborne novel, was developed and part-written alongside my debut crime novel, *The Taken Girls*, in which Ed Ogborne appeared for the first time. Hence, it should be no surprise that I wish to thank many of the same people.

First, and always, my thanks to Helen for her constant support and encouragement. Whenever I am unsure, her advice and comments on drafts continue to be invaluable.

My good fortune has continued with Jo Bell of Bell Lomax and Moreton as my agent, and Phoebe Morgan of Avon, HarperCollins as my editor. Thanks to them both for good advice, for patience with my questions and for being a pleasure to work with. These thanks must be extended to the team at Avon for their commitment and expertise in the production, publication, and promotion of my novels.

Some of the opening chapters of what is now *The Victim* were first written way back in 2013 when I was on the Curtis Brown Creative writing course where I benefited greatly from interactions with Nikita Lalwani, the lead tutor, and Anna Davis, the Director. Fellow CBC students from that time have become friends and, those of us who are able, continue to meet regularly. I am grateful for the support, encouragement, and comments on multiple drafts which I have received from Aliya, Antoinette, Chris, Ian, Louise, Swithun, Wendy and Ziella.

Tim Forte has been a generous source of advice on the information the police may and may not obtain from mobile phones for use as evidence in cases which go to trial. Of course, any errors in that respect are my own.

Finally, once again, my thanks to the many people, known and unknown, who, with phrase, image, or gesture, have unwittingly stimulated my imagination to develop ideas which have found their way into this novel.

If you enjoyed *The Victim*, why not head back
to where it all began and read the first book
in the series, *The Taken Girls*?

The Taken Girls

Time is
running out...

G. D. Sanders

Available now.